RED JULIE

J. A. WHITING

For Virginia and John, with love

1

Martin Andersen drove his black Mercedes 550 past the driveway of his beach house. His eyes scanned the darkness for people, cars, or anything that looked suspicious. The moon was high in the sky. The road was empty. He drove to the end of the quiet, side street and turned around, deciding that things looked safe.

His headlights illuminated the rising garage door and when it was fully elevated, the Mercedes eased into the middle bay of the three-car garage. Andersen immediately hit the button and waited for the door to close, and only then unlocked the car door and emerged into the blackness of his garage. Andersen stood in the hot dark, holding his breath.

Cold sweat caused his shirt to stick to his back. He could not detect anything out of the ordinary, so he entered the foyer of his four thousand square foot contemporary home but did not turn on any lights. He used a pen light to shine on the staircase that took him to the main living area on the second floor of the house.

Andersen could hear the ocean pounding against the rocks outside. He loved this house perched on a bluff of the rocky coast at Perkins Cove, Maine. The spectacular view, the layout, the grounds. He had worked hard and this house was one of the rewards of his financial good fortune.

But not tonight. Tonight he wished he was anywhere but here. He stood fixed at the top of the stairs, listening. His heart was hammering as his vision grew accustomed to the darkness in the room.

His eyes flicked about searching the shadows, making sure that he was alone. Sensing no one lurking, he hurried to the master bedroom to access the wall safe. A month ago he had fled without the contents of the safe. Andersen knew he was taking a chance returning tonight. His hands shook as he punched in the code, turned the knob, and swung open the small, heavy metal door.

Something to his right caught his attention and he turned to see the light on the security panel of his bedroom wall blinking red in the darkness, indicating that the door from the deck into the kitchen was open. He froze. A bead of sweat rolled down his forehead, traveled along his eyebrow to his temple and continued down the side of his face. Tension caused the membranes lining his throat to constrict so that he could barely take in any air.

He stuffed the cash and credit cards into his pants and rammed the gun into his jacket pocket. As his feet moved slowly across the plush carpeting, he was thankful that he had given in to Rodney's insistence to carpet over the wood floors in this room for maximum quiet.

He listened at the door. He had to get to his car. Hearing nothing he sucked in a deep breath and took a step into the hallway. Andersen stood stock still trying to sense any movement in the dark space of his own home. Nothing. Did the security system malfunction? His auditory system still on high alert, he moved his feet inch by slow inch, holding his breath now, and crept down the hall. Andersen edged into the living room.

White, bright light flooded the space and stabbed Andersen's optic nerve, the sudden transition from dark to light blinding him for half a second. Oh no. He squinted. Two men were standing near the far wall of his living room. Both were wearing suits giving the impression that they were businessmen, but Andersen knew better. Bile rose in his throat. His body coursed with adrenaline.

"Mr. Andersen," the shorter man said in greeting. "We noticed that you had come home."

The taller man had the hint of a smile on his mouth, but his eyes were cold and dead.

"How did you get in here?" Andersen said with forced indignation. His heart was beating like a jack hammer.

"You have something we want," the shorter man said.

Andersen's mind was racing. He knew what these men were capable of. He had to get to his car. He put his hand in his pocket and took a step towards the staircase that would lead back to the lower level garage.

"I would stay where you are, Mr. Andersen." The shorter man lifted a gun and pointed it at Andersen's chest.

From inside his pocket, Andersen adjusted his trembling hand and his index finger found and contracted against the small piece of metal. His gun fired through the fabric of his jacket into the man's stomach. Not what Andersen was aiming for, but it would do. The man jolted, dropped his gun, and slipped to the floor.

Andersen whirled for the door to the garage and, pulling his gun from his pocket, shot wildly at the taller man. His panic and inexperience caused the bullet to travel low, missing the man's core, but grazing him in the calf of his left leg which was enough to slow him down.

Andersen's foot missed the top step of the staircase and his feet scrambled in the empty air attempting to find something solid. His back cracked into the stair treads and he careened down fourteen marble steps to the foyer floor. Gasping, he half crawled, half ran into the garage and to the Mercedes. He flung the driver side door open,

4

but before he could get in, a hand caught his shoulder. The darkness of the garage shrouded the facial features of the man who gripped him, but Andersen knew who it was.

He twisted to the right and used the elbow of his right arm to smack the attacker in the throat. The attacker grunted and paused, but his hands were like iron and they clamped around Andersen's neck as the man's knee came up and caught Andersen in the groin. Andersen groaned and tried to contort himself away. He gripped his attacker's throat with his left hand while raising his right hand which still held his gun. A blast filled the air, but it was not from Andersen's weapon.

Andersen doubled over from the bullet that entered his gut just as he pulled the trigger of his own weapon. That bullet hit the attacker in the shoulder and sent him reeling back onto the floor of the garage. Andersen had a grip on the man's necklace, the chain twisted between his fingers, and it ripped off in his hand as the man hurtled backwards.

Andersen staggered to his car, punched the button to raise the garage door, and stomped the gas pedal, sending the car flying back, scraping the roof of the Mercedes against the rising door.

The moonlight danced over Andersen's car as it shot up Shore Road and veered onto Route 1 towards the highway. In minutes, the headlights of a speeding car showed in Andersen's rearview mirror and, wheezing and gripping the steering wheel, he pressed harder on the gas pedal. The loss of blood combined with the pain of the bullet lodged in his core caused his vision to blur and he fought to keep the car on the road.

A blast sent a bullet into the back window of the Mercedes, shattering the glass with a roar. Andersen flinched and his car swerved into the opposite lane.

He took the turn for the highway too widely going close to ninety miles an hour. A man in an oncoming vehicle had only a second to react to the black missile flying toward him. He jammed on his brake and pulled the wheel to the right, but this action only presented the driver's side to the Mercedes, which exploded into it, crushing the car and killing its occupant instantly.

The Mercedes flipped over twice and filled the air with a sickening screech of crushing metal as the car skidded on its roof to a stop.

The car in pursuit of Andersen jolted to a halt just in front of the smashed car. Two men jumped from the vehicle, one limping, the other clutching at his bloody shoulder. The limping man was the one with dead eyes who had earlier been standing in Andersen's living room. Blood soaked one leg of his pants. He stood next to the car while the other man strode to the overturned Mercedes.

Andersen was lying in the street on his back, his

blood pooling under him, his legs caught in the mangled wreckage. He opened his eyes as the man with the bloody shoulder approached. The man held a knife. The light from the streetlight glinted off the blade. He knelt.

Andersen's screams would have frozen the blood of anyone who heard them.

2

Olivia forced herself to sit straighter in the driver's seat as she turned the radio up and opened her window a crack to let the cool, late-night breeze flow against her face. She shook her head a bit to throw off the drowsiness that had come over her. The movement loosened some of the light brown, shoulder length hair from her ponytail.

She was glad that she had waited until midnight to leave Medford to make the trip north because she had the highway mostly to herself, but now her eyelids were feeling heavy as she traveled the final few miles to the off ramp that would lead her to Route 1. She always felt happy anticipation on the trip to Maine and she was looking forward to being in her aunt's house on the coast again. Only it wasn't her aunt's house anymore. It was

Olivia's house now, and this would be the first time she stayed there as the owner.

She breathed a heavy sigh. Olivia still couldn't believe that Aggie was dead, gone for a month now, and that she wouldn't be there to greet Olivia as she pulled into the driveway. Aggie had raised Olivia from the time she was a year old, and while Olivia was growing up they divided their time between Cambridge, Massachusetts and Ogunquit.

Just over a year ago, Aggie had given up her apartment in Cambridge when she decided to retire from her teaching position at Boston College law school. She made the Ogunquit beach house her permanent residence. Olivia rented an apartment with one of her friends near the Tufts University campus while she was a student there, but the beach house was where she called home. Olivia loved the house and the town of Ogunquit as much as Aggie had.

When Olivia saw the highway sign indicating the exit for Ogunquit and the Yorks, she put her blinker on and moved the car to the right lane to take the ramp. The headlights cut through the darkness, and Olivia's eyes widened as she slammed on her brakes, causing her Jeep to skid onto the right shoulder of the exit.

A car was overturned near the end of the ramp, resting on its roof. Another car with its side and front end crushed was facing the wrong way in the street. Olivia thought she could make out someone in the shadows running away from the overturned car. There were no other people in sight.

Olivia flung her door open, leaped from the driver's seat and ran to the overturned vehicle. A man was on his back in the road, half in and half out of the car, his legs tangled in the metal. His eyes were closed. Blood covered his chest, stomach, neck, and face. Olivia knelt beside him. She gingerly touched his shoulder. The man's eyes popped open. Olivia jumped.

"It's okay. You'll be okay," she said. The man grabbed at Olivia's arms.

"Hold on. I'll be right back," she told him. The man made grunting noises deep in his throat and shook his head. His eyes were wide and wild. Olivia pulled away as he was trying to grab her jacket.

"I need to get my phone. I'm going to call the ambulance." Olivia ran to her car and grabbed the phone out of her bag. She punched in '911' and reported the accident as she rushed back to the man.

"They're coming. Help's on the way." Olivia knelt. She glanced at the other crumpled car. No one emerged from it. No one else was on the road.

The man on the ground grasped Olivia's jacket lapels. His eyes bulged. He gibbered at her. Mouthfuls of blood spilled from between his open lips. Olivia's stomach lurched but she fought to keep her face neutral.

"You'll be okay," she told him with a shaky voice. The man tried to raise his head while still gibbering at her, his hand clutching the side of her jacket.

"Reh," he mumbled. "Reh...oo...ee." The man pulled at Olivia to draw her closer. She leaned down and put her ear near to his mouth.

"Reh...oo...ee," he managed between ragged breaths. "Oo...ee."

Olivia strained to understand him. "Julie? Are you asking for Julie?" She peered into the vehicle. She hadn't even thought to look inside the car for anyone else.

"It's empty. I don't see anyone," Olivia told him.

The man shook his head and repeated, "reh...oo...ee." He turned his face to the side as he coughed up blood.

Olivia heard sirens. "I hear them. They're coming. Help's coming." She gave the man a thin smile.

The man looked over Olivia's shoulder and horrible noises let loose from his throat. His eyes were frantic and he grabbed at her wildly, his shoulders rocking from side to side. Olivia turned her head to her right. She startled. A man in a dark suit stood just behind her. He stared down at the man on the road.

"I didn't hear you come up. The ambulance is coming," she told the person in the suit. He did not look at her, only down at the man in the road. His eyes were like cold steel. His right hand was in the pocket of his suit jacket. The man on the ground contorted trying to free himself from the wreckage. Roaring noises ripped from his throat.

Olivia looked from the man on the ground to the standing man. A chill ran down her back. Her heart thudded against her chest.

"Step back," Olivia told the man standing over them. He didn't look at her. He didn't move.

Olivia raised her voice and glared at him. "I said step back." The man in the suit took a step closer and Olivia noticed that his pant leg was wet. There was a tiny puddle that looked sticky and wet on the street where he had stood a moment before.

The man shifted his steely gaze to Olivia. Her heart stopped. As the man's right hand twitched in his pocket, a car heading down the ramp skidded to a stop and a young man and woman jumped out and raced towards them.

The man in the suit turned his head to look at the couple. His face was calm, expressionless, but the muscles of his jaw twitched. A police car, siren screaming, shot up the street to the ramp from the direction of Route 1 with two ambulances chasing behind.

Olivia turned back to the man on the ground. His eyes were wide but now they were transfixed. His hands had dropped by his sides. He was still.

A paramedic ran to them carrying his medical bag and crouched down. His gloved hand reached for the man's neck to check for a pulse. Olivia stepped back, her arms wrapped tightly around her body. Tears gathered in her eyes. She was trembling. A police officer was at her side.

"Were you in the car, Miss?"

Olivia blinked at him and shook her head. "No, no. I was driving down the ramp." She pointed back to her car. "It was like this already." She gestured to the over-turned car.

The paramedics were covering the man from head to toe with a sheet. Olivia's throat constricted. She blinked to keep her tears from spilling. Three or four people had gathered and stood off to the side of the exit ramp watching. Someone handed Olivia some alcohol moistened towels to wipe the blood from her hands.

"I'd like to take your statement, Miss," the officer told her and nodded to his car parked at the end of the ramp. Olivia walked with him to his cruiser. Her body seemed filled with ice and her hands felt numb. As she walked to the police cruiser, she scanned the people who had gathered to watch. The man in the suit was not among them.

Olivia gave her statement to the police officer. Other officers arrived and flares were placed on the ramp. The few cars exiting the highway were instructed to travel onto the grass just off the road shoulder in order to get around the accident scene.

Back in her car, Olivia inched down the street,

weaving around the safety personnel and the gawkers who had assembled. She glanced at the ambulance as she passed. Her hands twitched on the steering wheel.

Olivia was only seven miles from reaching her house but she was still shaking and the road seemed to swim before her. She removed one hand from the steering wheel and shook it, then did the same with her other hand.

Approaching a roadside café that was open twenty-four hours, she pulled into the parking lot and parked near the front entrance. Images of the accident scene flashed in her mind and she swallowed hard.

She rummaged in her bag for tissues. He died. I couldn't help him. She sat for a few minutes trying to calm herself. What did he say? Where's Julie? Red Julie?

Olivia could see some teenagers in one of the booths near the window, laughing and talking. She sighed, got out of the car, and walked into the café, where she ordered a takeout coffee from the girl behind the counter.

The girl stared at Olivia's jacket.

Olivia looked down and saw that blood was smeared over the front of the tan blazer. Handprints were outlined in blood on the fabric of the arms.

"I just came from an accident," she hurriedly explained.

The lights seemed too bright and hurt her eyes, and the cooking smells of the greasy late night breakfasts turned her stomach. The waitress returned, snapped the plastic lid over the coffee cup, placed it in front of Olivia, and turned to the cash register to ring in the sale.

Reaching into her jacket pocket for the twenty dollar bill she had put there before she left her Medford apartment earlier that night, her fingers bumped something small and hard.

Olivia pulled her hand from her pocket and her eyes went wide. She was holding a thick gold cross attached to a heavy gold chain.

The cross was elaborately carved and had a sunburst design in the center of it. In the middle of the sunburst was a small silver skull with a large diamond embedded in each of the eye sockets. The sunburst's rays radiated in gold and silver from the center skull and were decorated with diamonds of varying sizes. The initial "S" was engraved on the back. The clasp was broken off. There were tiny splotches of blood on the cross and chain.

Olivia gaped at the necklace in her hand like she had never encountered a piece of jewelry. What the heck? Reacting to instinct, she clenched her fingers over the cross to hide it from anyone who might be looking her way and shoved it back into her pocket. The man from the accident must have put it in my pocket.

Her eyes darted around the room to see if anyone had noticed what she was holding. No one was looking at her. She paid for the coffee and hurried back to her car, wiping the specks of blood from her fingers against her jeans.

~

It was two in the morning when Olivia turned onto Obed's Lane and drove slowly down to Whitney Way. The land in this area of Ogunquit had been owned by Aggie's husband's family for over one hundred years. In the early 1900s, parcels had gradually been sold off to other people.

Olivia's house was a three bedroom brick ranch. Its lot was small, but it sat overlooking the ocean, affording a magnificent view from almost every window. The Marginal Way edged along the front of the property. The Way was a mile and a quarter paved public foot path which wound along the cliffs and rocky shoreline of the Atlantic Ocean meandering between shrubs of rosa rugosa and bayberry. The path extended from Shore Road to Perkin's Cove.

Olivia turned into her driveway and parked in front of the one car garage. She walked around to the back lawn. There was a small stone patio with pots of red geraniums and pink and white impatiens scattered around. The moon lit up the night and made a path of silver across the ocean. Olivia took a deep breath of the sea air and stood for a long time, still, quiet, and alone, looking out over the Atlantic.

She shifted her gaze to her neighbor's backyard and smiled at the manicured lawn and the borders of flowers edging his property. Joe was a master gardener whose yard was always bursting with blooms in spring, summer, and fall. Tourists walking by on the Way often stopped to admire Joe's gardens, and if he happened to be out trimming or deadheading, people would engage him in discussions about what he had planted and how he cared for them. Joe was always eager to help and he patiently and good-naturedly answered the same questions over and over.

Joe had lived in the house next to Olivia's for over twenty years. Joe had been Aggie's best friend...more than best friends, and he had been like a father to Olivia since she was a year old.

Olivia returned to her car and took out a small suitcase. She turned the key in the lock of the house. Her house. She wandered from quiet room to quiet room without turning on lights. The kitchen where she and Aggie had cooked pancakes together. The dining room with the cut glass bowl in the center of the old oak table where they had played cards and board games and had done messy crafts that left glue residue and glitter all over the place. The living room where the afternoon light would spread over the puzzle table set up in front of the bay window. The oak bookcases that displayed photographs that Aggie had taken over the years.

Olivia walked down the hallway and into the bedroom that used to be Aggie's room. The moonlight cast a glow across the floorboards and over the double bed covered by the quilt that Aggie had stitched by hand. Each square had some importance. There was a square cut from the satin lining of Aggie's wedding dress, a fabric patch from the dress Olivia had worn on her first day of school. Aggie had embroidered dates and descriptions on some of the pieces. Olivia sat on the bed and ran her hand over the different colored squares.

She reached into her pocket and took out the cross necklace. Recalling how the accident victim had clutched at her, pulling on her jacket, she shuddered. Red Julie. What does it mean? Why did you put this in my pocket? Is it for someone named Julie?

The necklace looked old, maybe antique. Olivia wished she could show it to Aggie.

Aggie had been a lawyer by profession, but she knew all about antiques and, in retirement, ran a small, busy shop near Perkin's Cove. Aggie would go to Europe once a year and on road trips all over New England, Canada, the south, the Midwest, scouring yard sales, flea markets, and estate sales for treasures to sell in her shop.

The house was so quiet. A weight seemed to be

pressing down on Olivia's chest as she sat on Aggie's bed alone in the darkness. Her lower lip quivered. She lifted a pillow from under the covers and rested her face against the soft cotton pillowcase. She caught the faint smell of Aggie's perfume.

Tears tumbled from her eyes and she sobbed.

3

Olivia couldn't sleep and after three hours of tossing and turning, she decided to get up and go for a jog. She did four painful miles through the sleepy, early morning streets and as she turned the corner to her house, she saw Joe Hansen returning from his walk from the other direction.

Joe had turned seventy-two around Christmas time, but was still active and strong from years of working in construction. He was just over six feet, lean, with a full head of silver grey hair and light blue eyes. Olivia smiled and waved and jogged to meet him.

"Liv!" Joe's face was bright and happy. They hugged. "You made it. Get in late?"

"I got in around two," Olivia said. "But I couldn't sleep at all. I got up at six and went for a run." They walked back to their houses together, Olivia's arm linked through Joe's.

"Thanks for stocking the fridge for me," Olivia told him. "And for taking care of the flowers."

"Any time," Joe replied.

"You took your walk already?"

"I try to do my six mile loop early every day. Get it done before I head out to work. Oh, I got a new bike." He chuckled. "It's a tricycle."

Olivia laughed. "A what?"

"You need to see it. It's an adult bike but it has three wheels like a kid's tricycle. It's great for people with balance problems. Or for people who can't ride a regular bike." Joe smiled. "My sister sent it to me. She said I was getting too old to ride a regular bike. She worries about me. For no reason," he added. Olivia knew that Joe's sister must have sent him the bike because Aggie had died riding a bicycle, but she didn't mention it.

"You're in great shape," Olivia told him. "You don't need a bike like that."

"Yeah, well. I kept it. It makes her happy. She doesn't know I don't use it." His eyes twinkled.

"How's the project going?" Olivia asked.

"That one's done. Sold right away. But I have a new one. Got a beauty up in Wells. It's not a beauty yet, but it will be. It's right on the water."

"I'd like to see it," Olivia told him.

After graduating from college with a degree in history, Joe realized that historical renovation and restoration of older homes was how he wanted to spend his working life. He established his own company and, over the years, built a reputation for knowledgeable, high quality work. He was in demand all over the United States and Canada. He had written several books on the subject.

In retirement, Joe had taken up buying, renovating, and selling properties along the Maine coast and he was often invited to speak at historical societies and conventions. He had even been a guest lecturer at Yale and MIT. He said that he was busier now than he had ever been in his life.

"Oh, by the way, there's a new store in the center," Joe said. "A book shop and it has a little café in it too."

"Sounds nice," Olivia said.

"It is. And an old friend of yours is working there," Joe said.

"Really? Who is it?"

"You'll just have to go to the center and check it out one day."

"Joe, come on, tell me."

"Nope."

They reached their houses and stood at the end of Olivia's driveway. "How about I treat you to dinner?" Joe asked. "We never got to have a proper graduation celebration, with Aggie passing and all."

Olivia had graduated from Tufts University a few weeks after Aggie passed away. She had stayed in Medford for two extra weeks to finish some research she had worked on with one of the Tufts professors, to clean up her apartment and close out her lease. "I'd like that. Where should we eat?"

"Your choice. Where would you like to go?"

"Let's go down to Perkins Cove. Let's go early," Olivia said. "Before the crowd shows up. Want to leave around five?"

"Sounds like tradition." Joe smiled, but his eyes got all watery. Aggie, Joe, and Olivia always went early to dinner and sat outside on the patio of their favorite restaurant, surrounded by flowers, overlooking the harbor.

Joe swallowed hard trying to clear the grief out of his throat. "I'll be back at five. We can walk down to the cove on the Marginal Way." Joe stared at Olivia for a few seconds. "I'm glad you're back, Liv." He hugged her.

Olivia wrapped her arms around him. "Me, too."

"It'll be okay. We'll be okay," Joe whispered, trying to convince them both.

She nodded.

"I'll see you at five." Joe turned, but paused before crossing the lawn to his own house. "Liv, you do anything wrong by any chance?" he asked her.

Olivia looked at him with a puzzled expression.

Joe cocked his head to his right. Olivia turned to look.

A dark car was coming down the lane. "Looks like an unmarked police car," Joe told her.

It stopped at the end of the driveway.

A tall muscular man came around the front of the car. "Morning," he said.

"Morning," Olivia and Joe replied.

"I'm Detective Michaels." He opened a leather wallet and flashed his badge at them. "Are you Olivia Miller?" he asked.

"Yes, I am."

"Sorry to bother you, but I'm just following up on the accident report you gave last night."

"You were in an accident?" Joe asked, concerned.

"No, I saw an accident," she said. "Well, I didn't see it happen. I came on it afterwards. I was going to tell you about it tonight."

"Do you mind if I ask you a few more questions, Ms. Miller?" the detective asked.

"No, I don't mind. Would you like to come into the house?"

"No, thank you." The man shook his head. "This should only take a few minutes." He pulled out a notebook.

Olivia recounted what she had told the officer the night before.

"Did you notice anything unusual about the victim?"

"How do you mean?" Olivia asked.

"Did he say anything to you?"

She shook her head. "No. Well...he was trying to say something. Tell me something. But he ...there was blood in his mouth." Olivia tensed up recalling what she had seen. Joe put his arm around her. "I couldn't understand what he said. It was all just garbled."

"You're sure there was nothing you could make out?" the detective asked.

Shaking her head again, Olivia said, "Nothing. Sorry."

The man wrote in his notebook. "Okay then. Thank you for your time. Sorry to bother you so early." The detective shook their hands and went back to his car. He turned in Olivia's driveway, backed out and drove away.

Olivia's face was ashen.

"You okay?" Joe questioned.

She looked at Joe. "The man died at the scene."

"Oh, no." Joe looked down. "I'm sorry you had to see that." He took her arm and walked her to her door.

AT FIVE, Joe stood in Olivia's kitchen while she found her sandals and pulled them on. "I'm starving," she announced. "Can't wait to eat."

They headed out the door. "Wait, I want to get my

wallet." Olivia turned back and grabbed it off the kitchen counter. Joe stood in the open doorway.

"What the hell?" he muttered. He was looking out at the road.

Olivia came up beside him to see what had Joe's attention.

"Now what?" she asked when she saw what was outside. A police car had pulled up and parked beside her front lawn. An officer got out and started up her driveway. She and Joe looked at each other. Olivia sighed. They stepped out onto the walkway.

"Hello. I'm Officer Chapman. Are you Olivia Miller?" he asked.

"Yes, I am."

"Ms. Miller, would you mind if I follow up with you on the accident you saw last night?'

Olivia's face was stern. "Okay. But how many times do I have to answer these questions?"

The officer was polite. "We just sometimes need to follow up. It won't take long." He took out a small notebook. "Was the man conscious when you arrived on the scene, Ms. Miller?"

"Like I said to the detective this morning..."

The officer interrupted. "Detective?"

"The detective who came this morning," Olivia told him.

"What was his name?"

Olivia and Joe looked at each other. Joe shook his head.

"I didn't get his name." Olivia thought for a moment. "Wait...it was...Michaels. Detective Michaels."

"What did he say?" the officer asked.

"He asked about the accident. He asked me what the man said to me. Things like that."

The officer looked from Olivia to Joe. "Would you excuse me for a minute?" He walked back to his patrol car and got in. He sat there for a while talking into his radio.

"What's going on?" Olivia asked Joe.

"Not sure. But something isn't right."

The officer came back up the driveway. "Sorry to keep you waiting." He hesitated. "Would you mind coming down to the station?"

"The station?" Olivia's voice was high.

"What's this about?" Joe asked.

"No need for concern. It will only take a little while," the officer said. "The captain would like to have a word with you. Simply precautionary."

"Precautionary?" Joe repeated.

Olivia looked pained. "Am I in some sort of trouble?"

"No, no. Nothing like that," the officer responded. He hesitated again, almost said something else but thought better of it. "The captain will explain it all to you." He smiled.

Olivia and Joe exchanged glances.

"What should I do?" Olivia asked Joe.

Joe looked at the officer. "Guess it can't hurt to go down there. See what this is about. But I'm going along."

The three of them got into the police car and headed to the headquarters.

"So much for our early dinner," Joe complained.

"WHAT DO you mean you don't have a Detective Michaels here?" Olivia demanded.

"It appears that the man who paid you a visit this morning is an imposter," the captain informed them. "There is no record of a Detective Michaels at any of the departments in the area."

Letting to a breath, Olivia asked, "Could he have been a private investigator?"

"He should have identified himself as such," the captain said. "There are private investigators working in the area, but we know them and have a fairly good relationship with them."

"Couldn't he have been from out of the area? Hired by someone not living around here?" Joe asked.

"Certainly possible. But PIs usually identify themselves appropriately. This man who paid you a visit? As far as we know, he is not a legitimate member of any law enforcement agency. And he could be brought in for impersonating a police officer," the captain said. He directed his attention to Olivia.

"If he shows up again, refuse to speak with him. And as soon as you are away from him, call 911," the captain urged. "Do not put yourself in danger by confronting him in any way."

Olivia nodded.

"Ms. Miller...I hate to ask you...but would you be willing to speak with one of the state police detectives on Monday?"

"Is that necessary?" Joe asked.

"It would be most appreciated...because of a turn of events."

Joe and Olivia looked confused.

"What do you mean?" Olivia asked.

The captain hesitated. His expression was serious. He cleared his throat. "The victim...the man who died at the scene. He had been shot."

Olivia's and Joe's eyes widened.

The chief cleared his throat again and continued, "You couldn't understand him because he...his tongue had been cut out of his mouth."

Olivia gasped.

Joe shook his head. "Ugh, no," he said.

4

Joe and Olivia skipped the restaurant. They picked up a pizza and walked back to Joe's house. He made a fire in his fire pit and they sat in the yard munching on slices loaded with cheese, tomatoes, peppers and mushrooms.

Joe had a beer and Olivia was sipping iced tea. The sun was setting and the sky was a mix of blues, violets and pinks. The slight ocean breeze cooled the air from the unseasonable heat of the day. It was getting dark, but tourists still streamed by on the Marginal Way.

"Have you thought about what you're going to do with Aggie's shop?" Joe asked, leaning back in the Adirondack chair. He wanted to talk about something besides the accident.

"Yeah. At first, I was just going to put it up for sale, but now I'm thinking about opening it up. Maybe just limited hours this summer. It will keep me busy and give me time to think about whether to keep it or not. I don't know a fifth of what Aggie knew about antiques, but I'm willing to learn. And I could definitely use some income."

"Sounds like a smart plan."

"I want to keep the house, too," Olivia said. "It's my home."

"I'm sure that will break Magdalene Streeter's heart," Joe chuckled. "She'll be after you about selling it, you know. Visions of dollar signs must be dancing in her head. She'd been barking up Aggie and my trees lately about selling the houses. You know how she is, all sweet when she wants something. Any time we'd run into her, she would pour it on, 'You two should start thinking about selling those houses of yours. Wouldn't you like it better somewhere warm?'" Joe shook his head. "That woman is not subtle."

"That's her. That's why she is such a successful real estate broker, I guess," Olivia said.

Joe rolled his eyes. "Don't let her bully you, Liv. I'm sure she'll approach you soon to see if you're planning to sell."

"What do you think, Joe? Can I handle owning the house on my own?"

"Of course you can. I'm here. I'll help you if you need it."

"Aggie left some money that I can use for property

taxes and utilities," Olivia said. "I think it will be enough until I finish law school."

"It's your house, Liv. If you want to keep it, then we'll make it work."

"Thanks, Joe. I don't know what I'd do without you," she said softly. After a minute, Olivia said, "I need to talk to you about the accident."

Joe nodded. "Awful. When I got coffee after my walk this morning, I heard people in the bakery talking about it. I didn't know then that you had been at the scene." He took another slice of pizza from the box. "The victim owned the house at the corner of the point. He was some sort of financial advisor...investments, wealth planning, stuff like that. Name was Martin Andersen."

"I don't remember ever seeing him around," Olivia said.

"The guy lived in Boston. Owned the beach house for about three years but didn't use it that much. Guess he worked a lot."

"You ever meet him?" Olivia asked.

"No. Never knew his name. Until now. I understand he had a partner but no other family."

Olivia was quiet for a minute. "So what the hell happened? The accident...he'd been shot...the tongue?" She shuddered.

Joe shrugged and shook his head. "Nasty business. Gruesome."

"The man...Andersen...he was trying to tell me something. I couldn't make it out. I thought he was calling for someone else in the car. But the car was empty."

"Cops didn't find anyone else. They must have searched around in case there was a passenger. Thrown out of the car or whatever..."

"Andersen was so frantic...I assumed he was just in shock. He was pulling on me...like he wanted me to get him out of the car...or he didn't want to be left alone...just grabbing at me...pulling my jacket. His legs were all tangled in the metal. It was awful, Joe. I couldn't help him. I couldn't understand him."

Olivia wiped her hands on a paper napkin. "Now I think he was trying to tell me something. Something important."

"What did it sound like he was saying?" Joe asked. "Could you get any part of it?"

Olivia was quiet for a minute. "It sounded like he was saying something like...'red Julie'."

"Red Julie," Joe repeated. He thought about that. "'Julie'...Cops said he didn't have any relatives. A friend? Ex-wife? Co-worker? Pet? But what's the 'red' part of it?"

"I might've gotten it wrong. It was hard to make out. It's just what it sounded like."

Joe took a pull of his beer. They looked out over the darkening Atlantic.

"There's more," Olivia said.

Joe looked at her.

"Andersen started really panicking while we were waiting for the ambulance." She paused. "He was making these awful noises and trying to roll from side to side. Like he was trying to pull himself out of the car." Olivia rubbed her forehead. "I was scared." Her voice was soft.

"Naturally..." Joe said. Olivia didn't say anything else. She kept rubbing her forehead and started to massage her temples.

"What?" Joe asked.

Olivia lifted her eyes to him. "Andersen looked over my shoulder...his face was horrified...I turned. There was a man standing so close to me. I didn't even hear him approach. He said nothing. It was so weird, Joe. He just stared at Andersen. Just glared at him. His face was... mean, like nothing I've ever seen. Andersen was flipping out, making screaming noises and grunts." She shivered.

"So what happened? This man say anything?"

"Nothing. Just staring. I felt...I don't know...menace... something bad. I felt like I had to protect Andersen. I know it sounds crazy. It was an instinct, a feeling. Like this other man was...evil." Olivia's hand shook as she lifted her glass from the grass next to her chair. She sipped. "His pant leg was wet. I think he was bleeding, Joe."

"So what did he do? What happened?" Joe asked.

"I told him to back off."

Joe's eyes went wide. "You did?" He smiled and added, "I don't know why I'm surprised."

Olivia swallowed hard. "He looked me in the eye then. It was bad. His look. I thought he was going to kill us both."

Joe's face creased with worry.

"Some people pulled over just then. Ran over to us. The cops arrived too...and the paramedics. I ...I didn't see him anymore after that. He disappeared. The officer came right up to me and started asking questions."

Joe shook his head.

"There's something else," Olivia said.

Joe raised his eyebrows.

"I was wearing my tan jacket. After the accident, I was upset, shaking, so I stopped for a coffee. I reached into my pocket for my money."

She put her hand in the pocket of her shorts. "And found this." She opened her outstretched hand.

Joe leaned forward. "A necklace? A cross?" He picked it up and turned it in his hand a few times, inspecting it. "Looks valuable." He saw the engraved 'S' and traced it with his finger. "An initial." He looked at Olivia. "Not Martin Andersen's initial obviously."

"No," she said. "Why would he put it in my pocket, Joe? He's the only one who could have put it there. Why not just hand it to me?"

Joe stared at it. "He must have given it to you deliberately."

Olivia nodded. "I agree. But why? Why put it in my pocket?"

Joe kept staring at it as if he might glean some answer by looking. He raised his eyes. "I guess he didn't want anyone to see it?" Joe offered.

"So did he steal it?" Olivia asked. "Did he want me to return it to someone? To Julie, maybe? Whoever she is." She sighed. "Or did he want me to hide it from someone and that's why he slipped it into my pocket?"

Joe shrugged. "It must have been important to him since he made sure he gave it to you. In the midst of being trapped in the car and the tongue and the gunshot wound." Joe winced at the thought of the man's accident and injuries. "The guy's dying but he makes sure he gives you this necklace. In secret." He shook his head and passed the necklace back to Olivia.

"You didn't tell the cops this stuff," Joe said.

"No."

"Why not?"

Olivia shook her head. "Not sure. It doesn't feel right." She looked up at Joe. "It seems like I have an obligation. To do the right thing. To honor Martin Andersen's intention." She put the necklace back in her pocket. "But first I have to figure out what that intention is."

5

Olivia walked into town to meet with the manager of the bank about Aggie's accounts. On the way home, she wanted to pick up a few things at the food market. The store was small but it had an excellent array of products. She and Joe were planning on grilling chicken and vegetables for dinner and Olivia wanted to make a lemon marinade.

When she reached the town center, Olivia noticed the new book shop across the street. A man was out front sweeping the sidewalk. He turned towards the road continuing his cleaning. Olivia smiled in surprise.

Brad Walker. She hadn't seen him since she was fourteen. They had been friends from the time they were seven years old. They both spent every summer in Ogunquit until his family moved to the west coast and didn't travel to Maine anymore.

Every summer day, they would swim, bike, climb trees, kayak, read, and sit by Joe's fire pit at night and tell ghost stories. Brad gave Olivia a compliment once, telling her gratefully, 'You're as much fun as a boy and you're not afraid of snakes or spiders.'

Actually she was afraid of snakes but she wouldn't show her fear to Brad. Brad, his parents, and five sisters would come to Ogunquit around the twentieth of June and would stay for two months. As soon as Brad arrived, he and Olivia would pick up where they left off ten months before, as if they hadn't been apart at all.

When they were fourteen, a new girl came to town for the last few weeks of the summer. Brad was smitten with the girl and he spent days mooning over her which drove Olivia crazy. When Brad asked the girl to the movies one evening, Olivia was furious.

Every day for two weeks, he spent with the new girl. Olivia wanted to gouge her eyes out. Olivia would sit in Aggie's shop in the afternoons, moaning while Aggie tended the store. "Why would he want to hang around with her? She just does her hair and doesn't want to swim and wears makeup and she's so boring," Olivia would say.

Aggie just listened.

Some days, Olivia would ride with Joe to one of his house projects and would fume and rant while Joe painted or tiled or repaired. He tried to give Olivia a job to do to distract her but she was so angry she would only do it half-heartedly or with such rage that she risked ruining whatever task Joe had assigned her.

That was the last summer Brad and his family came to Ogunquit and, at the time, Olivia had resented that he had ruined their last weeks together in favor of some blonde pixie.

Olivia watched Brad for a few minutes. She hadn't seen him for seven years. He was tall now, with broad shoulders, but she would have recognized him from any angle or distance.

The best friend I ever had.

The sight of him warmed her with the sun of other summers, and of things that used to be but weren't any more.

She crossed the street. Brad looked up as she approached and recognition passed over his face. They smiled at each other.

"In the market for a new book?' he asked.

"I might be," she replied.

"Then you've come to the right place."

Olivia nodded. Brad stepped forward and hugged her. Olivia realized that despite all the summers they had spent together, they had never hugged before.

"You look good," he told her.

"You too," she said.

His face was serious. "I'm sorry about Aggie."

"Thanks," Olivia said. She blinked and changed the subject. "So, you're back and working here."

"Actually I own it."

"You do? Well, congratulations."

"Thanks. I'm going to try to make a go of it. I know everything's ebooks now but some people still want to hold the book in their hands. I have a little café inside too. I'm planning on having author readings and signings and sometimes some music in the evenings."

"Wow, I'm impressed," Olivia told him.

His dark brown hair flopped over his forehead. His eyes were the color of the sky and to Olivia's surprise her heart did a little flip. He leaned on the broom.

"I finished college a year early. Then I spent last year working in an independent book store while I developed my business plan. Decided to move back here and set up shop."

"I hope it works out, Brad. It looks great."

"I hear you're going to law school in the fall," Brad said.

Olivia looked surprised. "Yeah, I am."

"I see Joe a lot. He told me. Harvard. Wow, that's great. Just like Aggie."

Olivia nodded.

"She was always so proud of you," Brad said.

Some people approached and entered the store. Brad put the broom against the door jamb.

"Have time to come in?" he asked.

"Not right now. I have an appointment. Another time though," she said.

"Come by anytime. Maybe you'll even get a free latte."

"Really?"

"Yeah. I know the owner." Brad grinned. He took a few steps toward the entrance but stopped before going in and turned back to Olivia. "Sorry about that last summer. I was dumb."

"Yeah," Olivia said. "You were." She smiled at him.

SUNDAY NIGHT, Joe and Olivia made it to their favorite restaurant in the cove. They sat outside on the patio and had a fine meal while watching the boats in the cove. They raised their glasses and toasted their dear Aggie.

They walked home along the ocean.

"It's going to take a long time to go through Aggie's stuff," Olivia said.

Joe nodded.

"Anything you'd like of hers? To remember her by?"

Joe smiled. He shook his head. "I got all I need to remember her right in here." He touched his chest at his heart.

"How come you two never got married?" Olivia asked.

Joe laughed. "She never asked me."

Olivia laughed at that. "You could've asked her."

Joe looked at Olivia. "I was afraid she wouldn't have me."

"Right." Olivia shook her head. "I see I'm getting nowhere with this line of questioning."

"Maybe after your first year of law school is finished, your techniques will have improved. You can ask me again then." He winked at Olivia.

"I will," Olivia said. "Joe, do you have Aggie's laptop and cell phone at your house? I can't find them."

"No. Did you check her car?" Aggie's car was parked in one of Joe's garage bays.

"I did. They aren't in there. I've looked all over the house. Her computer backup drive isn't there either."

"Must be at the shop," Joe offered.

"Yeah, I'll go down to the store in the next couple of days. There's so much to do with closing her accounts, paying bills and all, I just haven't had a chance to get to the shop. What about her camera? Did she leave it at your house? I can't find that either."

"I don't think so. I don't recall seeing it. I'll look around for it," Joe told her. "If there's anything you need me to do to help, I'm here."

"I might take you up on that. I want to see what's down in the basement, but you know how I hate dark, closed in spaces."

"Yes, I do. Joe chuckled. "Think it has anything to do with getting yourself locked in that closet when you were little?"

Olivia rolled her eyes. "It could."

Aggie used to have an old walnut wardrobe in the basement where she kept winter coats and jackets. On a rainy day when Olivia was five, she was playing in the basement and decided it would be a good idea to hide in the wardrobe. The door locked when she pulled it shut. Her screams brought Aggie and Joe running to the cellar where Joe had to pull the old wooden door off with a crowbar. The wardrobe was hauled to the dump the next day.

Joe and Olivia walked along in silence for a while, then came to one of the many benches placed along the Marginal Way. They were almost to their houses.

"Want to sit for a bit?" Joe asked.

"Yeah, let's," Olivia answered. They sat side by side looking out over the sea. The first stars were dotting the sky.

"How can she be gone, Joe?"

"Don't know, Sweet Pea," Joe sighed.

"She was fine when I came up here for a few days on my March school break."

Joe nodded.

"You saw her everyday. Did she seem tired? Run

down? Did you notice anything different about her? Was she worried about something?"

Joe rubbed his palms on his pants and took a deep breath. "No...nothing. I guess when it's your time..."

"You don't believe that...neither do I."

Olivia turned to Joe. Tears were streaming down his face.

"Joe..." She put her arm around his shoulders.

He used both hands to brush away the tears. He forced a smile. "Big tough guy."

"It happens to me all the time," Olivia told him, her voice wobbly. "Everything's fine and then something, a scent, the breeze on my arm, a word, the way the light comes in through the window, makes me think of her and the thought of never seeing Aggie again punches me right in the gut and I almost double over. I'll be driving in the car or standing in the shower and the tears come pouring out."

Joe nodded, his shoulders slumped. They sat in silence.

"Does the pain ever go away?" Olivia asked.

"It turns into a big hard knot, a lump that stays in your heart forever. Time goes by and it doesn't hurt as much," Joe told her. "But that lump is always there."

When Joe was thirty-four, he lost his wife to cancer after ten years of marriage and was left to raise their two year old son alone. Joe's son was now a prominent oncologist working in Boston.

Olivia sighed and slipped her arm through Joe's. More stars twinkled in the sky.

"Thanks for straightening up the house and all. After Aggie died. Thanks for getting rid of the bike, too," Olivia said.

Joe nodded.

"I know it wasn't easy for you to do that. Thanks for taking care of everything so I could finish up school."

"It hasn't been easy on either one of us," Joe said.

Olivia looked back out over the ocean. "Why was she out so late? Where was she going? Why was she on my bike? She never rode that thing."

"I guess we'll never know for sure. The police assume she was heading to the shop. But it wouldn't have mattered if she was on that bike or not."

"How could she have a massive heart attack? She was in better shape than you are."

Joe cocked his head at her. "Thanks a lot. Does that mean I can expect to go at any time?"

"You know what I mean," she told him.

"Just don't remind me how old I am."

"She was active. Involved." Olivia shook her head. "She was only sixty-three. That isn't old." She stared at the waves pounding the rocks.

"How do they know she had a heart attack?" Olivia went on.

"Well...I don't know. They just know."

"They didn't do an autopsy. Maybe it was the fall from the bike that killed her. Maybe she got distracted. Maybe she lost control of the bike and ..."

"Liv...she had a heart attack...she fell off the bike but that wouldn't have caused the fatality." He was quiet. "Anyway, the result is the same."

Olivia's leg jiggled up and down. She ran her hands through her chestnut hair. The air was cooler now.

"Should we go home?" Joe asked.

"Not yet." Olivia didn't say anything for a few minutes. She sighed. "Something's not right."

"How do you mean?"

"Aggie died but there was nothing wrong with her."

Joe started to shake his head.

"Why would someone cut out someone's tongue?" Olivia asked.

"I don't know. So he couldn't speak...to stop him from talking,"

"Exactly. So what did Andersen know that someone didn't want him telling? Why slip that necklace into my pocket? What's 'red Julie' mean?"

Joe turned his palms up. "Don't know."

Olivia continued to fire off questions. "Who was that man who showed up and menaced me at the accident?

48

Who was that guy impersonating a cop that came to talk to me?"

Joe looked at her.

"Aggie didn't say anything to you before you went to visit your sister those last two weeks of April? She wasn't worried about anything?"

"No. She didn't tell me anything of the sort. We emailed back and forth during the two weeks I was in California. Just general chit chat."

"And then she dies," Olivia said. "Doing something she never does."

"What are you getting at, Liv?"

"She was in contact with you almost every day that you were away. But she never told you what was wrong. She was closer to you than anyone, besides me. Why didn't she say anything?"

"Maybe there was nothing to tell."

"Maybe she was trying to protect you...and me," Olivia said. "And why didn't she go to the police?"

"The police? For what? Protect us from what?"

"There's only one reason she wouldn't go to the police," Olivia said.

Joe stared at her.

"She didn't trust them."

"Liv, why would she go to the police? About what?"

"Something must have been worrying her. Something must have had her afraid."

"Like what?"

Olivia shrugged.

"Well, if something was worrying her, how do we know she didn't go to the police? Maybe she did go to the police. We don't know," Joe said, exasperated.

Olivia shook her head. "The chief would have told us."

"Why are you so sure that something was wrong?" Joe asked.

Olivia looked at him. "Come on. I'll show you."

OLIVIA LED Joe into the extra bedroom that Aggie had used as a den. She opened the closet door. Aggie had a small safe built into the closet wall where she kept important papers, some old jewelry that she never wore but couldn't part with, her and Olivia's passports, and a few hundred dollars in cash.

Joe and Olivia both knew about the safe and both had the combination. Olivia turned the knob, punched in the code, and opened the safe. She stepped back. Joe moved closer. His eyes widened.

He turned to Olivia. "A gun?"

She nodded. "I was going through her things. I found it this afternoon." She paused. "There's something else."

"Every time you say that, it's never anything good," Joe muttered.

Olivia led him to Aggie's bedroom. She opened the third drawer of Aggie's dresser and pushed some sweaters aside. Joe looked.

He shook his head. "What the hell?"

A butcher knife and some pepper spray lay in the drawer.

They looked at each other.

"This is why I think something was wrong," Olivia said.

6

Olivia had an appointment to meet with the detective, the real detective, on Monday morning. She told Joe that she would be fine meeting with him alone, so Joe went to Wells for the day to work on his house project.

The detective asked Olivia to meet him at a coffee shop at the edge of town. She arrived first, got tea, and took it outside to the patio tables overlooking the main street. The tables were crowded with early morning tourists and some locals scattered here and there.

Olivia watched the patrons who were approaching the coffee shop. She and the detective had swapped descriptions of each other over the phone. A man fitting the detective's description walked into the patio area and Olivia raised her hand to signal to him.

He nodded and headed over to her table. The detective was tall, lean, but muscular, and younger than Olivia expected. She thought he must be in his late twenties. He wore a pair of navy slacks and a fitted white collared shirt which left no doubt that this was a man who worked out. A lot. He got more than a few admiring glances from the women customers as he passed them.

Olivia stood.

"Ms. Miller?"

"Yes. Nice to meet you, Detective."

They shook hands and sat down.

"Jason Brown. Thank you for meeting me," he told Olivia. "I won't take too much of your time. As Captain O'Brien told you, the case has taken an unexpected turn with suspicion of foul play," the detective said.

"Suspicion?" Olivia asked.

Detective Brown met Olivia's eyes. "Yes. We can't be sure what we're dealing with until we look into things."

"He had his tongue cut out. He'd been shot. That sounds like foul play to me."

"True." Brown opened his leather folder and took out his pad and pen. "Would you mind recounting for me the events of the night when you came upon the accident?"

Olivia took a deep breath and looked down at her tea cup. She recalled what happened from the time she turned onto the exit ramp until she got back in her car and drove away. She left out a few things.

Brown's eyes met Olivia's. He didn't say anything.

"Is this the productive pause where if the officer doesn't say anything the interviewee will keep talking?" Olivia asked.

"It could be," Brown replied. He sat without saying anything.

Olivia just looked at him. She stayed quiet, then said, "If you're looking for something more, I guess you'll have to ask."

"Is there more to know?"

Olivia shrugged. "I don't know what else to tell you."

Brown wrote in his notebook.

"Ogunquit's a pretty small town. I'm surprised there's a detective on staff," Olivia said.

Without looking up, Brown said, "I'm with the State Police. Originally out of Portland but I've been working the York-Ogunquit-Wells area for the past year or so."

"This must be quieter than around Portland," Olivia said.

"There's trouble everywhere, I'm afraid."

Brown made eye contact with Olivia. "Did the victim say anything?"

"Nothing I could understand."

"What about other witnesses? Was anyone else around?"

"I thought I saw a man running away from the overturned car. It was very dark. I didn't see where he went.

No one else was around until just before the cops and paramedics arrived."

"So you didn't notice anyone else in the area when you came on the scene?"

"No." Olivia didn't know if she should tell him about the man.

Brown stared at Olivia. "I get the feeling you're not telling me everything, Ms. Miller."

Sweat beaded up on the back of Olivia's neck. "I..." She shrugged.

"Think back on the night. Just walk yourself through it all again in your mind. See if anything new comes up. Take your time." He went back to writing in his notebook.

Olivia felt unnerved. After a minute she said, "I remember that there was a man off to the side."

Brown lifted his eyes.

"The guy on the ground. He seemed upset by the man's presence."

"How so?" Brown asked.

"He seemed more than upset. He seemed terrified. The man gave me the creeps, actually."

"Did you just remember him now?"

Olivia shook her head. "No. I didn't say anything because...I don't know...it didn't seem relevant."

Brown said, "Just tell me what you saw. I'll decide if it's relevant."

Olivia didn't like his tone. She lifted her tea cup to her lips while keeping eye contact with Brown.

They were both quiet.

"Another pause?" Olivia asked with an edge to her voice.

Brown sat straighter in his chair and asked, "Had you ever seen this man before? Did he seem familiar in any way?"

"No. He wasn't familiar to me. I would have remembered him if I had seen him before."

"Can you describe him?'

"The guy was tall and slim. Muscular, but not heavy. He was wearing a suit. It was dark out so I didn't see that much. But he had a look on his face. Cold. Mean. It chilled me. I felt... in danger."

"Could you pick him out of a lineup?"

Olivia tilted her head. "A lineup?" She paused, thinking. "It was dark. We were under the streetlight, but, no, maybe not. No, I don't think I could."

"Did he say anything?" Brown asked.

"Nothing," Olivia said. "Really. He didn't."

"Did you notice a vehicle?"

Olivia shook her head.

"Was he still there when the officers arrived?"

"I didn't see him anymore after the authorities arrived."

Brown looked at the cars passing by on the street. He turned to Olivia. "Why were you afraid of him?"

Olivia thought. "A feeling. His eyes. His silence." She added, "I could imagine him doing that...with the tongue. Or worse."

Brown changed the subject. "How long have you lived on Whitney Way?"

"Well, ever since I was very little I would spend summers there, and some weekends, holidays. My aunt owned the house. I lost my parents when I was one. My aunt became my legal guardian."

"You know a lot of people in town?"

"Some."

"But not the victim?"

Olivia shook her head.

"Why not?"

Olivia cocked her head. It seemed a strange question. "Ogunquit's a small town, but obviously I don't know everyone here. As I said, I'm usually just here in the summers."

"Well it seems the victim knew you."

Olivia blinked.

"He had your name in his wallet. And your picture with your address in Medford written on the back."

A chill raced down Olivia's spine and her brow furrowed. She opened her mouth but nothing came out.

She closed her mouth. Her eyes were like saucers. "He... my name? Why?"

"That's what I hoped you could tell me," the detective told her.

"I have no idea." Olivia's eyes darted around. Her mind raced. She shook her head. "No idea at all."

7

Olivia walked home from the meeting with the detective as fast as she could. She sat at her computer and with hands shaking, typed the victim's name and the word "obituary" into Google. She hit enter.

She clicked on the listing that came up in the search. When the page opened, the man's picture was in the upper left corner of the write-up and his smiling face made Olivia jump.

She pored over the words. Martin Andersen. Age 52. Lived in Boston. Educated at Dartmouth. MBA Yale Business School. Relatives deceased. Owner of Andersen Financial. Long time environmental activist. Leaves his partner, S. Rodney Hannigan of Boston. Funeral would be Wednesday at 2pm.

Olivia re-read it. She leaned back in her chair. Why

was my picture and address in your wallet, Martin? Who are you? Who were you? Her eyes scanned the write-up again. She made a note. Rodney Hannigan. Looks like I'm going to a funeral, Olivia thought.

JOE STOOD next to Olivia's Jeep as she opened the driver's side door.

"I wish you'd let me go along," Joe pouted.

"It would be a waste of your time. I'm just going to talk to him. It'll be fine. No sense in you losing time on your project," Olivia said. "I'll be ok, Joe. Nothing's going to happen to me at a funeral."

"If the guy seems unreceptive then just leave. Don't push."

"I won't push."

Joe took a deep breath. "I'm uneasy, Liv."

"I know. Me, too. I'll be careful." Olivia hugged him. "I promise."

Olivia got into the Jeep, buckled the seat belt and started the engine.

"Call me when you're on your way back," Joe said.

Olivia rolled her eyes at him.

"I mean it," Joe told her. "Humor an old man."

Olivia smiled. "Okay, okay."

She waved as she pulled away.

I T T O O K an hour and a half for Olivia to make it to Boston. She used her GPS to find the church and pulled into the parking area in the back.

The lot was nearly full. Groups of people were congregating on the sidewalk and in front of the church. Olivia climbed the granite steps and took a seat in the back pew. She wanted to scan the crowd as they entered, but she wasn't sure what she expected to see.

People took their seats and music began to play. The priest and attendants led the coffin procession down the aisle. A slender, well-groomed man followed behind. His face was drawn and pale. His eyes were red.

Near the end of the service, the funeral director made an announcement inviting attendees to join Mr. Hannigan at a nearby restaurant for luncheon immediately following the ceremony. Burial would be private.

Olivia rose and quietly left the church. She walked to the restaurant and waited outside on the sidewalk. People began to arrive from the church. Two men were about to enter the restaurant when Olivia stepped forward.

"Mr. Hannigan?"

One of the men turned to Olivia.

"May I have a moment?" she asked.

The well-dressed man nodded and his companion went in alone.

"I'm sorry for your loss and I'm sorry to bother you at this time, but I wondered if I could ask you some questions? My name is Olivia Miller."

"Questions?" Hannigan asked.

"I sat with Mr. Andersen after the accident. Until the ambulance arrived. I was the first one on the scene."

Hannigan's eyes misted over. "I see," he managed. He swallowed and cleared his throat. "Thank you for staying with him. I'm grateful that he wasn't alone."

"Mr. Hannigan, my aunt passed away in early May. Under what I think...well, what I think are strange circumstances. These two deaths, so close together, they seem...suspicious." Olivia paused and went on. "Being at the scene with Mr. Andersen, the police took my statement and questioned me."

Mr. Hannigan nodded.

"The police said that Mr. Andersen had my name and address and picture in his wallet."

Mr. Hannigan's eyes widened. "You knew each other?" Hannigan asked.

"No. That's what's so puzzling. We never met. Do you have any idea why he had my name? Did he ever mention me to you?"

"No. Never."

"Did either of you know my aunt? Her name was Aggie Whitney."

Hannigan shook his head. "No. The name isn't familiar."

"I don't know what's going on," Olivia whispered. "Do you know anyone who would want to hurt Mr. Andersen?"

"No, of course not. Martin was kind, gentle. He was a good friend to everyone. Helpful. A good person. I don't know. I don't know how this happened." Tears started to run down Hannigan's face.

"I'm sorry," Olivia said and touched his arm. "Was anything different? Did he seem like anything was bothering him? Was he worried? Stressed?"

"No. He seemed himself for the most part. Martin was never secretive. He told me everything. He had been in Europe on business until the day before he died."

"How long was he in Europe?"

"Four weeks. He left May 2. I remember the date because it was my birthday. We had dinner at the airport just before Martin left."

Olivia's face was serious. Aggie had died on the night of May 1.

"Was it a scheduled trip?"

"No. In fact, it was quite last minute. Martin had been staying at the house in Ogunquit for about a month. He was working on a book on personal finance and was running his business from the beach house. He was planning on spending two more weeks in Ogunquit but he came home unexpectedly the night before he left for Europe. He said a client in London needed him right away, so he booked the flight for the next day."

"Do you know who the client was?"

"I don't."

"Was it unusual for Mr. Andersen to be called away like that?"

"Oh, not at all. Martin had many high end international clients. When they were in need, they expected Martin there immediately."

"When did Mr. Hannigan return from London?" Olivia asked.

"The day he was killed."

"So the very day he returned from Europe, he made a trip back to Ogunquit?" Olivia asked.

"He said that when he was called away so suddenly in May he had left another client's paperwork at the beach house," Hannigan said. "He said it was essential. He was planning to drive up that night from the airport, pick up what he needed, have dinner, and return the same evening."

Olivia nodded.

Hannigan said, "We both have demanding careers with many late nights, overseas travel, events we are expected to attend. I should have canceled my meeting the night he returned. I should have gone to Ogunquit with him. I should have been with him. I..."

Olivia touched his arm. "No one can predict what's going to happen," she said quietly.

"The police are investigating. But, so far, no leads." Hannigan let out a sigh and shook his head.

Olivia paused. Her mind was racing. "Where did Mr. Andersen stay when he went to London?"

"He always stayed at the Goring."

"The Goring? For four weeks?"

Hannigan nodded.

"Would you mind if I looked into Mr. Andersen's stay?"

Hannigan looked quizzical.

"Things just don't seem right to me," Olivia said. "Because of the unusual circumstances around my aunt's and your partner's deaths. Something was wrong. Although, I don't even know where to start or how I would find out anything."

"Yes." Hannigan spoke in a whisper and the burden of sadness caused his face muscles to droop. "You have my permission. It can't hurt for you to look into it. Do what you can. See what you can find out."

"Do you know the name of any of the clients that Mr. Andersen had in London?"

Hannigan closed his eyes for a moment and shook his head. "I know it sounds like I don't know anything about

Martin, but I have no idea who he went to see when he traveled on business," Hannigan said. "Perhaps you can contact his secretary, Paula Adams. She worked for Martin for years. She booked his flights, kept his calendar and appointments. Her email is on the company website. Tell her that we spoke and that she has my permission to answer your questions."

"I'll do that," Olivia said, then hesitated before saying, "I haven't told the police this. I don't know...I'm not sure I want to share this with them. Mr. Andersen said something to me at the scene...it was garbled...it was something like...'red Julie'. Do you know what he might have meant?"

Hannigan repeated, "Red Julie. I don't know."

"Did he know anyone named Julie? A friend? Someone at work? In your building?"

"Not to my knowledge. I can't think of anyone. Julie. I don't know." He looked at Olivia. "Olivia, why don't you want to tell the police this detail?"

Olivia took a deep breath. "My aunt seemed to know something...or fear something. She didn't tell her best friend what she was worried about. She didn't tell me. She didn't go to the police. It makes me wonder why."

Hannigan shook his head. "Please keep me informed. I'm going to keep our conversation in confidence." They exchanged cell numbers and email addresses.

A friend of Hannigan's emerged from the restaurant. "Rodney, are you coming in?'

Hannigan turned to the man. "Yes. I'll be right there." He looked back at Olivia. "Please join us."

"Thank you, but I need to get back," Olivia said. "I appreciate your time. I'm sorry for keeping you from your guests." Olivia was about to offer her hand to shake, but remembered the necklace and said, "Oh, just one more thing...did Mr. Andersen own a gold necklace? A cross necklace with diamonds?"

Hannigan looked surprised. "No. He didn't. He didn't care for jewelry of any kind. Why do you ask?"

Olivia glanced across the street. On the corner, staring across the street at them, was the man with dead eyes from the accident scene. Olivia held her breath. Adrenaline shot through her. She looked quickly at Hannigan.

"Mr. Hannigan. Look across the street. There's a man on the corner. Do you know who it is?"

Hannigan looked to where Olivia indicated, but the man was just turning the corner and was gone.

"I didn't see him," Hannigan told her.

"Thank you for your time," Olivia said quickly backing up towards the street. "I'm so sorry about what happened...and for barging in on you like this. I'll be in contact."

Hannigan nodded. "Thank you, Olivia."

Olivia darted into the traffic, weaving around cars,

and crossed to the opposite sidewalk. She ran to the corner. She craned her neck, but the man was gone.

~

OLIVIA SAT in her car talking into her cell phone.

"So it was a waste of time as far as learning why my name was in his wallet or what 'red Julie' means, but now I know for sure the cross necklace wasn't Andersen's," Olivia said. "Which just brings up more questions."

She paused and swallowed to steady her voice. Her fingers nervously twisted a strand of her hair. "And, Joe, that guy from the accident...he was watching us from across the street."

"Liv, maybe it just looked like the guy. A lot of people in the city fit his description. You were talking about the accident. Maybe you just thought it was him because he was on your mind," Joe said.

Olivia let out a big sigh. "Maybe, Joe. I'm not sure I guess."

"Are you leaving now?"

"Yeah. With the traffic leaving the city, I'll probably be back in two hours or more."

"Drive careful. I'll be leaving Wells in about an hour. Come over when you get back. I'll make spaghetti. We can talk."

"Sounds good. See you later."

Olivia started the car and pulled out of the parking lot into the street. She headed for the highway. On I-95 she sat in bumper to bumper traffic for ten miles. She kept switching radio stations every few minutes. Nothing suited and she turned it off.

Her thoughts wandered. Images of the accident flashed through her mind. The desperation. Feelings of helplessness. The tongue. A necklace placed in her pocket by someone who didn't own it. Aggie. Aggie's gun. The detective who wasn't a detective who showed up asking her questions. The man at the accident. The man on the sidewalk across from her today. Her name in the victim's wallet.

What's going on? She wanted to write everything down and stare at the words on the paper so that maybe they would shift into order and reveal something to her.

The traffic picked up speed and she glanced in the rearview mirror to change lanes. She moved the Jeep into the middle of the highway. She checked the rearview mirror again. Her heart started to pound.

A dark sedan, a few cars behind her, switched lanes right after she did. Olivia brushed her hair behind her ear with shaking fingers. I'm imagining things. She forced herself to take a deep breath.

Noticing that she had sped up and was going too fast, Olivia eased up on the gas pedal. She switched back into the right hand lane. Her eyes flicked up to the rearview mirror again. The dark sedan was still a few cars behind, now also in the right lane. Olivia set her jaw.

She sped up and switched lanes again, this time to the far left. As soon as she could, she switched back into the middle. She continued these maneuvers for several miles keeping her eyes on the road ahead. She pressed harder on the gas pedal, forcing the car faster than she felt comfortable with.

Olivia gripped the steering wheel, determined to keep on like this for a few more miles. The highway was crowded but all of the vehicles were moving along rapidly. She weaved in and out between them.

She slowed a little and looked into the mirror. Her heart pounded like a jack hammer. The sedan was three cars behind her. It was too far back to make out who was in it. Olivia's mind raced. Was it following her or not? She had to find out.

A rest area was coming up in a few miles. Olivia switched to the middle lane again. The sedan moved into the middle.

Just as she approached the rest area, Olivia swerved into the right lane and took the exit leading into the parking lot without slowing. The sedan jerked to the right and followed.

Instead of turning into the lot, Olivia floored it and shot ahead to the roadway leading back to the highway.

Sweat beaded on her forehead. The sedan was coming up fast behind her just as she merged back onto the interstate. Whoever was in the sedan had to know that she was aware she was being followed.

Olivia glanced at her phone on the console. Her hand moved for it but she changed her mind and took hold of the steering wheel again. She had another plan.

Knowing that on weekdays the state police usually had a speed trap set up a few miles ahead, she pushed on the gas pedal to cover the distance as fast as she could.

The speedometer needle touched 85mph. Her breath was coming quick. Her sweaty hands slipped on the wheel. Her friends usually teased her because she drove like a little old lady. They wouldn't recognize her today.

Olivia prayed that the police were in their usual place. She pressed harder on the pedal and shot past the spot where they often hid. A State Police car flew after her. Relief flooded her body. She slowed and pulled over to receive her ticket. As the cop pulled in behind her, she saw the sedan drive past.

Olivia knew the sedan would slow and wait for her up ahead, so as soon as she got her ticket, she took the first exit off the highway to avoid them. After traveling the back roads for a half hour, she pulled into a McDonald's.

She went in, used the bathroom sink to splash water on her face, and ordered a coffee. She returned to her car, her limbs feeling shaky and rubbery, and found the entrance back to the highway. She felt sick to her stomach for the remainder of the ride home. No one followed her. I lost him.

Olivia parked the car in her garage, grabbed her wallet, and strode across the lawn to Joe's house. His truck was in his driveway.

She knocked on the screen door and called, "Joe?" She opened the door and stepped into his kitchen. Joe wasn't there. She walked into the living room. His cell phone was on the coffee table.

"Joe?"

She flung open the French doors that led to his patio. He wasn't there. Olivia's heart started to pound. She turned and went back into the house. She rushed to the master bedroom. Empty. She raced to the bathroom. No one.

Olivia's stomach was churning. She ran through the living room again and out through the French doors into the yard.

"Joe!" Olivia screamed.

"What the hell?" Joe called down to her from the roof.

Olivia ran to the side of the house and saw the ladder leaning there. She looked up and saw Joe fiddling with the chimney.

"Joe." She smiled, tension draining out of her. "I thought something happened."

"Something almost did. Almost fell off the damn roof. You scared the hell out of me."

Olivia sucked in a deep breath and blew it out. She put both hands on her head while Joe edged to the top of the ladder and made his way down to the lawn. Olivia was as white as a ghost.

"What the heck is wrong?"

Olivia's eyes brimmed over with tears. Joe stepped forward and enveloped her in his big arms. She cried into his shoulder.

8

Later that night, Olivia sat in her pajamas, curled up on the sofa with her laptop. Joe had urged Olivia to report the incident on the highway to the police, but she refused.

Being back in Ogunquit and talking it over with Joe made her feel like she was overreacting and she wondered if she misperceived that the car was following her. She admitted that the man in Boston may have just reminded her of the man with the dead eyes at the accident scene.

Feeling much better after relaxing, eating dinner with Joe and talking through things, she went home, showered, watched some reality television, and made a cup of tea.

Olivia pored over internet articles about Martin Andersen and Rodney Hannigan, trying to find a 'Julie' who was connected to either of them. She reviewed Andersen's company website, looking for any Julies or Julias who worked there. She did the same for the firm that Hannigan worked for.

She came up empty.

Olivia typed in addresses of the properties surrounding Martin's brownstone in Boston's Back Bay and his beach place to see if she could find out if any Julies were neighbors of his. She searched Facebook to see if Martin had an account. Everything was a dead end.

How am I supposed to find this Julie? Olivia stood up and started pacing. She decided she would pay a visit to Andersen's secretary sometime in the coming days.

OLIVIA LEFT the house early the next morning. She hadn't gone for a run for a few days and hoped the exercise would shake off some of the tension and confusion she was feeling. The first mile was torture and her legs were burning, but she pushed on until she fell into a rhythm and her breathing smoothed out. Just as she was completing a four mile loop of the town, a companion joined her.

"Hey," he said, smiling at her.

"Hey," Olivia grunted. The guy was gorgeous but she hoped he wouldn't strike up a conversation as she needed all of her air at the moment to remain upright and finish the last mile. And besides, she was drenched in sweat. Not the time to make a best impression.

He ran the last half-mile alongside her. They matched strides until they reached the center of town and Olivia stopped to cool down. Mr. Handsome stopped with her.

"Nice run," he said.

Olivia nodded. Accent. Eastern European?

His blonde hair was cut short and showed off his tan to advantage. He didn't have that skinny look of a long distance runner. The guy was in good shape and his arms and legs were toned and muscled. His dark brown eyes held Olivia's as he extended his hand to her. "Alexei Sidorov," he introduced himself.

Olivia wiped her sweaty hand on her sweaty shorts and shook his hand. "Olivia Miller."

"I've seen you running around town," he told her. "But I could never catch you." He smiled.

Olivia laughed at that. She wasn't the swiftest thing on two legs but she could hold her own. They walked down the hill to the beach.

"Vacationing or local?" Alexei asked her.

"A bit of both. I've been coming every summer since I was little," Olivia answered. "You're here for a visit?"

"I'm a bit of both as well. My father recently

purchased a place here."

"Oh, really? Whereabouts?"

"Out on the Marginal Way. The old Victorian."

Olivia's eyebrows went up. "Nice place. You've done a lot of renovating." That was an understatement. The place had been turned into a palace.

Alexei nodded. "Maybe you'd like to see it sometime. It has turned out quite beautifully."

Smooth, Olivia thought. "That might be nice." They turned onto the walkway that would lead back up to the main street. "Are you spending the summer here?"

Alexei paused in the middle of the wooden walkway that spanned a section of the shoreline. He leaned on the railing and gazed at the sea. Olivia stopped next to him.

"For the most part," he told her. "I'll be back and forth. Travel is required as part of my work."

"You travel quite a bit?" Olivia asked.

Alexei nodded.

"What do you do?" Olivia asked.

"I graduated from Harvard a few years ago...the business school," Alexei told her.

Olivia didn't like Alexei's Harvard name-dropping, which was obviously intended to impress her and she wondered what kind of business was supplying the wealth to nearly tear down the Victorian and create such a grandiose structure. Clearly this was only one of the Siderovs' homes.

"Now I'm involved in the family business," Alexei added.

"Doing?" Olivia inquired.

Alexei smiled. "This and that."

"I see. Well, if I knew 'this and that' paid so well I would have majored in that," Olivia said.

Alexei laughed and changed the subject. "So, are you spending the summer here this year or do you have to return to work?" he asked her.

"I'm staying for the summer." She didn't want to tell him about the antiques shop.

"And after that?"

"I'll be starting law school at the end of August."

"Ah," Alexei replied. "A clever girl, are you?"

"I try to be."

"How old are you?" Alexei asked.

Olivia narrowed her eyes. "Do you ask that question of everyone you first meet?"

"Only the ones I'm interested in," Alexei said with a smile.

"It's not the best opening line," Olivia told him. "I'm twenty-one."

"You have a young face. Although a beautiful one." He tried to hold her eyes as he stepped closer to her, but Olivia looked away, embarrassed. A young face? What the heck did that mean?

"Where will you be attending law school? Somewhere here in Maine?"

Olivia was confused by what she felt were mixed messages from Alexei. One minute he seemed to be flattering her and the next he gave off an air of superiority that she found unattractive. She didn't want to tell him the truth about attending law school at Harvard, so she lied. "Oh, just a small school. I'm sure you've never heard of it."

Alexei seemed about to press the point, but Olivia asked, "Where are you from?"

"All over," he replied.

"Where did you grow up?" she asked.

"We lived in many different places."

Olivia wondered why he was being so evasive.

"I'm going kayaking this afternoon," Alexei said. "Perhaps you'd join me?"

Olivia was intrigued, but she felt a hesitation. This was a handsome man and she liked that he was paying her attention, but something felt prickly. Something about him seemed off.

"It's such a beautiful day. It would be nice to have company. Especially yours," Alexei said. He held Olivia's eyes in his gaze.

Oh, why not, Olivia thought. "I was planning on kayaking this afternoon as well," she said.

"Excellent," Alexei replied. "I can pick you up."

"Not necessary." Olivia wasn't ready to give him her address. That felt too much like a date, and she needed more time with him to decide where to go with this. "I'll be on the river around two. Maybe I'll see you there."

They parted ways when they reached Shore Road. Alexei was going in the direction of Olivia's house, but she turned right and headed back into town. She didn't want a stranger walking her to her house, so she took the scenic route home.

She knew she was being overcautious, but she believed in following her gut. And her gut was urging her not to let this man push his way into her life.

"You know, Liv, people would say you were a rich girl," Joe told her. He was up on the roof again and Olivia was sitting in the grass near the base of the ladder.

She rolled her eyes at him but he couldn't see it. "Oh, come on. Look at that place. Those renovations have turned it into some kind of a palace. A Taj Mahal. It's ridiculous. It looks completely out of place."

"You're being critical of the man because he was born into a wealthy family."

"Yes, I am."

"That doesn't seem fair," Joe went on. "Did you notice

that your inheritance from Aggie has made you a millionaire? On paper anyway. If you sold the house."

"I'm not selling the house, so basically I'm still poor. And I'd never be in his financial league, anyway. Far from it. And the way he name-dropped that he had graduated from Harvard. I don't know, I can't pinpoint it, but he seems kind of entitled and arrogant."

"You're going to go to Harvard," Joe pointed out.

"But I don't brag about it. Jeez. And I'm not arrogant."

"No?" Joe teased.

"Joe!" Olivia protested. "Why are you defending him? You haven't even met him."

"Exactly. And you talked to him for a few minutes. You should give him a chance. Get to know him before passing judgment. There aren't exactly a bunch of suitors banging down your door."

"Ugh. How rude," Olivia said.

"Just sayin'." Joe straightened the shingle and nailed it into place. "So, are you going kayaking this afternoon?"

"Yes," Olivia muttered.

OLIVIA HAD on her cutest bikini and a soft blue fitted t-shirt. She chided herself for doing it but she had put on some pink lip gloss. She put on her life preserver, got into the kayak, and slipped into the ocean river that cut along behind Ogunquit beach.

Moving her paddle smoothly in and out of the ice cold water, the kayak glided over the surface. White puffs of clouds dotted the bright blue sky. She passed sea birds and marsh grasses. The contrast of nature's greens and blues was breathtaking.

The stress and worries of the past few days moved to the back of her mind. She stopped stroking and let the kayak drift in the current. Closing her eyes, Olivia leaned against the seat back with the sun warming her skin.

"Don't fall asleep or you'll drift out to sea," someone called.

Olivia startled and turned toward the voice, shading her eyes from the glare of the sun.

Alexei stroked swiftly across the river, closing the distance between them. He was lightly tanned and his pearly white teeth gleamed in the sun.

Olivia was sure they must be veneers. No one had such perfect rows of teeth. Either that or he had spent a fortune on braces and whitening products. She watched his arm muscles ripple as he moved the paddles in and out of the water.

As he approached he flicked some water at her off the end of his paddle.

"Hey," Olivia protested, but she gave Alexei a smile.

"There's a beautiful spot up ahead. Why don't we

paddle there and take a swim?" Alexei suggested.

"It's early June, Alexei. The water's freezing," Olivia told him.

"But it's so hot today. It will feel good to cool off."

"We'll see," Olivia told him as she started to paddle up river.

When they reached the area of dunes near Footbridge Beach, they landed the kayaks and pulled them up on shore. Olivia straightened and caught Alexei's eyes lingering over her body in a way that made her uncomfortable.

"So, ready to jump in?" she asked and stepped into the sea up to her ankles.

"Not so fast," he told her. "I think I know a way to heat things up a bit more."

Alexei took Olivia roughly by the arm and spun her around to him. He pressed in close to her and ran his hands over her shoulders before putting one hand on her back and pulling her to him. His other hand touched her chest. He leaned down and put his mouth over hers.

Olivia put her hands on his chest and pushed hard against him, and at the same time she jerked her head to the right to remove his lips from her mouth.

The result wasn't so much pushing Alexei away as pushing herself back from him. But as far as Olivia was concerned, she had achieved her goal of disengaging from Alexei.

Olivia retreated a few steps into the water. It was so cold her ankles ached, but she was determined to keep distance between them. She glared at him.

Alexei grinned at her. "Ahh...what? Come here." He reached his hand to her.

"I don't think so," Olivia told him. She held his eyes, her face stern.

His expression hardened. "You prefer to be cold?"

"I prefer to be treated respectfully," Olivia said.

He waved his hand in the air, dismissing her words, and shook his head. "When a man finds you attractive, you should respond. You act childishly."

Olivia's eyes widened. "You act like a spoiled brat. Do you always get what you want?"

"Of, course. Why wouldn't I?"

Olivia turned and dove into the ocean. She swam under the surface for several yards, her skin tingling with pain from the icy sea. Her feet numb, she stood up, shook the water from her hair, and walked to her kayak.

"Olivia," Alexei said.

"Time to go," Olivia replied.

"Come back. Stay."

"You talk to me like you're issuing commands to a dog," Olivia said as she pushed off from the shore and paddled away without looking at Alexei.

She was furious. How obnoxious could a man be? So

self-centered and egotistical. The paddle slashed at the water and moved the kayak up the river.

Olivia banked the kayak at the Sea Shore Hotel on Ogunquit Beach, where she had arranged with the owner to keep her kayaks. She latched it to one of the pilings on the hotel's dock and nearly jogged up the street to the center of town, propelled by her lingering anger.

As Olivia rounded the corner to the market, she crashed into Brad, who was just coming out of the store with a grocery bag full of cartons of milk.

"Whoa, woman in a hurry," Brad said.

"I'm so sorry, Brad. I wasn't paying any attention," Olivia apologized. "I'm just distracted."

"By the look on your face, it's not anything good that's distracting you."

Olivia made an even sourer face.

"Oh, that's much better." Brad smiled, but when she didn't respond to his joking his smile disappeared. "You're shivering. How about some coffee? Or maybe some tea. My mom says tea makes everything better."

The corners of Olivia's mouth turned up into a tiny smile and she nodded in agreement. They crossed the street to Brad's store.

"Here, sit outside in the deck chairs and warm up in the sun. I'll go in and make you something. What'll it be?" Brad asked.

"Surprise me," Olivia answered as she settled into one

of the chairs.

Brad stared at Olivia for a few seconds. "Okay, judging by the situation here, I have determined just the thing to make you feel better." He grinned and headed into the store, but paused and looked back at Olivia. "I will work my magic," he said in a silly, deep voice. Olivia smiled and shook her head in mock disgust.

It felt good to lean back in the chair and let the sun warm her. The sun dried her swimsuit and she stopped shivering.

Brad emerged from his store carrying a sweatshirt and wooden tray. The tray was lined with a placemat and on it was a china pot of tea, a cup and saucer, a silver bowl of sugar cubes, a pot of cream, and a small plate cradling a scone and some raspberry jam. A silver teaspoon and knife were tucked into a blue linen napkin.

Olivia sat up straight and her eyes widened. Her face brightened. "What's all this?" she marveled.

"We aim to please," Brad said. He handed Olivia the sweatshirt and set the tray on the side table next to the deck chair she was sitting in. After pouring tea into her china cup, he said, "Enjoy. I have to go in and get my two employees going, but I'll have a few minutes to sit after that if you have time to stay."

Olivia nodded as she slathered the jam on her scone and took a chomp out of it. She laughed and wiped her mouth with her napkin.

"Yum," she managed.

"I'll bring you another one when I come back," Brad laughed.

~

OLIVIA AND BRAD sat side by side in the deck chairs on the patio next to his store and watched the cars drive by and the tourists strolling along the main street, browsing the shop windows. Olivia had filled him in on her kayaking adventure.

"So this Alexei guy is quite the charmer," Brad said.

"Ugh," Olivia answered.

"You'll make a good lawyer, Liv. Very articulate and verbal," Brad teased.

Olivia ignored him. "How can anyone think that a person wants to be groped a few minutes after meeting? What about finesse? What about wooing? No, just act like a caveman."

"Ah, the lost art of wooing," Brad said. "That's not a word that comes up often."

Olivia rolled her eyes at him. "You know what I mean."

"I'll have to remember that. Wooing." He smiled at her, his blue eyes twinkling.

Olivia felt warmth flow through her body and it

wasn't the sun that was heating her.

"Hey, you two," someone yelled, and they looked up. "Must be nice to be able to just sit around all day soaking up the sun," Joe called to them from his pickup truck. He was waiting in traffic on the street in front of them. Olivia waved.

"Can't fault people for knowing how to enjoy life," Brad called back to Joe.

The traffic started to move and Joe followed the cars up Route 1 to Wells. He waved.

"Joe's okay, huh? While I was working on the store to set it up, he would come by some nights to lend a hand. We'd sit outside afterwards and talk. He sure misses Aggie. I haven't had much chance to have a good conversation with him since I opened the store. How's his place in Wells coming?" Brad asked.

"The Wells place will be done soon. Then he'll be on to the next project. He keeps real busy," Olivia said. "I'm lucky to have him." They watched the traffic.

"Do you have employees in the evening working at your store?" Olivia asked Brad. "Can you get away? Want to come to dinner tonight? Joe and I were planning on making some cornbread and chili. Meat chili for him and vegetarian for me," Olivia said. "We can all catch up with each other."

"That would be great," Brad said. "I'm getting tired of my own cooking."

Someone coming towards them from across the street caught their eyes and they looked up. They stifled groans.

Bustling at them was Magdalene Streeter. Her hair was cut short and the effect of the combination of the length and the bright red color created the illusion of flames shooting out the top of her head. She was panting from the exertion of moving her bulk. Wearing a long flowing dress that barely contained her, Magdalene's flesh bulged in ripples creating hills and valleys all over the fabric.

"Olivia. Brad. I'm glad I caught you together," she said.

Brad stood up, but she waved him to sit.

Magdalene was the town charitable organizer. A role she had appointed to herself. Whenever she came at you, you knew it would be for money or some volunteering thing. She also ran one of the most successful real estate agencies in Maine.

The townspeople all knew she did a good deal for the area, but her manner was grating and most people thought she took on all the work in order to ingratiate herself with the wealthy. She was always in everyone's business, especially those with some cash. Olivia and Brad braced themselves.

"As you know...or maybe you don't," Magdalene began her spiel. "We are raising funds for the York Hospital and this year we are planning a ball as the fundraiser. We are hoping that businesspeople in town might feel the urge to donate something for the silent auction...a gift certificate or an item of worth."

She paused to take a deep breath. The sparkling diamond hanging from her silver necklace was like a ship rising up and down on the waves of her heaving chest. "Oh, this heat does not agree with me." She dabbed at her brow with a handkerchief.

"Can I get you a cold drink?' Brad offered.

Magdalene dismissed him with a wave of her hand. Two of her chubby fingers were encircled with bands of platinum cradling huge diamonds that flashed in the sunlight. There was no stopping her speech once she got going.

"In addition, we are asking all businesspeople to attend the ball as a show of unity," the woman went on. "There will be a small charge to business owners of one hundred dollars each to attend, of course. Much less than the cost to the general public. It will be quite the gala and you should feel very fortunate to be able to take part at such reduced cost to you...and your donation to the silent auction is good advertising for your businesses. It's win-win all around. I know I can count on you both." She batted her eyes.

"Olivia, you will be re-opening Aggie's shop, wont you?" she asked, and did not wait for a reply. "Aggie put so much love into that shop, it would be a sin not to honor her by keeping it open this summer." She rummaged through her oversized bag, searching for her clipboard.

"Oh, yes, I'm sorry for your loss," Magdalene managed, not looking up. She paused in the search through her bag and straightened up, a fake smile on her face. "What are you planning to do with the house?" she asked sweetly.

"Live in it," Olivia answered flatly.

"I understand you are going to law school," Magdalene said. "I know how expensive that will be. I could get you a good price for the house, even though it needs a good deal of updating." She prattled on. "Nevertheless, the location is what it has going for it and the lot is a decent size. We could also market it as a tear-down. Someone could build a lovely home there."

"No." Olivia was seething. How does Magdalene know if the house needed updating? And how does she know I'm going to law school?

"I can make you a very wealthy young lady. You won't have time to come up here with your studies and all. The house will be a burden. And for heaven's sakes, Olivia, once you graduate, you certainly won't be practicing law in this area. You'll be living in a city."

Olivia was silent.

"You think about it," Magdalene told her. "We'll talk again. Oh, here it is." She yanked the clipboard out of the bag and brandished it in front them. "Here are all of the shop owners who will be taking part so far." She handed the clipboard to Brad. "Please sign that you will be attending. And here," she indicated with a pudgy finger, "here is where you state the amount you will be pledging." She tapped the page.

Brad and Olivia looked at the list.

"We are expecting one hundred percent participation," she announced.

Brad cleared his throat and signed the page.

"Excellent!" Magdalene exclaimed. "Now Olivia," she said.

Brad handed the clipboard to Olivia.

"I'm not sure..." Olivia began.

"Nonsense. You are Aggie's heir. You have a responsibility," Magdalene clucked.

Olivia sighed. She signed and handed it back.

"Wonderful!" Magdalene said. She put the clipboard back into her bag. "The town always comes together for a good cause. We will send your invitations to you shortly." She started away, and called over her shoulder, "I forgot to tell you. The gala is being held at the restored Victorian. The new owner has graciously offered the use of the grounds to the committee at no charge."

Olivia looked at Brad and groaned.

9

A ggie's antique shop was on Shore Road just before the turn in the road that led down to Perkin's Cove. It was a good spot, Aggie always said, because she got the foot traffic to and from the cove, but she could make the hours as she wanted. If the store was in the cove next to all the other shops, she would have felt obligated to stay open early and close up late.

Her shop contained a variety of different antiques, music boxes, jewelry, photographs, paintings, china, and sterling silver flatware. Aggie also sold online through a website she had set up.

Olivia stood at the door of the shop. She had helped Aggie with the store since she was a little girl. She peered inside through the wide plate glass window and saw the crystal chandelier, the wooden display cases, and the desk in the corner where Aggie worked on broken jewelry.

Olivia swallowed hard. She put the key in the lock and pushed open the door. A little bell tinkled when the door swung open. The air inside was hot and still from being locked up for weeks. Walking from case to case, she ran her hand over the smooth wood of the counters and noticed a gold bracelet and some small tools on the desk. Aggie must have been fixing the clasp.

Olivia brushed tears from her eyes.

Some of the display cases had been pushed away from the wall and had been covered with drop cloths. Aggie had been in the middle of painting the walls a soft mocha color.

Olivia peered among the tools and papers for Aggie's cellphone, and bent to see if Aggie had placed her laptop under the desk. She opened all the drawers of the desk and searched the display cases and cabinets. Stepping into the back storage room, she checked the file cabinets, the closet, under the sink, under the small wooden table where Aggie would eat her lunch. She even opened the small refrigerator to see if the laptop or phone was inside.

Olivia put her hands on her hips and, standing in the middle of the cramped room, turned in a circle, gazing over every inch of the space to decide if she had overlooked any spot that might hold the items.

Aggie kept a small safe in the closet and even though

she knew it couldn't fit the laptop, Olivia opened it anyway to check for papers that might indicate inventory, receipts, names of buyers and sellers, and any pending sales that needed to be taken care of. It was empty.

With a sighed, Olivia took off her sweater. She would have to search through the house again. She returned to the front room of the store. There was lots of work to do, starting with finishing the painting of the shop ... and Olivia was determined to finish what Aggie had started.

JOE CAME HOME EARLY SO he could get cleaned up and get started on dinner since Brad was coming. Olivia heard his truck and took her bag of groceries over to Joe's house so they could work on the chili together. She also took her laptop.

"So, I told you how Andersen went to London the day after Aggie died and was only back in the US for a day when he was killed," Olivia said. Joe had showered and was in the kitchen chopping onions and peppers. Olivia was cooking ground beef in one pan and bulgur wheat in another pot.

"Strange," Joe said.

"There must be a connection between Aggie and

Andersen. He had my picture in his wallet. They must have known each other and were on to something," Olivia surmised. "Something dangerous obviously, since someone killed them."

Joe looked up. "Who would want to kill Aggie?"

"The same person who cut out Andersen's tongue?" she asked. "The person who shot him?" She paused. "Why did Aggie have a gun?"

Joe ignored that last part. "This is all speculation," he said.

"Someone shot Andersen," Olivia said. "Why was Aggie on that bike...and so late?"

"This is all too much for me," Joe said. He stopped chopping and looked off into space.

"And Andersen took off for London out of the blue," Olivia said.

Joe turned towards Olivia. "But he often left unexpectedly. Hannigan said so," Joe said.

"Yeah, Andersen takes off right after Aggie is killed. And then he returns and dies the very same day. Something else must have been going on besides his work commitment."

Joe sighed. "I'm having a beer."

"What about chopping?" Olivia asked.

"Task master," Joe muttered.

Olivia added spices and tomato paste to the meat and

stirred to mix it together. She scooped it all from the frying pan into the large crock pot.

She mixed mushrooms, spices, and tomato paste into the bulgur wheat for the vegetarian chili and poured that mixture into the smaller crock pot.

"I'd like to look into what Andersen was doing in London," Olivia said.

Joe was sipping his beer, leaning against the island counter. "How?"

"Are you done with those peppers and onions?" Olivia asked.

Joe lifted the cutting board and divided the chopped vegetables equally between the two crock pots.

"Well, to start with, I thought I would send an email to the hotel where Andersen always stayed to confirm that he was a guest there for the four weeks."

"They won't tell you. Confidentiality," Joe said.

"I'll say I'm with the police."

Joe's eyes widened. "You can't do that, for heaven's sake. That would be impersonating a police officer."

"Would it?" Olivia said slyly.

"Of course it would. You'd be arrested."

Olivia was preparing a salad. She glanced at the clock. "Joe, maybe you should get started on the corn muffins." Joe walked around the kitchen island and pulled out the mixing bowl from under the counter.

"Well, I could email the London hotel and say that I

was hired by Rodney Hannigan to investigate the events of Andersen's death," Olivia said. "I could attach the newspaper story reporting the accident so they could see that it was legitimate."

"So now you're a private investigator? You need a license for that, you know." Joe cracked two eggs into the bowl.

"I don't intend to claim I'm a private investigator," Olivia said. "I intend to imply."

Joe chuckled. "Go ahead. Give it a try. I'd be surprised if they tell you anything."

Olivia went to her laptop and sat in the kitchen chair.

"Hey," Joe said. "Not now. We're cooking here."

"It'll only take a minute." Olivia's fingers tapped on her keyboard. "Here's the hotel contact information." She did a bit more tapping. "There. Sent."

"How'd you write that so fast?" Joe asked, adding cornmeal to the mix.

"I wrote it before I came over. I just wanted to run it by you. I changed the police part to 'hired to investigate' and then I sent it," Olivia said. "If there's any trouble, I'll blame you since the email was sent through your wireless network connection." She smiled.

"Thanks a lot," Joe said.

"I'll visit you in prison," Olivia told him.

BRAD ARRIVED for dinner with a bottle of white wine, a homemade blueberry cake, and a bouquet of pink Gerber daisies. They sat outside at Joe's patio table over-looking the Marginal Way and enjoyed the chili, salad, and cornbread while reminiscing about what mischievous children Brad and Olivia used to be.

"I don't know why I let you talk me into so much trouble," Brad said to Olivia.

"You instigated an equal share," Olivia protested.

"How about the time we cooked up the scheme to see how far north we could ride our bikes on Route 1?" Brad chuckled.

"Yeah," Joe said. "Only you both forgot that you had to ride back home. I get the telephone call at nine at night to come pick you up in the truck because you were both exhausted. Never mind we're all worried senseless."

"What did Aggie used to say to us?" Brad said. "All brains and no sense?"

"Plenty of brains but no common sense," Olivia clarified.

They laughed.

"If the shoe fits..." Joe said.

"Hey!" Olivia playfully punched his arm.

After dinner they took out kayaks, hauled them across

the lawn and launched them from the rocks in front of the house. They paddled up the Ogunquit River which wound around behind the beach.

The sun was setting and it cast a red, pink, and violet glow across the sky and sand. A few people walked along the beach, flew kites, and rode flotation devices in the river's current. The air was dry and comfortable. When they returned from kayaking, they made a fire in Joe's pit and sat in the Adirondack chairs munching Brad's blueberry cake with whipped cream.

"Ahhh, this is delicious, Brad," Olivia said, closing her eyes in delight after shoveling in another forkful.

"Brad, you're welcome to bring dessert over any night," Joe said.

"This has been one of the bookstore's most popular desserts," Brad told them. "It's a modified version of my mom's."

"Do you make all the desserts you serve in the bookstore?" Olivia asked.

"Oh, no, I order most of them from the bakeries in town. Occasionally I'll bake something to serve. I enjoy baking, but I just don't have the time to provide everything we need. It's a heck of a lot of work running the business. This is my first night off," Brad said. "In fact, I'm going to give the store a call to see if everything's okay. Excuse me a minute. Be right back." Brad got up and walked closer to the house to make his call.

"It's nice to have Brad around again," Joe said, leaning back in his chair. "He's a lot of fun. Great guy."

Olivia nodded as she licked the last crumbs and a smudge of cream off her plate.

"Nice manners, Liv," Joe said. "There's plenty of cake, you know. You don't have to get every last crumb."

"Waste not, want not," Olivia said with a laugh, tossing one of Joe's favorite sayings back at him.

"Liv, would you like another piece?" Brad asked as he came back to the fire pit.

She looked up with a sheepish grin. Brad touched his nose, indicating that Olivia had a dot of cream on the end of her nose. She wiped it off with her napkin.

"I can't believe we have to go to that gala this weekend," Joe grumbled.

"Maybe it will be a good time," Brad offered.

"I'm kind of looking forward to getting dressed up," Olivia said.

"You? Want to get dressed up?" Joe asked in mock surprise.

Olivia made a face at him and said, "Well it's not often I get to wear a gown."

"You have a gown?" Joe asked.

"Joe!" Olivia said. "Did you think I was going in jeans? Aggie has gowns from all of the events she had to attend for the college and the charity things she went to. I found a pretty one in the closet that fits me. I just had to buy some shoes." She took a sip of her coffee. "I just wish the gala was somewhere else. It will be very awkward to see Alexei again."

"We'll be with you, Liv. We'll act as buffers," Brad said. "I am looking forward to seeing the Siderovs' place, though. So many people in town talk about the renovations and addition. I bet there'll be a huge turnout just because of the curiosity factor."

"Construction buddy of mine, Mike Sullivan, was telling a group of us about the addition," Joe told them. "He got called in for a day to do some masonry after one of the regular workers got hurt. Sounds like no expense was spared. Everything is the best that money can buy. Siderov wants things a certain way, too. Mike said one of the guys told him that they had to pull walls down and redo them because one tiny thing was off. He said Siderov has a massive temper. Everybody's afraid of the guy."

"Sounds like a real jerk," Olivia said, rolling her eyes. "Guess the apple doesn't fall far from the tree," she added, referring to Alexei.

"Time for me to retire to my bed," Joe said, yawning. "Stay as long as you want. Put the fire out before you leave." He got up from his chair, kissed Olivia on the head and patted Brad on the shoulder. "Goodnight, you two."

"Goodnight, Joe," Olivia and Brad replied.

"I can't stay long. I'm up early tomorrow. But how about a glass of wine before I go?" Brad asked.

Olivia said, "Okay, sure." She was eating her second piece of blueberry cake. "I don't drink very much but one glass of wine would be good."

"Good thing you don't drink like you eat," Brad teased.

Olivia made a face at him. "I enjoy good food, but alcohol...well, you know how I feel about that."

Brad nodded while struggling to open the wine. When Olivia was a year old, her mom, dad - who was Aggie's brother - Aggie and Aggie's husband were returning from a Fourth of July outing to a lake where they enjoyed a day of swimming, games, and a picnic lunch. It was two o'clock in the afternoon, heading south on Route 495 on their way back to Boston, when the nineteen-year-old drunk driver fell asleep at the wheel, lost control of his car, hit two cars, crossed into the middle lane and plowed into Olivia's father's car.

Olivia's dad and Aggie's husband were in the front seats and were killed instantly. Aggie, Olivia's mom Suzanne, and Olivia, strapped into a car seat, were in the back. Suzanne died of massive head injuries two hours later in Massachusetts General Hospital after being airlifted there.

Aggie was eight months pregnant with her first child, a baby boy, who arrived stillborn four hours after the accident. Olivia had some cuts from flying glass, but other than that she was unhurt.

Four people killed. Six people's lives changed or ended from an accident caused by a drunk at two o'clock in the afternoon.

The young man was convicted of involuntary manslaughter but because of Aggie's appearance in court pleading leniency for the young man, he was ordered to perform one hundred hours of community service and take part in an alcohol education training class. He also lost his license for a year. Aggie believed in forgiveness.

Aggie became Olivia's legal guardian and never re-married. When Olivia was eighteen, Aggie told her that if she hadn't had her to care for and love, she would have crawled into a hole and never come out.

Olivia didn't remember her parents, but she kept a picture of them on her nightstand.

Aggie had been a public defender before the accident, but afterward she decided to teach at Boston College law school so that she would have a more flexible schedule to be able to get home earlier to their apartment in Cambridge. The Ogunquit house had belonged to Aggie's in-laws and because her husband died in the accident and there were no other living relatives, the house went to Aggie.

Aggie and Olivia lived at the Ogunquit house all summer long, at Christmas, during spring breaks, and for many weekends each year. And that's how Joe entered their lives.

"Here, Liv," Brad said, handing her a glass of wine. They clinked their glasses together. "To happy, healthy days," Brad said. They watched people walking on the Marginal Way and the fireflies appearing and disappearing in the growing darkness.

"I'm not working on Wednesday. Interested in a bike ride?" Brad asked.

"Should we see how far north we can ride before we have to call Joe to come get us?" Olivia said.

"I'd like to see his face if we did that again," Brad chuckled. He took a sip of his wine. "It's nice to be back in Ogunquit."

"How did you decide to come back here, Brad?"

"I looked at places up and down the California coast but nothing suited. When I thought about where I really wanted to be, the answer was here. Even though I only came here for summers as a kid, it seems like this is where I belong."

"Yeah, I feel the same way," Olivia said. "Your whole family is still in California?"

"Yeah. So I have a good place to visit in the winter." Brad smiled.

"How's the store doing? Are things going well so far?"

"Things are going better than I had hoped," Brad said. They sat quietly looking at the stars.

"I'm glad you're still here, Liv," Brad said. "And Joe, too. You both make me feel like home."

Olivia's heart filled with warmth. "I'm glad you're back." She smiled. "I need someone I can get into trouble with."

Brad leaned forward in his chair. "Liv, remember that day we both leaped off the jumping rock, but the tide was too low and we hit the smaller rocks?"

"Yeah, you had twelve stitches and I had ten. All the stupid things we did and still survived."

"No wonder Aggie said we had no sense," Brad laughed. "Thank heavens for you, Liv. My summers would have been so dull if you weren't with me. My sisters would never have done the crazy things we did."

Olivia chuckled.

After a few minutes Brad said, "Joe told me you had a tough time last fall."

Olivia sighed. "Yes, I did. Very unexpected. Really, that guy broke my heart, which actually hurt more than the gunshot. I'll tell you about it another time. It's a story for another day."

Olivia had met a Boston University graduate student during the fall semester of her senior year. He was handsome and athletic and he was intent on dating her. Lavishing her with attention, he took her out every weekend in his red Porsche, and talked about how he wanted her in his future.

She fell for him. Turned out he was a master manipulator who had lied about everything. He had claimed to have completed an undergraduate degree at MIT, published papers in academic journals, and achieved perfect 800s on his SATs.

All of it was made up.

Olivia's suitor had married a young woman in Vermont the year before he started his graduate work at BU and promptly took off on her. The wife found out where he was, tailed him when he dated Olivia, and decided to put an end to his antics. She shot him in the head, killing him instantly - which wasn't her plan. She would have preferred that he suffer before taking his last breath.

The woman shot Olivia, too, but the bullet only grazed her shoulder. Olivia lay on the sidewalk bleeding, pretending to be dead. As the wife stood over Olivia, aiming to put a bullet into her head, Olivia raised her leg and slammed it into the woman's kneecap, knocking her to the ground.

The woman got life in prison with no chance for parole. Olivia later found out that while her Romeo had been dating her, he had also been busy with a good number of other girls on campus.

So much for falling in love.

Olivia balanced her wine glass on the arm of her chair. "What about you, Brad? Are you seeing someone?"

Brad shook his head. "Not any more. I dated the same girl for the last two years of college, but we split up."

"Grew apart?"

"In a manner of speaking," Brad said. "She cheated on me."

"Seems to be a lot of that going around," Olivia said. "At least you didn't get shot."

Brad almost choked on his swallow of wine. "You should write a book, Liv."

"But there would be too much bad stuff in it."

"That's why it would sell," Brad told her. "Listen, I'm sorry about that accident the other night. Joe told me you were the first one there."

Olivia filled him in on the details of what had happened the other night and how Martin Andersen said "red Julie" to her. She told him about the mysterious guy that showed up at the accident, the necklace in her pocket, the fake cop that came to her house, her suspicions about Aggie's death and the gun in her house.

"What?" Brad asked. "This is ridiculous. How could all of that have happened?"

"Unfortunately, it did. And it's not over." She paused in thought. "Brad, I need to figure out what 'red Julie' means. How all of these things connect together."

"I think you should let the police handle it," Brad said.

Olivia gave him a serious look. "Aggie didn't die of a heart attack. I know it. But I'm the only one who thinks so. I can't leave it to the police."

"Liv..."

"I just can't." Olivia leaned forward. "Aggie was riding my bike, late at night, in the dark." Olivia's forehead was furrowed. "Why? Why would she do that? She never rode a bike.

"Maybe she needed something from the store?" Brad offered.

"She would have walked. Or taken the car. Not the damn bike." Olivia slumped in the chair for several seconds then her eyes widened and she leaned towards Brad. "Maybe she was trying to get away from something. Someone."

Olivia's thoughts tumbled out. "Maybe she was trying to get away quietly. Without being seen. Maybe she couldn't get to the car. Walking would be too slow. So she took the bike from the shed."

Brad thought it over. "Maybe. But who? Who was she trying to get away from? Who'd be after her?"

"That's what I need to figure out," Olivia said. "But I need help." She held Brad's eyes.

Brad sighed. "Sounds like you're about to drag me into this mess."

Olivia's face brightened.

"Why do I let you talk me into these things?" he said, shaking his head.

10

After Brad left, Olivia sat at her kitchen table reading her emails and searching the internet. There was an email from Martin Andersen's secretary replying to Olivia's request to meet. She would be in the office on Friday before noon if that would be a convenient time for Olivia.

Olivia tapped out her response, agreeing to meet at the end of the week. The cross necklace was on the table next to her laptop. She checked eBay for anything that might look similar but found nothing.

She Googled 'gold cross necklace diamonds' and got thousands of hits of items for sale. None of the necklaces looked like the one in her possession.

Picking up the gold cross, she brought it close to her eye to inspect the elaborate workings of the piece.

It was two inches in length with the sunburst

extending out an inch around the center. It was heavy and looked old.

Olivia wished that Aggie was there to give her opinion about it.

Why did you give this to me, Martin? What am I supposed to do with it?

11

On Wednesday, Olivia rode her new bike into town to meet Brad at his bookstore. He wanted to be sure things were in order with his employees before he took off for the day.

Olivia stopped in at the food market for some granola bars, and as she was putting them into her bike's saddle bag, she saw Brad and a cute blonde standing in front of his store chatting.

The young woman was short, curvy, and in good shape. She was wearing little shorts and a tank top that showed off her curves to full advantage. Smiling and laughing, the woman stepped closer to Brad. He didn't seem to be minding the attention.

A flash of jealousy jolted Olivia's body. She always felt common and plain and awkward around girls like that. Busying herself with her bike's saddle bag so she didn't appear to be spying, she took a glance across the street to see if the blonde had moved on, but the young woman was still making eyes at Brad, her chest all high and perky.

Olivia decided she wasn't going to wait all day, so she crossed the street with her bike.

"Liv. Hi," Brad said. "I'm all set to go." His cheeks looked flushed.

Brad's bike was leaning against the wall of the bookstore and he turned to get it, saying, "Liv, this is Jen. She works here. Jen, this is Olivia."

The blonde eyed Olivia, sizing her up, and turned away disinterested and smiled at Brad with a look of confidence that indicated that she didn't consider Olivia a threat.

"When will you be back?" The blonde batted her eyes at Brad.

"Not sure. Call my cell if you have any questions." He straddled the bike.

Ugh, Olivia thought. Miss Perky Chest working for Brad.

"Ready?" Brad asked Olivia.

Olivia managed a smile. "Yes, let's go."

Starting up Route 1, they biked for miles, stopping occasionally to photograph whatever caught their eyes. The two rode along the coast until they were hot and sweaty and decided to stop for lunch and a swim. After buying sandwiches and drinks, they sat on top of some rocks overlooking the ocean.

"This is great," Brad said. "I haven't exercised for weeks. It feels really good to be out and riding."

Olivia nodded. "I know," she mumbled between chews of her sandwich. "I needed it. It helps to clear the head and get away from things for a while." She had a drop of pesto sauce on her chin and Brad reached over and wiped it off with his napkin.

The touch of his hand made her heart flutter and she looked down at her sandwich, hoping that her cheeks weren't pink.

"You always ate with gusto," he chuckled. Olivia swallowed and grinned.

"Look who's talking," she said. "Aggie used to say you ate her out of house and home."

Brad stretched out on the warm rocks and closed his eyes. "This is the life. Maybe the bookstore will do really well and I can hire someone to run it while I just lay around."

Olivia laughed. "I can't see you just lolling around. You'd go crazy after a while. You seem real laid back but your mind is always racing. When we were kids you were always cooking up schemes, inventing stuff, starting businesses that I had to work at."

Brad laughed. "Which business was the worst one?"

"Let me think," Olivia said. "Oh, I know. The summer of mowing lawns." She rolled her eyes.

"I knew you'd say that," Brad chuckled.

"You got all those clients and then you broke your wrist so I had to do all the mowing while you sat there and ordered me around. And then you kept two-thirds of the money because it was your business, you said." Olivia shook her head. "I should have quit."

"Why didn't you?" Brad asked.

Olivia crumpled up her face. "I don't know why. I guess I was a wimp."

Brad chuckled. He was still laying back on the rock with his eyes closed.

"You, a wimp? Not a chance."

Olivia reached over and poured the cold water from her bottle all over his stomach. "That's for being a brat."

Brad yelled and lurched up. He reached for Olivia but she scrambled away down the rocks to the beach below. Brad chased after her as she ran in and out of the waves.

They ended up body surfing in the ocean for an hour before returning to their bikes. Brad checked his phone and discovered a message from Jen at the bookstore - aka Miss Perky Chest - saying that the evening employee had called in sick and that they would be shorthanded unless Brad came back to work that shift.

"It's okay," Olivia told him. "Let's head back. If we start now, you'll only miss an hour of the last shift."

Brad nodded and sighed. "It's gonna be a long night."

Olivia thought, I'm sure Miss Perky Chest will keep you company. An ache settled around Olivia's heart and squeezed.

∾

WHEN SHE RETURNED to her house, Olivia showered and turned on her laptop to check her mail. There was a polite reply from the Gorham Hotel, citing confidentiality, declining Olivia's request for information regarding Martin Andersen and whether or not he had been a guest at the hotel. Joe was right.

Olivia sat on the sofa, tapping a pencil on the coffee table wondering what to do next. She put the tea kettle on and paced around the kitchen. The credit card.

Olivia rushed to her laptop and typed an email to Rodney Hannigan asking him to check Andersen's credit card statement to see what he had done in London and if he had stayed at the Gorham for the entire four weeks, and if not, to see if there were any other charges indicating where he had traveled. She hit enter and sent it.

∾

OLIVIA WAS GOING through folders and documents that Aggie kept in the safes and in the file cabinets. There was insurance to file and final bills to pay. She was sitting at the kitchen table writing checks when her phone beeped. It was Rodney Hannigan.

"Olivia," he said. "Is this a good time to talk?"

"Yes, I'm just paying bills, so I'm glad for the interruption."

"I went through Martin's credit card statement and it's not what I was expecting. It seems that he stayed at the Gorham, but he checked out at the end of the third week. But there are no charges for the fourth week in London."

"Are there charges made to a different hotel?" Olivia asked.

"No," Hannigan told her. "There are only charges for the first, second, and third weeks. Nothing else at all for the last week he was there. Not for food, purchases, nothing at all. It seems Martin was only in London for those three weeks, not four."

"Did Martin have a friend in London or nearby who he might have stayed with?" Olivia asked.

"No. At least, no one I knew of. He always stayed at the hotel."

"He could have done some traveling, couldn't he?" Olivia asked.

"Martin always told me his plans. He told me if he was going to travel somewhere else. In case of emergency."

"There are no other charges to the card? For train travel or airline?" Olivia asked.

"Nothing," Hannigan said.

"Did he have another credit card?" Olivia said.

"He did, but rarely ever used them. I've been checking them but none have had activity in ages." Hannigan sighed into the phone. "This is a mystery, Olivia. Where was Martin during that fourth week?"

Olivia stood up and started pacing around her kitchen and living room. "Do you think it possible that he was trying to hide from someone? That he went to London to run from something? To get away from some danger?"

Hannigan was quiet.

"I'm just speculating here," Olivia said. "I know you aren't sure. I'm just thinking out loud. Did he seem nervous? Out of sorts?"

Hannigan said, "He did seem a bit snappish when I spoke to him on the phone the week before he left for London, but I assumed it was just the stress of trying to finish the book and handling some difficult client cases he was working on. When we had dinner at the airport, he seemed quieter than usual, but I didn't think anything of it at the time. When he was in London we exchanged a few emails, but they contained nothing of substance. I have been extremely busy the past two months. I should have been more in tune to Martin's feelings and moods. I should have pressed for details."

"Did Martin email you during his fourth week away?" Olivia asked.

"Yes, but I thought he was in London and he didn't say anything to the contrary."

"Rodney, is it possible that he used cash during the other week? Was there a large cash withdrawal from his savings or checking accounts?"

"We had joint accounts. There wasn't any unusual activity," Hannigan said.

"I'm stumped," Olivia said. "Are you able to check Martin's emails? I wondered if he ever corresponded with my aunt. Her name was Aggie Whitney. Maybe they knew each other. Or maybe there are emails that can indicate where he was staying during the other week in London. Or wherever he was."

"That's a good idea," Hannigan said.

"How did he pay his credit card bills?" Olivia asked. "Did he get paper statements or did he pay online?"

"He paid online. I'll look into our bank statements more closely to see if there are payments from the account to a different credit card company," Hannigan said.

"Rodney, have the police done any of this already? Looked at Martin's laptop or computer accounts?"

"I don't know. Not to my knowledge anyway. Martin's laptop was destroyed in the car accident."

"I ask because I can't find my aunt's laptop. All of the paperwork for her business would be on there. I can't find the hard drive that she backed up her files to either. I wondered if the police took them as part of an investigation of her death."

"If that were the case, the police would have informed you, wouldn't they?" Hannigan asked.

"Yes, you're right. I would think they would have to let me know if they had confiscated her personal property. In fact, there really wasn't much of an investigation at all when Aggie died. A heart attack is what they believe. Case closed."

"Olivia, I know Martin's email password, so I will look for anything that might help us find out what went on during the weeks he spent in Ogunquit and London. And I'll look into whether Martin was using another credit card," Hannigan said.

"Do you have Martin's cell phone?"

"I don't know where it is," Hannigan replied. "It wasn't recovered from the accident, as far as I know."

"I can't find my aunt's cell phone either. I wondered if you had Martin's phone. We could look at his received and sent calls to see if he phoned my aunt."

"What about phone bills?" Hannigan suggested. "They would indicate contacts made during the month."

"Okay, right, good idea. I'll check my aunt's phone bills," Olivia said. They exchanged cell phone numbers for Aggie and Martin. "Rodney, have you thought of any Julies in Martin's life? His tailor, his hair stylist, his tax preparer? I don't know. Anyone from the past?"

"I'm completely blank. I've stayed awake at night thinking about it. I just can't think of any Julies at all." His voice was tinged with hopelessness.

"I'll keep thinking," Olivia said. "I know I asked you before, but did Martin have any enemies? A client angry about something?" Olivia asked.

"No. There's nothing like that." Hannigan was quiet for a few seconds. "Just the beach house neighbor."

"What do you mean? Who?"

"The Siderovs. The owners of the Victorian. They were relentless in their desire to purchase Martin's beach house. One offer after the other. Martin wasn't interested. He became angry with their obsessive pursuit."

"Did they threaten him?" Olivia asked.

"No. It was more like harassment. They had never actually met. Proposals were made through an inter-mediary."

"It doesn't sound like a reason to kill him," Olivia commented.

"No, no. It wasn't like that. Just a major annoyance," Hannigan sighed.

Olivia absentmindedly poked at the pile of papers she

had been going through that she had removed from Aggie's safe. Aggie's passport slipped from under some documents. "Rodney...do you have Martin's passport? If he left London and entered the European Union there would probably be a date stamp."

"That's a great idea" Rodney's voice was excited. "The police gave me a box of Martin's personal effects that they recovered from the accident. I haven't gone through any of it. Can you hold, Olivia? I'll go to the other room and see if the passport is there."

"Yes, I'll hold on." Olivia paced back and forth across her kitchen. Several minutes passed before Rodney returned breathless.

"Olivia, his passport is here. There is an entry stamp that indicates that Martin left London at the end of the third week and went to Munich. Why didn't he tell me?"

"Munich?" Olivia asked.

"I'll keep digging through his credit card information," Hannigan said. "I'll call you if I discover anything else."

Olivia kept pacing after she and Hannigan ended their call. She wondered why Martin Andersen had gone to Munich and why he didn't tell Rodney. Could he have been running from something?

Olivia wondered where Aggie's laptop and cell phone could be. That laptop had all the shop's receipts on it, the customers' information, and the information regarding recent sales. Olivia had searched the house, the shop, and Aggie's car. Joe had looked through his house for them as well.

How could they just disappear?

Olivia stopped pacing. They would need help to disappear. A chill ran down her spine. Someone must have broken into the house. Or the shop. Someone must have taken the laptop and the backup drive and maybe the cell phone. Everything else in the house and the store seemed to be in place.

What was on the laptop that someone would want? What were they looking for? Olivia's hand started to shake at the thought that intruders had been in her house. She hurried to the front door and turned the deadbolt.

12

When Olivia called Detective Brown to report Aggie's missing laptop and cell phone and Martin Andersen's unexpected business trip to London, he asked Olivia if she was a fan of crime television.

"I'm not," Olivia replied. Her voice carried a tone of indignation.

"I don't see the laptop's relevance to your aunt's death," Brown explained. "Perhaps it will turn up. You say that there isn't any sign of forced entry into your home or the antique shop, nor is anything else missing. Is that correct?"

Olivia wanted to groan. She knew how it sounded. Like some nervous girl imagining connections that weren't really there. "That's right," she told Brown.

"And Mr. Hannigan reported that Mr. Andersen was

called out of town frequently. And unexpectedly. So I don't see how him rushing off to London has any significance either," Brown said. "Am I missing something?"

Olivia held the phone to her ear but didn't reply right away. "I guess not." She didn't report that Andersen went to Munich unexpectedly and without telling anyone and that there were no charges on his credit card for his last week away. She figured Brown would shoot holes in that too, and she already got the sense that he thought she was playing detective.

"Why don't you go down to the Ogunquit police station and file your concerns about the missing laptop," Brown said. "Then there will be a record of it in case it turns up as part of recovered property."

Olivia knew he was trying to placate her. "I will," she told him, even though she didn't think she would. "Sorry to bother you," she said.

"No bother," Brown said. "If you need to get in touch again, you know where to find me."

Olivia ended the call feeling small and unsettled. Brown wasn't any help. Intuition told her the laptop was stolen.

Aggie always told her to listen to her intuition.

13

Olivia wore a soft rose colored sundress that was fitted to the waist. The skirt was full and knee length. She wore beige strappy flat sandals and carried a bottle of white wine.

Alejandro Callas was having a party at his grandmother's Ogunquit home. Brad and Olivia knew Alejandro and his sister Esme from when they were all kids, but they hadn't hung around together because the Callases were several years older.

Alejandro had been in to Brad's café and he told Brad to invite any friends of his to come along to the party. There would be a DJ, beer and wine, and tapas. Brad had invited Olivia and two of his employees, and Olivia was meeting the others at Brad's store after closing so that they could all walk to the Callases' together.

Brad, Miss Jennifer Big Chest, and Sean, a new

employee of Brad's, were just coming out of the bookstore when Olivia arrived. Jennifer batted her eyes at Olivia in mock friendliness and turned to talk to Brad. Sean and Olivia walked side by side making small talk.

The Callases had a big sprawling white Colonial off of Shore Road which overlooked the Atlantic Ocean. As the group approached, they could hear music and people's chatter coming from the back yard.

The back lawn had tiki torches lit along the edges of the property, and colorful paper lanterns hung from tree branches. Some guests were dancing and others were clustered in groups, talking and laughing. The girls' spring dresses and the lights and music created a festive atmosphere.

Olivia and the others mingled and danced with the guests, and she ran into several people that she used to know when she was a child.

After several dances with different friends, Olivia carried a glass of white wine to the stone terrace overlooking the festivities and she stood watching the party.

Brad was dancing with a shapely redhead who was wearing a tight mini skirt. His face was flushed from beer and dance and he was smiling and laughing with his partner.

Olivia smiled watching him. A tingle jumped through her body. She realized that she wanted to be the one that Brad was smiling at and, for only a moment, her feelings surprised her. The song ended and the redhead said something to Brad and then headed toward the drinks table.

Earlier in the evening, Alejandro had brought his grandmother out to watch the festivities, and the elderly Mrs. Callas sat in a wheelchair off to the side of the dancers, smiling and slightly moving her upper body to the rhythms of the beat.

Brad spotted Mrs. Callas and headed over to her. He bent down and hugged her and she reached up and touched Brad's cheek, her face beaming. Brad knelt beside her as the music started up again and they placed their heads close together so they could chat. Olivia had no idea what they were saying, but the elderly woman was clearly enjoying it.

Alejandro came back to wheel his grandmother into the house, and Brad hugged her sweetly before she left, his eyes happy, crinkled with kindness. The redhead returned and pulled Brad back to the dance floor.

"Hey," a soft voice spoke from Olivia's right side. She turned to see Esme Callas next to her.

"Esme...hi." Olivia smiled.

Esme was petite and shapely with long beautiful legs. Her hair was nearly black, with soft waves falling below her shoulders. Her olive skin was perpetually lightly tanned and her yellow linen dress showed off her coloring to advantage.

Even when Olivia was young, she thought that Esme was like a creature from another planet who moved through the world with elegance and grace. Esme was the one that all the girls wanted to be and all of the guys wanted to be with.

Because of the age difference, Olivia and Esme were never friends, but Esme was always friendly and sweet whenever their paths crossed.

"Who are you watching?" Esme asked.

"Everyone," Olivia answered.

Esme tilted her head. "See anyone you like?"

Olivia laughed.

"Hmm..." Esme said. "I think so." She held Olivia's eyes. Her gaze was kind. "I see how you look at Brad."

Olivia flustered. "Brad?" she chuckled. "He's my friend."

"More than a friend, I think." Esme's voice was like water.

Olivia turned away to look out at the dancers so that Esme wouldn't see the blush on her cheeks. "Brad and I have always been friends. Anyway, I'm not his type."

Esme watched Brad dancing with the redhead.

"That girl isn't his type," she said. "But you are."

Olivia sighed and shook her head. Esme leaned on the granite rail of the terrace. "Tell him how you feel," Esme said. Olivia kept her attention on the dancers.

"No," she whispered. "If I said something and he didn't...well..." Her voice trailed off.

"Olivia," Esme spoke. Olivia was about to protest but she saw that Esme's face had become serious.

"I'm sorry about your aunt," Esme said softly.

"Thank you, Esme."

"You're doing okay?"

Olivia nodded.

"Grief takes its time," Esme said. "Sometimes it feels like it will never let go." Olivia blinked. When Esme was ten, she lost her mom to a sudden heart attack. "But its grip loosens eventually." Esme's voice was soft and kind.

Olivia wondered how long she would feel the hard, cold grip of grief around her heart.

"My brother told me you're working on opening Aggie's shop."

"I'm going to open it limited hours this summer. I didn't realize it would be so much work to get things organized. Not just the shop. The paperwork to settle the estate, get the house transferred into my name. There's a lot to do," Olivia told her.

"I'd make a wager that Magdalene Streeter has asked you about your house and the shop. Whether you plan to sell them," Esme said.

"Oh, yeah. She went on about how the house would be such a burden to me."

"Not surprised. She's been after my grandmother to

sell this house. Gram just comes up from Boston for the summer months. And now that Alejandro and I live on the west coast, she's alone a good deal here."

"Will she sell?" Olivia asked.

"She hates to let the house go but she knows its time to sell it. But I don't want her to sign on with Magdalene." Esme's voice had a harsh tone.

"Why not?" Olivia questioned.

"I don't like her tactics. She has been visiting my grandmother quite a bit. Is working very hard to win Gram over, pretending to be her friend, concerned about what is best for Gram. She isn't sincere. She only wants the profit."

"I understand. Your grandmother would probably get a very good price for the house though if Magdalene represented her. She's the most successful agent around," Olivia said.

Esme was quiet for a moment. "I heard Magdalene speaking harshly to my grandmother one day when she thought they were alone. I didn't like it. Gram brushed it off, but I think she was upset by whatever Magdalene said to her."

Esme faced Olivia. "My husband, Jack, works for a hedge fund. He has friends in the Boston area who work in the financial world. Some have told him that Magdalene has overextended herself. She is the main investor in two massive building projects on the coast. One up in

Kennebunkport and one in York Harbor. Most of her money is sunk in those projects. Things haven't gone as planned and she is on the verge of financial ruin. She needs some big real estate sales very soon to keep the projects afloat and avoid bankruptcy. Once the projects are complete, she is going to make a killing, but right now her finances are in peril."

"I had no idea." Olivia was stunned. "Joe told me Magdalene had been pestering him and Aggie about selling their houses."

"I'm not surprised," Esme said. "I'm also wondering how far a desperate woman would go to keep her fortune and her reputation intact."

"What do you mean?" Olivia asked.

Esme shrugged but her eyes held Olivia's. "My grandmother refuses to speak to Magdalene now. She gets visibly anxious if that woman calls or shows up at the house."

"You think she threatened your grandmother?"

"I don't know. But after the party tonight, Gram is closing up the house and returning to Boston. I think she's afraid to stay here anymore with only her attendants and no family around."

"Should you mention this to the police?"

"I can't. What would I say? I think Magdalene Streeter is threatening my grandmother? I have no proof. I'm only going on intuition since Gram won't talk about it."

Olivia nodded.

"Keep this between us, Olivia, will you? It's okay to tell Joe but otherwise would you keep it quiet? I wanted to tell you because Aggie just passed away. I'm afraid Magdalene might try to prey on you...you know when someone is in a more vulnerable state they might get talked into things they regret later. I didn't want her convincing you to sell and then have you be sorry. And I just don't trust her. Be careful of her. None of us are going to be around Ogunquit anymore. I thought someone in town should know of my suspicions. Keep your eyes and ears open. I'll have Alejandro give Brad our contact information. Call me if you need to."

"I will but why tell me, Esme? Isn't there someone else in town you should share this with?"

"I always admired you, Olivia," Esme said.

"Me?" Olivia's mouth gaped.

"You were always so athletic and fearless...the way you used to jump off the rocks into the ocean." She shook her head. "My god, I wanted to do that. And when the kids all got together and someone was being teased or left out, you always stuck up for them or invited them to join in. You were so brave."

Olivia's eyes were wide. "Me?"

Esme threw back her head and laughed, the sound of it warm and deep. "Yes, you."

A skinny balding man came up behind Esme. He was

about six feet five with a long narrow face and a sharp nose. The combination of his features gave him a bird-like appearance. He bent and kissed Esme tenderly on the cheek.

"Jack." She took his arm and drew him to her. "Olivia, this is my husband, Jack. Jack, this is Olivia." They shook hands. Esme looked at Jack like he was the only man at the party, like he was the only man worth looking at. Olivia would never have placed the two together: Esme, so graceful and beautiful, and Jack, so gawky and gangly, bordering on ugly. But the two of them seemed like two parts that created a whole. Olivia couldn't stop smiling at them.

"Can I steal you away?" Jack asked Esme. "The caterer has a question."

Esme nodded. "I'll see you later, Olivia. Remember what we talked about." She and Jack stepped away arm in arm.

Olivia watched them go musing about what Esme had told her about Magdalene Streeter. A hand touched her shoulder and she jumped. She turned to see Brad standing beside her.

"Brad. You startled me."

"Sorry. I was looking for you." He had a goofy grin on his face helped along by several beers.

Olivia smiled.

"Dance?" Brad asked and held his arms open.

Olivia stepped into his arms and they moved to the slow beat of the music. Brad's hand on her back sent electricity sparking between them. The warmth of his arms around her was good and right and they stepped closer together creating a place on the terrace that seemed just for them.

"Olivia!" Chad Andrews, an acquaintance from childhood, interrupted Brad and Olivia. He shook Brad's hand. "Brad, I hear your bookstore is doing great. Congratulations. Glad to hear it." He turned to Olivia. "You promised me a dance about an hour ago." He smiled at her. "How about it? Can you excuse us, Brad?"

Brad nodded. Olivia held Brad's eyes for a second before she and Chad walked down the stone steps to join the dancers. Brad's gaze was glued on Olivia as she danced with Chad. Then he sighed and turned away.

BRAD, Olivia, Sean, and Miss Jennifer Big Chest walked along the quiet night streets of Ogunquit. They were among the last to leave the Callas' party and everyone but Olivia was feeling the effects of too much alcohol. When they reached the center of town, Sean offered to walk Jennifer the rest of the way to her rented cottage and they parted ways with Brad and Olivia.

"I'll walk you home," Brad said to Olivia.

They stepped off the curb and Brad lurched forward, his body flailing as if his muscles were made of rubber. Olivia grabbed his arm to steady him and keep him from falling.

"Whoa. I missed the curb," Brad slurred. Olivia stifled a giggle.

Brad swayed a bit and his eyes looked glassy and unfocused.

"You okay?" Olivia took his arm again.

Brad raised his eyes to Olivia and squinted. "Liv. I don't feel so good." He coughed and started to dry heave. Olivia pushed him a few steps towards a trash can back on the sidewalk and held his shoulders. Brad, making horrible retching noises, deposited the contents of his stomach into the bin.

Brad moaned. "I'm sorry." Olivia handed him a tissue from her purse and he wiped his mouth.

"It's not the first time you've retched in front of me." Olivia smiled at him.

"I'm so gross."

Olivia laughed. She held his arm again. "I think I'll walk you home."

They crossed the main street and headed to Brad's book store.

"Good thing you're only a block away," Olivia told him. "I don't think you'd make it much further."

With Olivia steering Brad along the street, they made it to the side entrance of the book store building. Brad's hand fumbled in his pocket trying to dig out his key to the second floor apartment. Olivia took the key from his hand and unlocked the door while Brad leaned against the wall.

"But I need to walk you home," Brad protested.

"I think I can manage better on my own." Olivia chuckled as she opened the door for Brad. She started to help him up the stairs.

"I can do it." Brad swayed a bit and grabbed the hand rail. "I'm sorry I drank too much." He put one foot on the first step.

"Here's your key." Olivia placed it in his free hand. "Put it in your pocket. Have a glass of water and go to sleep. You'll feel better tomorrow." Maybe she thought to herself thinking about the raging head ache Brad would probably wake up with. She turned the bolt in the doorknob so it would lock when she pulled the door shut. She waited until Brad was at the top of the stairs.

"Goodnight," she called to him.

"Thank you, Liv," Brad's feeble voice quavered.

Olivia closed the door with a tug and headed down the dark, silent streets to her house. Esme's concerns about Magdalene Streeter floated about in Olivia's mind. She couldn't come to terms with Magdalene threatening an old woman. Magdalene was single- minded in her pursuit of money and was probably unscrupulous in some of her dealings but

Olivia never saw the woman as threatening or dangerous. Joe, Aggie, and Olivia wondered sometimes how a real estate broker could have amassed the type of fortune that allowed her to live such a lavish lifestyle.

Magdalene had a massive home, collected cars, took exotic trips, and had jewelry that could rival that of any Hollywood star. Joe suspected an inheritance had added to Magdalene's own accumulation of wealth, but none of them knew much about her except that she worked like a dog and never mentioned any family.

Aggie always felt badly for her and would often say what good is all that money if you have no one to share it with.

Olivia tried to imagine if Magdalene could resort to desperate tactics if she was in danger of losing her fortune. She just didn't know. She guessed that people could surprise you and not only in good ways. She wanted to talk to Joe about Esme's concerns.

Olivia turned down the side street that led to her house. Moonlight filtered through the trees and lit the road in spots. Olivia hadn't thought she would stay out so late and wished she had left the front door light on so it would be easier to see the lock.

As she approached her house, something caught her

eye at the side of her yard. She stopped short thinking she saw movement near the back corner.

Olivia sidestepped to the left and moved closer to her neighbor's bushes. She peered to the back of her property.

She thought she could see the beam of a flashlight cross her lawn. Her breath caught in her throat and her heart hammered her chest. She flicked her eyes to Joe's house. It was dark. All of the houses on the street were dark.

Olivia reached into her purse and pulled out her phone in case she needed to call 911. She tried to slow her breathing, wondering if the movement was just the moonlight flickering across the lawn. Maybe a raccoon had caught her eye.

She took short steps along the hedge that separated her property from the neighbor's house on the left, being careful not to step on any branch or twig that would crack and give her approach away. She hugged the hedge.

When she was almost to her back yard, the silhouette of a man moved towards her from the rear of the house.

Olivia pressed against the branches and stood stock still holding her breath as the sweep of the man's flashlight caught her in its beam.

"Alexei," Olivia gasped, her hand tightened its grip on her phone.

"Olivia." Alexei startled. He directed the beam away from her face.

"What? What are you doing here?" Olivia tried to keep her voice steady.

"I came to drop something off." Alexei took several steps towards Olivia. She pressed herself closer to the hedge and the branches scratched her back and shoulders.

"At this time of night?" Olivia's voice had a higher pitch. A mix of fear and anger rose in her throat. "It's kind of late."

"I couldn't sleep."

"What do you want?" Olivia stepped away from the hedge but her index finger hovered over the screen of her phone in case she needed to place an emergency call to the police.

"I feel badly about the other day. I wanted to talk. I wanted to give you these." Alexei lifted his right hand. He held flowers out to Olivia.

Olivia shook her head. "It's after two o'clock in the morning."

"I know. I'm sorry. I was looking for somewhere to leave the flowers. I didn't plan to wake you. There's a note."

"Why didn't you just leave them on the front porch? Why are you in my backyard?"

"I wanted you to see the flowers first thing in the

morning. I thought you might go out the back door first, so I was going to leave them on the patio."

Olivia groaned and started for the front of the house. "This is weird. I don't like you snooping around my house at night." Alexei trotted after her.

"I apologize. It was stupid."

Olivia stopped at the front door landing and wheeled around. "I don't want you doing this again. I swear, I'll call the police."

Alexei tried to hand her the flowers. "I'm sorry. I've been under stress. It was a stupid thing to do. I'm sorry that I startled you." He held the flowers out to Olivia. "I won't do it again. But please, read my note."

"I need to go to bed. I need to get up early. You need to go."

"I will." Alexei took a step closer. "Please. Take the flowers."

Olivia sighed and took them. "Go, now." Her voice was firm.

Alexei backed away. "I'm sorry again. Please forgive me."

He strode down the driveway.

Olivia watched him until he was out of sight. She took her key out of her purse and pushed open the front door, sighing. She was exhausted.

Why on earth would he come to her house so late at night with flowers?

She hated the idea of him lurking around the outside of her house ... and with a flashlight. She couldn't help but feel violated.

She considered notifying the police, but then wondered what crime it was to bring someone flowers. Heading into the dark kitchen, she filled a glass with water and took a long drink.

Olivia put the flowers on the kitchen table and as she reached to turn on the small lamp she kept there, her hand froze in mid-air.

That light was on when I left. She let out a long breath. *The bulb must have burned out.*

She flicked the lamp switch and the light blazed. Adrenaline coursed through her veins. Olivia stared at the lamp and stepped away from the table.

I always leave it on when I go out. Did I turn it on before I left?

Olivia rushed to the backdoor and checked that it was locked.

She turned on the kitchen's overhead light and stared back at the lamp. Her hands shook.

Did someone turn it off while I was out? Was Alexei in here?

14

Olivia didn't sleep all night. She sat up in the living room chair with every light in the house blazing. She was at Joe's door at 6am. She told him about Esme's concerns and about finding Alexei in her backyard.

Joe was angry and threatened to go to the Siderovs' house to have a talk with "the fool" but Olivia calmed him down.

"He's probably harmless," Joe said, "but it shows very poor judgment on his part. He's a guy you should steer clear of. Sounds like he has problems."

Joe and Olivia concluded that she had probably just forgotten to turn the kitchen table lamp on when she left for the party. Joe scolded her for not coming directly to his house last night after seeing something in her back-yard. He decided he would install a security system in

Olivia's house and some motion detection lights around the perimeter of her property so that no one could lurk in the shadows.

"I'll start the work this afternoon," Joe told Olivia. "I'll be leaving some tools in your garage. Don't run over them when you pull in."

Olivia was grateful and said she would feel a lot more secure with the alarm system in place. As for Esme's concerns about Magdalene, Joe and Olivia weren't sure what to make of it all and decided it would be best if they both kept alert for any news about her that wasn't above board.

"I always liked the Callas family," Joe said. "They're good people. Something would have to be done if Magdalene threatened Mrs. Callas in some way."

Olivia and Joe considered that because of her poor health and advanced age, Mrs. Callas may have misinterpreted some things that the real estate broker said to her. Still, they decided that they would keep alert to the possibility that Magdalene may be desperate enough to do anything.

"Could she be behind Aggie's and Martin Andersen's deaths?" Olivia revealed her fears to Joe. "Could the cross necklace belong to her? You know how she loves jewelry, the more expensive the better. Could the "S" on the back stand for "Streeter"? Could she have killed them with the hopes that it would be easier to get their houses if they were dead?"

Joe rubbed his face.

"Did Aggie and Martin suspect her?" Olivia continued. "Did they know each other? Is that how my name and address and picture got into Martin's wallet? Did Magdalene Streeter kill them?" Tears welled in Olivia's eyes.

Joe reached across his kitchen table and took her hand. He didn't have any answers.

OLIVIA DROVE to Boston even though she was feeling exhausted. She didn't want to sit around and brood. She had to do something to figure things out and she hoped speaking with Martin Andersen's secretary would shed some light – any light - on the goings on.

Olivia found the building that housed Andersen Financial not far from Boston's Beacon Hill area. She took the elevator to the tenth floor and the doors opened directly into the reception area of office suites.

The décor was understated modern with walls of glass, polished wood floors, and a stainless and glass reception desk. Abstract artwork hung on the walls in muted yellows, blues and browns. The reception area seating included soft leather chocolate sofas and chairs.

The effect was one of wealth, luxury and confidence, and Olivia thought that if she had any money to invest she would feel very comfortable with this company's advice.

The woman behind the desk was wearing a white blouse and navy jacket with a necklace of blue and rose beads. Her hair was light brown parted on the side and cut into a neat bob. She smiled and asked, "May I help you?"

"Yes." Olivia stepped to the front of the desk. "I'm Olivia Miller. I have an appointment to meet with Paula Adams."

The receptionist indicated one of the brown sofas. "She'll just be a moment."

Olivia sat and picked up a copy of Forbes magazine and flipped through the pages.

"Olivia?" Olivia almost dropped the magazine, surprised at how quickly and quietly the woman appeared.

A short, strong looking woman with silver gray hair stood before her. She was dressed in black pants and a red cardigan.

"I'm Paula Adams." The woman extended her hand and led Olivia to Martin Andersen's office. It was decorated almost exactly as the reception area with the exception of more whites, grays and blacks in the color scheme.

The two women sat opposite each other in matching white club chairs.

"I've worked for Martin for over twenty years," the secretary told Olivia. "I really can't believe he's gone and won't be coming right through that door."

Olivia nodded. "I understand," she said, thinking of Aggie.

"I heard that you were with him at the end. I was glad to hear he wasn't alone."

Olivia nodded again. "Mr. Hannigan suggested that I speak with you about Mr. Andersen's last business trip. My aunt lived in Ogunquit too and she died the night before Mr. Andersen left for London. Then Mr. Andersen is killed the same night he returns to Ogunquit from overseas."

"Was your aunt's death suspicious?" Paula asked.

"I feel that it was, but the official reason given was a heart attack," Olivia said. "The two deaths within a month of each other seem suspicious to me. I wonder if there is some link between my aunt and Martin. And the violence of Martin's death - well, that never happens in our small town. I don't believe that it was random. There has to be a reason behind it."

"How can I help?" Paula asked.

"I'm not sure, but I was wondering if you know the name of the client Martin went to see?"

"Honestly, I don't know, Olivia. Martin left unexpectedly. He didn't contact me to make the travel arrangements, which was very strange. I have always made his arrangements. Always. He did it himself. Martin was in contact with me every day for the past twenty years, but when he went to London this time, I didn't hear from him for several days. I didn't even know he had left the country. He asked me to transfer his work to the other advisors here until he returned. I pressed for details but for the most part he was mum. I was concerned to say the least."

"Did you have any idea why he was acting that way?"

"My reaction was that he was under too much stress and needed some time alone to think things over...maybe he had health issues...maybe he was considering retiring and putting the company up for sale. I didn't know what to think. I had to put out a lot of fires here. His clients were irate. Some threatened to take their accounts elsewhere. I was baffled that Martin would behave this way after years and years of building this business. I was worried."

Paula clasped her hands and continued. "I never imagined that Martin would be murdered. At first I thought it may have been one of his disgruntled clients who killed him, but then I wondered how anyone would know he had returned and gone up to Ogunquit. I certainly didn't know he had come back."

"So what do you make of it?" Olivia asked. "It sounds like Martin was in a hurry to get to Europe, but maybe not on business?"

"It could've been business. But he didn't share any of the details with me."

"And that was unusual?" Olivia asked.

Paula Adams snorted. "Very. For over twenty years I knew who his clients were, when he saw them and where, what he needed to do his work. Certainly not the details of the work, of course. I'm not a financial advisor, but I was Martin's support services. We were a good team. This trip to London? I was completely in the dark. I have no idea what he was doing there or why he was ignoring his long-time clients. It's inexplicable."

"Unless," Olivia started. Paula straightened and looked at Olivia keenly. If Olivia had an explanation, she was eager to hear it. Olivia continued, "Unless he was in danger."

"How do you mean?" Paula asked.

"Perhaps he was running from something. Perhaps the trouble didn't start when Martin returned from the trip. Maybe the trouble started before he left. Maybe going to London was an attempt to escape from trouble."

Paula looked across the room, her eyes unfocused, considering Olivia's words. "It makes sense." She nodded.

"When we spoke, he was cryptic. He said he was planning to meet with some colleagues in London to plan some new financial strategies. When I pressed him for more information, he was evasive and cut the phone call short. After that, he sent a few emails just to check in but that was all. I admit I was concerned and it crossed my mind that maybe Martin was unhappy with me and that was the reason he seemed to be behaving strangely. I wondered if he might be planning to replace me. I could not figure out what I had done wrong. Now I'm ashamed that I wasted time worrying about myself. My focus should have been on Martin's welfare."

"There was no way to explain it," Olivia said. "You couldn't know what was going on. We still don't know what was going on."

"No," Paula said. "But the purpose of the trip had to be to get away from something. He must have been hiding out in London. How awful." Paula blinked back tears. "Why didn't he tell one of us? We could have helped him."

"He probably didn't tell anyone for the same reason my aunt said nothing," Olivia said. "They didn't want to put anyone else in danger."

Paula's face seemed to relax. "That's the first thing about all this that makes any sense," she said. "That is exactly like Martin. Thinking of others before himself."

"It seems from his passport that Martin also went to Munich while he was away," Olivia said.

"Did he?" Paula responded, surprise on her face.

"Do you know why he might have traveled to Munich?"

"Martin often traveled after conducting business in London. He loved collectibles. He enjoyed buying and selling old things. There was a dealer in Munich that he trusted and did business with. But if Martin felt he was in danger, why would he risk his safety by going there?" Paula asked. "If he was afraid of something, then indulging a hobby seems like it would be far from his mind."

"I agree," Olivia said. "It doesn't fit." She paused, thinking. "Do you know the name of the dealer he worked with?"

"Yes, I have his contact information in a file. Martin sometimes asked me to email him about certain items he was interested in."

Olivia brightened. "Could you email the dealer and ask if Martin visited him that week? And, if so, why?"

"Yes, of course. I'll do it right now." Paula went to the coffee table to pick up her laptop.

While Paula was preparing the email, Olivia said, "At the accident scene, Martin said something that sounded like Julie. Did he know anyone with that name who was important to him? He seemed desperate for me to find Julie."

Paula looked up from the keyboard. "Julie? I can't think of anyone. Let me just finish this email to the dealer and then I'll bring up a list of Martin's clients." After a minute of tapping and scrolling, she raised her eyes from the screen. "No Julies here. No Julias either. What other variations are there?"

Olivia thought. "Julianne? Juliet? Julianna?"

Paula leaned over the laptop, her eyes intent on the screen. She sat back. "No. None."

"I was afraid of that," Olivia said. "There's something else. Martin had a gold cross necklace in his possession the night he was in the accident. Had you ever seen him with something like that?"

"A necklace? No. Martin never had it here. Not that I ever saw anyway. He was never fond of jewelry."

Olivia wasn't sure what else to ask. Everything seemed to be a dead end. "Can you think of any reason that someone would want to kill Martin?"

"Martin was the best person I've ever known," Paula said. "He was smarter than anyone I ever knew, but what stood out was that he was honest, caring, warm, kind. People were drawn to him." Paula shook her head. "He must have crossed paths with a crazy person. That's the only explanation."

15

Olivia stood in front of the full length mirror. She was wearing a long, cream colored gown made of silk. The sleeveless dress followed her curves and flared out slightly from the knee to the floor. Tiny buttons covered in cream silk traced down the middle of her back, lending an air of elegance. The neckline dipped slightly and a tiny bit of cleavage showed.

Wearing her hair half up and half down, the soft chestnut waves fell just below her shoulders. Her makeup was understated. She had lined her lids with dark brown eye pencil and had applied several coats of black mascara which caused her blue eyes to pop. After putting on a soft pink lipstick, she smiled and walked out to the living room where Joe and Brad were waiting in their tuxedos.

When she entered the room, Brad gasped and Joe whistled. They gaped at her.

Joe said, "Excuse me, Miss, have you seen Olivia?"

The three of them laughed.

"You look stunning," Brad told her. She suddenly felt shy in front of him.

"We," Joe said, "will be the luckiest men at the gala." He offered his arm to Olivia and the three of them went out to the car.

Brad drove up the long, winding brick driveway edged with perennial beds. The sun was setting and lent a gorgeous glow over the property. The Victorian sat perched high on the bluff, overlooking the ocean.

Old fashioned lamplights lined the driveway. Lights were blazing inside the mansion and tents were set up on the expansive lawn. They could hear live music playing. Turning along the circular drive, Brad stopped the car at the front of the Victorian.

A butler stepped forward and opened Olivia's door. "Welcome to Bianco Pace," he said.

The valet walked around the front of the car and handed Brad a claim ticket. Joe emerged from the back seat.

Another butler carrying a silver tray bowed slightly and offered them flutes of champagne.

A red carpet had been placed on the brick and stone walkways and it stretched out, leading along the side of the building to the lawns in back. The butler gestured to the red carpet, indicating that they should follow the path.

Joe leaned in and said, "Bianco what?"

Brad said, "I think it means something like 'white peace' in Italian."

"Why Italian? I thought they were Russians," Joe asked. Brad shrugged.

Hundreds of people were already mingling on the lawn. An eight piece orchestra was playing under one of the tents and people were dancing on the wooden floor that had been placed over part of the lawn.

Tiny white lights sparkled in the trees and on the underside of the tops of the tents. Urns of flowers and potted plants were scattered all around the area. Another tent held long tables laden with meats, salads, fruits, and desserts.

Waiters carried trays of drinks and hors d'oeuvres between the crowds. Ice sculptures of Roman emperors stood overlooking the festivities.

"Yikes," Olivia whispered.

"Someone's showing off," Brad said.

The back of the Victorian soared above the bluff. A large veranda ran the full length of the mansion. There were glass French doors open from the house to the porch and two burly men with shaved heads wearing dark suits stood sentry beside the doors. They gazed out to the sea, indifferent to the gathering of people.

"Look at them," Olivia said.

"Not very friendly looking. What are they expecting? An attack?" Brad laughed.

Magdalene Streeter swept over to them huffing and puffing, sweat beading on her upper lip. "Well, is this not the grandest event in the history of the area?" she boasted as if she was the one who was hosting. She made a beeline for Joe and took him by the arm. "Look at this handsome one," she crowed. "How nice you clean up, honey." She batted her eyes at him.

"You look very nice, Magdalene," Olivia said.

Magdalene had an enormous diamond hanging around her neck. The diamond was held at the center of her throat by strands of yellow and white gold chains.

"What a beautiful necklace," Olivia observed.

Magdalene's hand went to her necklace and she puffed up her chest.

Olivia decided to try something. "You have such fine pieces of jewelry. I love that cross necklace I've seen you wear."

Magdalene's forehead wrinkled. "Cross necklace?"

"Yes. The one that has a skull in the center with the large diamonds."

Magdalene's lip curled and she huffed. "Skull? I would never wear such a thing. No matter how large the diamond."

"I'm mistaken I guess. I must have seen it on someone else." Olivia caught Joe's eye and shrugged.

"Well if you see it again, tell the person what poor taste they have." Magdalene's eyes swept the finery about them. "Look at this place," Magdalene said. "Have you ever seen anything like it?" She was nearly breathless over the extravagant display of wealth. "You know, people are saying the owner even had a safe room designed for the basement. With ventilation systems and video surveillance cameras. Very elaborate. A safe room. Can you imagine? Who needs a safe room?" she asked. "Only someone very important, that's who." Magdalene adjusted the straps of her gown. "I have to see it. As soon as Mr. Siderov makes his appearance, I will introduce myself to him."

Olivia, Joe, and Brad exchanged amused glances.

Brad leaned closer to Joe and Olivia. "Poor Mr. Siderov," he joked.

Magdalene seemed to emerge from her reverie of watching dollar signs dance in her head. She turned to Joe.

"You come along with me and let me introduce you to a few people. And we can have a nice chat." She started herding Joe into one of the tents. "Let the young people do whatever it is they do."

Olivia and Brad saw the look of dread that crossed

over Joe's face like he was being led to the slaughter-house. They stifled laughs and gave Joe a little wave.

"Her reaction about the cross necklace seemed sincere," Olivia observed.

"Can't be hers then." Brad sighed. "So many loose ends."

Olivia and Brad strolled around the party goers. They sampled some of the food and danced under the tent. Brad went to get some drinks and Olivia stood apart from the crowd, looking out over the water. Brad handed her some champagne.

"What's wrong?" he asked.

"That's Martin Andersen's house. Now it belongs to Rodney Hannigan." The Victorian was surrounded by lawn, a buffer of trees, and the ocean on three sides, affording a great measure of privacy. The fourth side shared a property boundary with the house that had been owned by the accident victim.

The house was perched on its lot at an angle so as to provide the best possible views of the sea. This caused its orientation to slightly face the Victorian. The contemporary house was tall and had walls of glass. There were wide decks projecting out from each of the three levels facing the Victorian.

"Its location must really bug the owner of this place," Olivia said. "Andersen had quite a nice view of these grounds and the Victorian."

"Yeah," said Brad. "From what I've heard, this Siderov guy values his privacy."

A murmur went through the crowd and Brad and Olivia turned their attention back to the tents. A short, stocky middle-aged man had appeared on the veranda. He had blonde short hair and was wearing a well cut dark suit with a white shirt and blue tie. He moved with confidence. The two body guards fell in with him but stayed a step behind.

"Must be our host," Brad said. Olivia nodded.

Another man emerged from the Victorian through the French doors. Olivia recognized the man as Alexei. He strolled along the veranda and down to the lawn behind the first man and the bodyguards. Siderov moved through the crowd, shaking hands and pausing to speak to some of the guests. Alexei followed along, greeting the people.

"This guy really thinks he's something special," Olivia said.

"How about we go dance instead of gawking at his grand entrance?" Brad asked.

Olivia and Brad were enjoying the music and had been dancing together for about a half hour when someone touched Brad on the arm. "Excuse me," a voice said. Olivia and Brad stopped in mid-step.

Alexei stood to Brad's side and gazed at Olivia. Ignoring Brad, he said, "May I have a dance with the lovely lady?" Without waiting for a reply, Alexei slid into dancing position and shouldered Brad away. He moved Olivia across the dance floor. She was stiff in his arms.

"You are the most beautiful woman at this gala," Alexei whispered into Olivia's ear. "No need to be tense. I am a very good dancer."

Olivia let out a sigh of exasperation.

Alexei continued. "I'm sorry our time together on the river was so short. I apologize again for my behavior. I appreciate a woman with energy and spirit. Perhaps we can start over. Did you like the flowers I left with you the other night?"

Olivia glared at him. "Have you ever been in my house?"

Alexei looked quizzical. "Why would you ask me that?"

Olivia tried to remove her hand from his, but he held on and pulled her closer with the hand that rested on her back. "I hope you're not going to be rude to your host."

"Alexei..." Olivia started.

"Alexei," a deep voice spoke from behind them. "How do you manage to attract the most beautiful women? And then lose them?" Alexei and Olivia stopped and turned. They were facing Alexei's father.

"You must introduce me," the father commanded.

"Of course," Alexei said. "Father, this is Miss Olivia Miller. Olivia, this is my father, Dmitri Siderov."

Siderov took Olivia's hand. He bent slightly forward and nodded. "Miss Miller, it is a pleasure."

"Thank you," Olivia told him. "It's nice to meet you."

"Would you honor me with a dance? I'm sure my son would not begrudge me." Siderov waved his hand dismissively at Alexei. "Go," he told him. Siderov moved into position and maneuvered Olivia in a slow dance around the floor. Olivia glanced over Siderov's shoulder, trying to find Brad and hoping for rescue. He was not in sight.

"So, what do you do, Miss Miller?"

"I'm a graduate student," Olivia answered.

"And what do you study?"

"I'll be entering law school in the fall," Olivia said. Siderov slid his hand slightly lower on Olivia's back. Like father, like son, Olivia thought. She gritted her teeth.

"Excellent. Alexei did graduate study at Harvard. We were pleased with the education. Will you be staying in the area? Where will you be going to school?"

"Stanford," Olivia lied. She enjoyed telling the Siderovs untruths.

"Very impressive," Siderov said. He was quiet for a minute as he moved Olivia around the dance floor.

"I hear you had a date with Alexei the other day."

"I wouldn't call it a date," Olivia said.

Siderov ignored her statement. "And Alexei said that it ended quite quickly. What called you away?"

Olivia bristled. "Rude behavior."

"Yes," Siderov said. "Rude behavior on your part."

Olivia's face went red with anger. She stopped following his lead and rooted her feet to the ground, which threw Siderov off balance. He caught himself from stumbling.

"Don't you..." Olivia began, rage constricting her throat.

From behind Siderov, Magdalene Streeter stretched out her hand to take Siderov's arm. Olivia was never so glad to see that flaming red head of hair.

"Oh my," Magdalene said. "Clumsy girl nearly tripped you." Magdalene elbowed Olivia out of her way and offered her hand to Siderov. "I'm Magdalene Streeter and I'm one of the committee members who helped organize this gala. I must thank you for your generosity in hosting our event."

Olivia took the opportunity to make her exit. "Excuse me," she muttered and strode away past the crowd of dancers. Siderov glared at Olivia as Magdalene prattled on. Olivia stormed out of the dance tent and collided with Alexei.

"Olivia," he said.

"Not now," Olivia answered. Her eyes were flashing as she tried to move past him.

Alexei caught her arm and she swiveled to him. "What's wrong with you? You tell your father everything?

Why? So he can intervene and get you whatever you want?"

Party goers heard the angry tone and cast glances at Alexei and Olivia.

"It's not like that," Alexei said, lowering his voice. He steered Olivia away from the crowd. "My father is very overbearing. He demands perfection. Everyone lets him down, especially me. He says what he says and then you just have to ignore him. That's what I've tried to do all my life."

Olivia did not respond.

"Olivia, please. You should pity me. I have to live with him every day."

Olivia sighed.

"Did you read my note? That I left with the flowers?

"Yes."

"You didn't call me."

"No, I didn't." Olivia rubbed her forehead. "I've been preoccupied."

"Have a drink with me," Alexei said. "Let's talk. Come on. Just one drink and then I'll leave you alone for the rest of the night."

Olivia groaned.

Alexei gestured to one of the waiters. The waiter came over and Alexei removed two flutes of champagne from the tray. He handed one to Olivia.

"Walk with me a bit?" he said. "Please. I need a break

from all of this." He seemed defeated.

Olivia weakened. She almost felt bad for him. They headed away from the tents.

Alexei sighed. "Such a pretty night."

Olivia glanced at him out of the corner of her eye.

"These events can be exhausting." Alexei sighed again. "Olivia..." he started. "I apologize for..." He waved his hand. "You know...for being a jerk."

"Just leave it," she answered. She did not want to discuss it. They looked at the sweeping vista before them. Olivia felt angry and exasperated, but she also felt a tiny bit sorry for Alexei. Olivia got the impression, even from the little time spent with the Siderovs, that they were dissatisfied, defensive, and troubled people. She tried to think of something to say.

"This is a perfect location...the view, the privacy," Olivia said. "The best spot in the entire town."

"Hmmm. Well, it would be, if not for that," Alexei said as he gestured to the house to their right. "It's like a sentry watching over us. A monstrosity." His voice had turned cold. He glared at it with his jaw clenched. Olivia was taken aback at how quickly Alexei's mood could shift from pleasant and conversational to angry. He was almost like a split personality.

Alexei turned his attention to Olivia. "I heard that you were at the accident scene of our poor neighbor's demise."

"I was," Olivia answered.

"Was he alive when you arrived?"

Olivia nodded.

"Did he speak?"

"I tried to comfort him," Olivia said.

"What did he say?"

"Nothing that made any sense. He must have been in shock."

Alexei's eyes held Olivia's and he took a step closer. "What did he say to you?"

Olivia didn't like Alexei's intense interest in the accident. "Nothing."

"But you said he spoke."

"I said he didn't make any sense." Olivia's voice was firm.

"But what words did he say?" Alexei pressed.

Olivia wondered why on earth Alexei was so keen on this topic. "He was praying," she lied.

"You said he wasn't making sense."

"Why are you asking me this?" Olivia demanded. Flickers of anger flashed in her eyes.

"He was my neighbor."

"Had you met him?"

Alexei shook his head.

Olivia held up her hands. "Then your interest seems morbid." Her tone was sharp with anger. "The man was incoherent. He was dying. I tried to comfort him, Alexei.

That's all." She faced the ocean. As far as she was concerned, the conversation was over.

"I've upset you. I'm sorry. I didn't mean..."

Olivia shook her head and put her hand up. "Stop."

They stood in silence for several minutes.

"Come. Let me show you the house," Alexei said.

Olivia started to protest. Being with Alexei was like riding a mood swing merry-go-round, and she wanted off the carousel.

"The work is really wonderful. I think you'll like it. Please, come see." He started across the lawn and beckoned to her with his hand.

Olivia looked over her shoulder at the crowd. "I should get back. I haven't seen my friends for a while."

"They'll be fine. We won't be long. Come see how nice it turned out." He smiled and walked backwards. "Please."

Olivia was curious about the renovations to the old house and she knew Joe would love to hear about what they had done to it. "I guess, but just for a little while," Olivia told him.

They climbed the steps to the veranda and entered the house through the French doors. They stepped into a massive living room furnished with beautiful white sofas, oriental rugs, impressive paintings, and two shimmering crystal chandeliers. The wall was expanses of glass, bringing the manicured lawn and the sea beyond into the room. The effect was breathtaking.

Alexei pointed at the paintings. "These are Matisse. My father prefers the Dutch masters, but he chose these because of the color scheme."

Olivia noticed security cameras poised at different points in the rooms. They entered a long dining room with stained glass windows along one wall. There was a huge mahogany table which easily seated twenty-four. Pale yellow walls were illuminated by another crystal chandelier.

"This is Venetian crystal, Murano. We found it in Venice last summer," Alexei said. "And my father had to have it for this room."

He continued the tour, showing a billiards room, a media room, two kitchens, a library, a den, and a ballroom. Each room was meticulously decorated with the finest furnishings, paintings, and finishing touches. Alexei relayed tidbits of information regarding several pieces in each of the rooms. He indicated a long hallway that he said contained his father's office suites and staff rooms, but they did not enter there.

As they came back to the living room where they had started the tour, Alexei said, "And upstairs there are eleven bedroom suites, each with its own sitting room and private bath. In addition, there is another living room, media room, small kitchen, library, and office suite on that floor. There are two elevators as well; one for staff and one for family."

"Well," Olivia said. "It's all very grand and beautiful. Your family did a masterful job of restoring and expanding the house. A lovely new home."

"Thank you," Alexei said. "It will be used primarily in the summer."

"Where is your main residence?" Olivia asked.

Alexei chuckled. "Wherever we happen to be at the time."

Olivia held his eyes and tilted her head at his evasive answer.

"Where do you call home?" Olivia asked.

"Wherever my father tells me to be."

"That's a strange answer," Olivia told him.

Alexei ignored the comment and took Olivia's elbow, steering her toward the French doors leading to the veranda, when Olivia remembered something. "Oh wait. You didn't show me the room everyone is talking about."

Alexei cocked his head. "What do you mean?"

"The safe room," Olivia said.

Alexei's face clouded over and he kept walking. "Gossip."

"Really?" Olivia peered at him. "So many people claim that your father built one here."

"Ridiculous." The muscles of his jaw twitched.

"Even some of the construction workers talk about it."

Alexei wheeled to her. "What? Who?"

Olivia startled at his strong reaction. "I don't know who. People talk."

"Exactly," Alexei said. "They talk about things they know nothing about."

"Why does this anger you?" she asked.

"It doesn't," he said sharply and strode through the French doors ahead of Olivia.

Instead of following him along the veranda, Olivia walked to the rail of the wide porch and stood looking out over the lawn.

"May I help you, Miss?" A butler stood at her elbow. "Is there something you wish?"

Ugh, Olivia thought. Are we watched every second? She shook her head.

"Olivia." Alexei had stopped at the top of the veranda's stairs. "It's time to rejoin the party."

As Olivia strolled over to where Alexei waited, she noticed surveillance cameras at different points on the roof.

"May I?" she asked formally with a touch of sarcasm, questioning if she might descend the stairs before Alexei.

Aware that she asked this because he had strode in anger through the French doors ahead of her when they left the house, he collected himself and said, "Yes. Please." He offered her his arm and they walked down the stairs together.

At the bottom of the stairs, Alexei said, "Thank you for indulging me with your company."

Olivia said nothing, but she held his eyes with her own for several seconds, her face expressionless.

"Perhaps we can get together soon," Alexei said. "A drink? A swim?"

Olivia nodded slightly, and as she turned away she said, "Yes, Alexei. We can get together sometime." She looked over her shoulder at him. "Sometime when you grow up."

OLIVIA, Joe, and Brad sat together in three of the garden chairs that were scattered about the Siderovs' lawn. It was nearly midnight but the party continued in full swing with no signs of ending any time soon.

"The house sounds magnificent," Joe said. "I'm jealous you got to see it."

"It is magnificent," Olivia told them. "But there's something weird about it too. There's such a vibe and feeling of being watched. There are surveillance cameras strategically placed all over outside here. And there are cameras inside as well."

"The way Alexei questioned you about the accident was strange. What was that all about?" Brad said.

"I don't know," Olivia said. "It was concerning how he pushed for answers about what Andersen had said to me at the scene."

"And you didn't reveal anything that Andersen said, right? You're sure?" Joe asked.

"No way. I wasn't telling him anything. You should have seen his face when he talked about Andersen's house. 'A monstrosity', he said. He looked like he was going to explode."

"I wonder if he or his family had some sort of run-in with Andersen?" Joe said.

"Nothing like that came up." Olivia was deep in thought. "It's very weird how Alexei's mood fluctuates so wildly. One second he is trying to be all charming and nice and the next second he's so angry that he seems like he could become violent. But with a father like that one..." Olivia flushed with anger recalling the dance with Mr. Siderov. "Can you imagine him berating me for what happened when Alexei and I were kayaking? What would he do? Threaten me to keep me dating his son?"

"Pathetic," Brad said.

"It worries me. They worry me," Joe said.

"No need." Olivia patted his hand. "He's all bluster."

"Sounds like that safe room conversation you had really set Alexei off," Brad said.

Olivia nodded.

Joe said, "Construction people were dying to get some

work on this place. I would have loved to have been part of the renovation team. But instead they flew in experts... so they claimed."

"But you're the well-known expert in antique renovation. They never approached you about working on it, Joe?" Olivia asked.

"No. They seemed like they didn't want any locals involved in the construction. Had to have their own people working on it. Occasionally they hired a guy from the area to do something minor, but even those guys had to sign a non-disclosure agreement."

"Meaning what?" Brad asked.

"No one was allowed to talk about what they saw at the house. Nothing about the construction was to be discussed with anyone outside the project."

"That's strange isn't it? It's not usual, is it?" Olivia asked.

"No," Joe replied. "It's not usual, but it's not completely unheard of. Many wealthy people guard their privacy with a vengeance. Or some fear that their homes will be copied and believe doing so will cheapen the value if the design is compromised and repeated."

"Alexei was furious when I told him that some construction people had been talking in town about the renovations here," Olivia said.

"You didn't mention Mike Sullivan's name, did you, Liv?" Joe asked, concern written on his face.

"No, absolutely not. Anyway, it isn't only your friend talking about this place. Magdalene Streeter was just talking about the supposed safe room earlier this evening. Rumors run wild, especially when things are shrouded in such mystery," Olivia said.

"Something seems very off with these people," Brad said. "What does this guy do?"

"International businessman," Joe replied.

"That's pretty vague," Olivia stated. "But not as vague as Alexei's answer when I asked him where he called home. Why so secretive? It's just a simple question...'where are you from?' But he wouldn't answer."

"I don't know," said Brad. "Seems to me there is more going on here. International businessman? Maybe international thief? International smuggler?"

"Brad," Olivia said. "Keep your voice down. This outside space is probably bugged too."

"You ever hear the saying...'behind every great fortune are even greater crimes'?" Joe asked.

"These people give me the creeps," Olivia said.

"I think I've had enough of the Siderovs' hospitality," Brad said. "How about we call it a night?"

Joe and Olivia agreed and the three of them walked to the front of the house. Brad handed the car claim ticket to the valet and they were home in under ten minutes.

16

They changed clothes and made coffee and carried their mugs into the yard to sit by Joe's fire pit. They leaned back in their chairs and watched the stars shining in the night sky.

"Did you have a nice time with Magdalene Streeter?" Brad asked, smiling.

"Thanks for letting her get her claws into me. I'll remember how you deserted me," Joe said. "It was the usual. Trying to get me to sell. Also trying to get me to convince Liv to sell. The woman is relentless." Joe let out a deep breath. "She didn't seem to know anything about the cross necklace."

"No she didn't," Brad said. He glanced at Olivia. "Are you awake?"

"I'm thinking."

"Uh oh," Joe said. "Means trouble."

"What are you thinking about?" Brad asked.

"The past couple of weeks...all the things that have happened," Olivia said. "I feel like I need a chart to keep things straight. All these loose ends...they must be parts of a common thread." Olivia continued, "Aggie is connected to the mess of it all."

"Liv..." Joe started. "Nothing seems to add up. Magdalene Streeter can't be behind it. It's just too far fetched. How could Aggie be connected to Martin Andersen? How could their deaths be connected in any way?"

"Joe, nobody gets murdered in this town," Olivia said. "And then there are two murders within a month."

"Aggie had a heart attack."

Olivia cut Joe off. "Then why did she have a gun in her dresser? Why was my picture in Andersen's wallet? My name and address? Aggie could have given it to him."

Joe didn't answer.

"Somebody killed her," Olivia said. "And I'm going to find out who and why. Somehow." She shifted her gaze to the darkened sea. "If only she hadn't been cremated. We could ask to have her body exhumed. Make the coroner inspect the body for foul play." Olivia let a long sigh. "All of this. It's like scenes in a dream. I just need to pull it together." She paused. "But the more I think about everything, the more I feel like its just water running through my hands."

"I think you're right, Liv," Brad said. "The circumstances of the two deaths…and just a month apart…it has to be more than coincidence."

Olivia nodded at Brad. "I need your help. To figure this out."

She looked across the fire pit to Joe. "I need you're help too, old man."

"I was afraid of that," Joe replied. "And don't call me old man." Joe took a deep breath. "Well, it's way past my bedtime anyway. We may as well stay up all night." Joe stood up from the chair. "Come on, children. Why don't we go inside and write down what we know. Maybe putting it on paper will help shed some light on all of this."

Olivia bolted upright and knocked her coffee mug off the arm of her chair onto the grass. "Dmitri Siderov," she exclaimed.

"What? So?" Brad said.

"Dmitri Siderov. The cross necklace. The letter 'S' is engraved on it. Could it be his necklace?" Olivia asked.

The three stared at each other.

"Siderov?" Joe said, sitting back down.

"How would Andersen have had it if it belonged to Siderov?" Brad asked.

"He lived next door. The Siderovs wanted Andersen's house. Things got testy between them. I don't know. Somehow Martin got hold of it. It's possible, isn't it?" Olivia said excitedly.

"So what happened? Siderov gave Andersen the necklace?" Brad asked, confused.

Olivia stood up and walked back and forth, her mind racing. "No, no. It wouldn't have been a gift. They hated each other," Olivia said.

"Rodney Hannigan said that Andersen and Siderov never met," Joe said. "There was an intermediary who made the offers for the house."

Olivia paced faster. "Yeah, Rodney said they'd never met," she said to no one in particular. "But...the necklace could belong to Siderov. It's clear that Andersen slipped the necklace to me. He didn't just hand it to me. He needed to hide it."

Joe said slowly, "Liv, maybe the necklace was in Andersen's hand at the accident. Maybe when he was clutching at you, it just fell into your pocket. Maybe he never intended to drop it. Or give it to you."

Olivia stopped and stared at Joe. She was quiet. She had never considered the option that Joe proposed. She sat back down. "That's possible." She turned her head to the ocean. "So maybe this necklace thing means nothing at all. Maybe he didn't pass it to me in secret." She looked down at her hands. "Maybe Aggie just died of a heart attack like the police said." Olivia's shoulders were hunched.

Brad piped up. "But why was Andersen's tongue cut

out? He had been shot, for Pete's sake. Why did that guy at the scene scare Andersen so much?"

Olivia lifted her eyes to Brad's.

Brad went on, "What if...what if that guy at the scene was there before you?"

Olivia leaned forward. "I thought I saw a man there when I got to the accident. I thought I saw someone running away from Andersen's car. But it was so dark and I was focused on Martin. I can't be sure if I saw someone or not."

Brad's talked faster. "What if that guy was the one who cut out Andersen's tongue?" He stood up. "That's why Andersen panicked when the guy showed up again."

Olivia straightened up. "What if the necklace belonged to that guy? Maybe Andersen didn't want him to get it back, so he slipped it into my pocket."

Joe's voice was weary. "I don't know. Maybe you two have seen too many detective shows."

"It makes sense, Joe. As soon as the guy appears, Andersen freaks," Brad said. "He didn't want that guy to get the necklace. Or he was afraid the guy was going to kill him."

Olivia nodded. "You're right, Brad. The guy at the scene...he's a link. Why didn't I think of this before?"

Brad was excited. "Maybe the guy caused the accident. Maybe he was chasing Andersen. Maybe he shot Andersen. Maybe he was after the necklace. What if he saw how badly hurt Andersen was, cut out the tongue, then came back again to check to be sure he was dead?" Brad's eyes widened. "What if the guy is working with Siderov?"

"This is crazy," Joe said.

"It fits, Joe," Olivia told him.

"I could come up with a number of scenarios that fit," Joe replied. "You two are going off half-cocked. Just because the cross has an 'S' on it doesn't link it to Siderov. It could belong to anyone." He leaned forward. "We wondered if it belonged to Magdalene Streeter. Her last name starts with an 'S'. She loves jewelry. She's supposed to be in financial distress. She had a run in with Mrs. Callas. She wants us to sell our houses. She must want to sell Andersen's house too. Maybe she represents Siderov. Let's list everyone in town whose name starts with "S". I bet we can come up with any number of reasons why they could be behind all this."

Olivia and Brad stared at Joe, processing what he suggested. A shadow of uncertainty flickered over Olivia's face. "That guy who showed up at the accident was frightening, Joe. I felt in danger. Mortal danger. The way Martin Andersen reacted to him tells me there is reason to suspect him."

"We need to find out who he is," Brad said.

"How?" Joe asked.

Brad turned to Olivia . "You think you saw him in Boston."

Olivia nodded.

"You were followed on the highway," Brad went on. "Maybe this guy was watching you. He might have wanted to frighten you...or find out what you were up to... find out what you knew."

"Yes. That could be," Olivia said.

"You haven't seen him since?" Brad asked.

"No. I haven't. We need to find out who he is."

"Maybe we could draw him out again," Brad said.

Olivia's face was questioning.

"Maybe we could do something to get him to show himself again," Brad thought out loud.

"How?" Olivia asked.

"What if we put an ad in the town paper? Describing the necklace. You know, like a lost and found ad. Say you found it and are looking for the rightful owner."

"No." Joe's voice was loud. "I don't like this. You could be putting Liv in danger."

"Joe, I thought you believed this was just our imaginations?" Brad asked.

"Well, if it isn't..." Joe said more quietly. "No one knows you have that necklace. It could put you in danger to make it public knowledge."

Olivia touched Joe's arm. "This whole thing is upsetting to all of us. You know that I feel an obligation to

Andersen. That I need to find out if he was trying to tell me something...or not. He and Aggie were connected somehow. Maybe Aggie gave him my name. Maybe that's how he had my name in his wallet." Olivia shifted her eyes to the ground. "The most important thing of all... maybe I can figure out what happened to Aggie." She raised her head. "I need to find out, Joe."

"I know." Joe's voice was soft. "But I'm afraid." Joe's eyes pierced Olivia's. "I'm afraid we're getting in this mess too deep." He paused. "I'm afraid of losing you, too," Joe said, his voice cracking.

Olivia knelt next to Joe's chair and wrapped him in her arms. "I'm not going anywhere. Nothing's going to happen to me." Joe blinked at her. "You're stuck with me," she said.

Joe cleared his throat and sighed. "Okay, come on. Let's go inside and use the laptop. Let's see what we can find out about Siderov. And maybe we can write up an ad together for the newspaper...about that damn necklace."

INSIDE JOE'S HOUSE, the three sat around Joe's laptop and Googled Siderov's name. "How can there be nothing of importance about this guy?" Brad asked. "Especially if he is an international businessman."

"Only pictures and articles about him at charity events, country clubs, golf tournaments." Olivia said.

Joe shrugged. "What do we expect to find?"

"Why don't you Google Martin Andersen and his company," Brad suggested. "Maybe there will be a link between him and Siderov somehow."

Joe keyed the name into the search engine.

"I did Google him, Brad. Nothing like that came up," Olivia said.

"Well, here's a picture of Andersen and Hannigan at some charity event," Joe said squinting at the screen. "Caption says, 'Martin Andersen of Andersen Financial of Boston and S. Rodney Hannigan of the law firm Hannigan, Windsor and Riley of Boston attended the...'"

"Wait," Olivia said. "Did you say 'S. Rodney Hannigan'?" Olivia peered over Joe's shoulder to get closer to the computer screen. She stood straight. "'S'?" She and Brad exchanged looks. "S. Rodney Hannigan?"

"Did the cross necklace belong to Hannigan?" Joe asked.

"When I spoke with him, he didn't acknowledge the necklace. I asked him about it. I asked, did Martin own a gold cross necklace? He said 'no'."

The three of them stared at each other, each one considering.

"Do you think he lied to me?" Olivia asked quietly.

"That's a good question," Brad said.

"You asked him if Andersen had a necklace, you didn't ask Hannigan if he owned a necklace," Joe pointed out. "Maybe he omitted that information. Conveniently."

"What if Hannigan is behind all of this?" Brad asked. "What if he killed Martin Andersen?"

"Ugh." Joe whispered. "His own partner?"

Olivia's eyes went wide, and she shook her head. "No, I don't believe Rodney is guilty. What connection would he have with Aggie's death? He seems too sincere in his loss."

"Maybe he's a good actor," Brad suggested.

"It's just a coincidence that his name starts with an 'S'," Olivia told them. "But, I'll make an appointment with him to speak face to face. I want to ask him where he was the night that Martin was killed. And I want to see his reaction when I show him the gold cross necklace."

"Maybe that's not a good idea. If he's involved..." Joe cautioned.

"I'll meet him at his Boston office," Olivia said. "Nothing can happen to me in the offices of that large law firm."

17

The next day Olivia was back at work in the antique store. The painting of the shop walls had gone much more slowly than Olivia had thought it would. The store space wasn't that large, but the walls had windows on two sides, crown moulding along the ceiling, and some built-in cases attached to the walls that required precise and careful painting around many edges. Olivia had been painting and cleaning for a full week.

It was just before ten at night when Olivia completed the last display case. She was pleased with the way the shop looked. Tomorrow she would tackle assessing the inventory and cleaning the interior of the cases. She thought that she would be able to open the shop in another week.

She took the brushes and paint cans to the back room

and put the brushes in the sink. After wiping off the excess paint around the rim of the can, she put the cover in place. She used paper towels to squeeze out extra paint from the brushes, and turned the faucet on to let water run through the brush bristles.

Glancing out the little window above the sink, Olivia noticed that a plain white van had stopped at the corner to let some people cross the street on their way back from the restaurants in Perkins Cove.

The back door of the van opened with a jolt and a young woman who looked to be in her late twenties, wearing a cotton shirt, jeans, and flip flops, jumped out and started to run to the sidewalk.

The passenger door flew open and a man lurched for the woman and caught her by the arm.

A chill ran down Olivia's arms and she turned off the sink water, anticipating that she might need to call 911.

The woman stood in a stance of defiance and yanked her arm out of the man's grasp. He slapped her across the face, the force of it knocking her back a step.

The woman stood still and slowly turned her face back to the man, her hands clenched by her side. She spit onto the sidewalk in front of him.

The man's arm twitched as if he might strike her again, but another group of people turned the corner and walked past them. The man said something that Olivia couldn't hear.

The woman reached for the rear passenger side door, slid it back, and climbed into the van. As the man turned to take his seat in the front of the van, the streetlight illuminated his face.

Olivia dropped the brush she was holding. It was Alexei.

The van drove away just as a knock sounded on the front door of the shop. Olivia jumped and her heart thudded against her chest. She peered around the corner from the back room and saw Brad at the front door. She let out a big sigh and went to let him in.

"Hey," Brad said. "I knew you'd be working late, so I ..." Brad's smile vanished. "You ok?"

"Yeah," Olivia said stepping back so Brad could come in. "I just saw something strange though." She led Brad to the back room and indicated the small window over the sink. "I was cleaning brushes in the sink and looked out the window. A van stopped at the corner. A woman jumped out the back of the van. She looked like she wanted to get away. A guy got out of the front...the passenger side, and he grabbed her, very rough and mean." Olivia paused for a breath.

"What happened?" Brad asked.

"The woman didn't fight or anything. It was hard to see her face because of the dark, but she seemed kind of...defiant, I guess. She pulled her arm out of the guy's hold. He hit her across the face, Brad. Then she spit on the sidewalk in front of him."

Brad looked out the window to imagine what took place.

"Then she just got back in the van," Olivia told him.

"She did? Maybe it was a lover's quarrel or something?' Brad asked.

"It was Alexei. The guy who grabbed the girl was Alexei."

Brad's mouth opened but he didn't say anything.

"Should I have called the police?" Olivia asked.

"I don't know." Brad thought about it. "She got back in on her own. He didn't force her. Right?"

"No, not physically."

Brad shook his head. "I guess not. She would have to press charges and if she got back into the van on her own...I mean, she could have yelled if she was afraid... there are always people around here. So I guess not then." He shrugged. "But what the hell is up with that Alexei?"

"I don't know. But it shook me up. There's something wrong with that guy."

Brad nodded. They went back to the front of the shop. "Listen, I came by because I saw Joe in town when I was closing up the store. He said he needed to talk to us. He's down in the cove right now...meeting with some guy about a house to renovate. He said he'd be done a little after ten and could we meet him at the bar in the cove."

"What's it about?" Olivia asked.

"He said he heard something of interest today and wanted to talk to us about it."

"Well, I'm done here. Let's go see what he has to tell us," Olivia said.

OLIVIA AND BRAD headed down to the cove.

"Did you see our ad about the necklace in today's paper?" Brad asked while they walked.

"I did see it. No one has called or emailed about it so far," Olivia told him.

"Maybe tomorrow. Or maybe the person in question won't reply so as not to call attention to himself," Brad suggested. "You armed your burglar alarm when you left the house, right?"

"Yeah, I did."

"Listen, Liv. I know you're a big girl and all..." Brad started.

"What?" Olivia asked.

"I just wonder if maybe you should stay at Joe's for a while...you know, in case someone breaks into the house when you're asleep, looking for that necklace."

"I have the alarm system. It'll be okay."

"Now I wish I didn't suggest the ad," Brad said.

"Don't be silly. It's a possible way to get that guy to show himself," Olivia said. "It's okay, Brad. Really. It had to be done."

"I'm worried. That's all."

"Are you turning into Joe?" Olivia asked. "He worries for all of us."

"I'm thinking he has good reason," Brad muttered.

Joe was sitting on the deck of the bar, overlooking the cove. He was nursing a beer. He waved to Olivia and Brad.

"How'd the painting go?" Joe asked Olivia.

"It looks good. I finished. Now I need to look over the inventory and clean up and I'll be ready to open." The waiter came by and Brad ordered a beer and Olivia asked for iced tea.

"So what's up, Joe?" Brad asked.

"I was up in Wells at the coffee shop this morning. A lot of construction guys hang out there before they head to their jobs. Turns out the guy that I mentioned to you the other night, the guy who worked on the Siderov place. Mike Sullivan. Well, he's disappeared. The police found his car crashed into a tree last night. A few miles from his house in Concord." Joe paused. "But there's no sign of him."

"What happened?" Olivia asked.

"Not sure. They speculate that he lost control of the

car. Hit a tree. But it's like he vanished...disappeared into thin air. They can't find him." Joe lowered his voice and leaned closer to Brad and Olivia. "Remember I told you this guy was a talker? He had worked on the Victorian, just for one day. The only guy from the area who had done anything there. Well, he talked about it...even though he had signed the agreement not to discuss the job. Trouble was, he said too much. He talked about the design, the materials they were using. He even leaked the word on the safe room," Joe said.

"But Alexei said there is no safe room," Olivia said.

Joe raised his eyebrows. "Who should we believe? The guy working at the place or Alexei?"

"Did he claim to see the safe room?" Olivia asked.

"Not sure if he saw it himself or one of the other workers told him about it," Joe said. "So this Mike Sullivan gets called again," Joe continued. "Day before yesterday. Siderov wants him for something else. Tells Mike to come by yesterday morning to complete some masonry work," Joe said. "No one's seen him since yesterday."

This is a weird coincidence," Brad said. "Guy works on the place and winds up missing."

"Do you think the Siderovs had something to do with this? Because Sullivan talked? It can't be. It's too unbeliev-able," Olivia said.

Joe rubbed his chin. "I don't know what to think. But

as Brad says, it's a strange coincidence."

"How old is he? Mike Sullivan," Brad asked.

"Late twenties," Joe responded. "And here's where it gets stranger. The guy who told me about Mike...he went over to Mike's house earlier this morning to see if his wife needed anything. Nobody answered the door. So he looked in the back door window and there were supper dishes on the table. Like the family got interrupted and just got up and took off. He said he called the house several times and no one will answer," Joe said.

"What do you make of it?" Brad asked.

Joe shrugged. "I don't know. The wife and kid didn't go with Mike. It seems the wife's sister stopped at the Sullivan's house yesterday around dinner time to drop off a sewing machine she had borrowed. Says she talked to Mrs. Sullivan for a few minutes and left. Everything seemed normal. According to the timeline, the police found Mike's car around the time the sister was at the house. So Mrs. Sullivan was at home when Mike hit the tree. But no one's seen or talked to the wife or kid since then."

"I don't like this," Olivia said. "I don't like it."

Joe squeezed her hand.

Olivia said, "Too many questions. Could there really be a link between Siderov and Sullivan? Would Siderov hurt Mike Sullivan because he talked about the Victorian?"

"Tell Joe what you saw from the store window tonight," Brad suggested.

Olivia told Joe what she had seen. Joe leaned back in his chair. "That guy is trouble. Maybe the whole family is trouble."

"All of this mess started up after the Siderovs moved here," Olivia said.

"We can't jump to conclusions," Brad answered. "We need to think things through." He ran his hand through his hair.

They were all quiet for a few minutes.

"I was thinking that tomorrow I might take a ride out to the Sullivan's house... to see if maybe the wife showed up," Joe said. "Maybe she's back. She could have gone to stay with someone. I'd like to ask her if her husband was threatened by Siderov."

"How about we go with you, Joe?" Brad asked. "I have the morning off. I don't think you should go out there alone."

"I agree," Olivia said. "I'd feel better if we came with you. If she's there, we can sit in the car and wait while you talk to her, if you think that's best. If she's not there, well, then we can have a look around."

Joe said, "I'd like to have you along."

"I'll come by and pick you both up in the morning," Brad said.

18

The morning sky was clear and blue and the weather had been perfect for the past several weeks. Everyone hoped it was the beginning of a warm, dry summer that would bring plenty of tourists to Ogunquit.

Joe and Olivia were being chauffeured by Brad to the Sullivan house in Concord; about twenty-five minutes drive from Ogunquit. The car wound along a country lane lined with mature trees whose branches framed a canopy over the road. The houses were spread far apart and every few miles, they passed a small ranch or cape. Some had barns in the backyard.

Brad pulled onto the road's shoulder in front of a well-tended, gray, shingled Cape Cod style house with a white picket fence around three sides of the front yard. The lawn was mowed and flowers bloomed in beds next to the fencing. There was no car in the driveway and no sign of anyone around.

"Pretty place," Olivia said.

"Yeah, nicely taken care of," Joe remarked. "I'll go to the front door and ring the bell. I'll see how things go. If she's willing to talk to all of us, I'll wave you up."

Joe followed the brick walkway to the front door. He waited a couple of minutes but no one answered. He turned towards the car and shook his head. Joe and Olivia got out of the car and joined Joe at the front of the house.

"Nobody home," Joe said.

Olivia stretched her neck to try to peer into the living room through the big glass window at the front, but the glare on the window made it impossible to make anything out.

"Let's go around back," Joe said.

A detached two-car garage was at the end of the driveway. There was a wide deck on the back of the house. A vegetable garden was off to the side and the plants looked like they could use a drink. Joe and Brad looked through the small glass windows of the garage.

"No cars," Joe said.

Olivia walked up the steps to the deck and looked out over the back yard. There was a swing set near the vegetable garden. A kid's bike was lying in the grass next to the garage. Joe and Brad joined her on the deck.

"I rang the back doorbell," Olivia said.

"Obviously no one's here," Brad said.

Olivia gestured to the clothes line in the yard. "The wash on the line is dry, so it probably wasn't hung this morning."

They were quiet as they looked over the backyard. Olivia went to the back door and peeked in the window. "The dirty dishes are still on the table."

"So I guess no one has been here since the night Mike disappeared," Joe said.

"Dead end," Brad said.

"Maybe I'll wander over to the neighbors' house and ask if they know how to reach Mrs. Sullivan," Joe said. "Why don't you two stay here? I'll be right back."

Brad and Olivia sat on the deck's steps.

"The kid must go to school. The bike isn't a tricycle, so the boy must be in elementary school. Maybe we could go over to the school and ask if there was a way to contact Mrs. Sullivan?" Olivia said.

"The school probably wouldn't give us any information. You know, privacy laws and all that," Brad told her. "Mrs. Sullivan could be staying with family or friends. She might not want to be at home right now. Maybe she just doesn't want to be alone here."

Olivia nodded. "I can certainly understand that." She knew it was going to take her a long time to get used to living in her house without Aggie.

"Are you doing okay, Liv? On your own?" Brad asked gently.

"I'm okay," Olivia said. "Most of the time."

Joe came towards them ducking under the tree branches as he crossed the patch of lawn that separated the Sullivan's driveway from their neighbors.

"Nobody home there, either," he reported.

The three started down the driveway back to Brad's car. A flicker of something caught Olivia's attention and she glanced up, but quickly moved her eyes straight ahead and kept walking. "Guys," she said. "Keep walking and looking forward while I tell you something, okay? Don't look up."

Joe and Brad kept walking to the car. "Okay," Brad said. "What is it, Liv?"

"I think I saw the curtain in the upstairs window move back. I think someone is watching us," she said. "Let's stand by the car for a minute and figure out what to do next. Let's not spook them."

When they reached their parked car, Brad opened the driver side door, crossed his arms and leaned on top of the car door facing Joe and Olivia, who stood on the passenger side. "We can pretend to be casually talking. Who the heck is spying on us?"

"I don't know. I'm pretty sure someone's in there. If we ring the bell again, it's not going to make them answer the door. What should we do?" Olivia asked.

"If it's Mrs. Sullivan, she obviously doesn't want any visitors," Joe said. "On the other hand, if it's not Mrs. Sullivan, why the heck are they in her house if she isn't home?"

"I think we should get in and drive away," Olivia said. "Then park a bit down the road and come back on foot."

"We can watch the house from a distance," Brad said. "There's plenty of cover around here with the trees lining the road."

Joe nodded. "Let's go."

BRAD PARKED the car on a small dirt entrance to a trail way. Two other vehicles were parked there and Brad pulled in and placed his car further from the road so that it would be less noticeable to anyone driving past. The three got out.

"Once we get up by the house, why don't we position ourselves so that we have three different viewpoints of the place? We can text each other if we see anything," Brad suggested.

"I don't know how to use the text feature on my phone," Joe said.

"Really, Joe," Brad said. "You need to come into this century."

"We'll all put our phones on vibrate and talk softly to each other," Olivia said.

"Come on, we need to hurry in case whoever's in the house decides to vacate before we get back," Brad said.

They jogged up the road. Brad stepped into the brush directly across from the house. Olivia decided to take her place behind a group of pines that stood a few yards in from the road across from the Sullivan's neighbors' house which gave her a view along both houses and down to the Sullivan's garage. Joe went into the woods on the right edge of the Sullivan's property so he could watch the back of the house.

Olivia pushed through the brush and branches. She tripped over a big root. Mosquitoes buzzed at her eyes and ears. Her tank top was stuck to her sweaty back.

Worrying that she had ticks all over her legs, she swiped at the mosquitoes and horse flies. Olivia came to a fallen pine tree and used it as a seat to perch on as she watched the front and left side of the house.

Watching the upstairs windows for any movement behind the curtains, she thought about Liz Sullivan and her missing husband. Olivia wondered how Mrs. Sullivan broke the news to her son that his daddy had been in an accident.

Her heart contracted as she thought about the call informing her of Aggie's passing. The phone ringing late in the night waking her from a deep sleep. Her hand fumbling over the side table trying to locate the phone in the dark. Joe's voice cracking.

She took a deep breath and let her gaze wander around the Sullivan's front yard. The toys, the neatly tended house and property.

She thought about the hard work that went into making a life. A family of three, with one missing now. Lives yanked from their brightly humming orbit. Olivia hoped that Mike Sullivan had just hit his head, had amnesia or something, and would be found wandering in the woods off of Route 495. Please just let it be a simple accident.

An hour passed. Nothing happened. Olivia got a text from Brad: are we wasting our time?

Olivia sent a return text: maybe.

She sat for fifteen minutes more before another text came from Brad: called Joe...no answer...you call him.

Olivia called Joe's number. He did not pick up. She texted Brad: maybe he doesn't feel the phone vibrate.

Brad replied with, maybe we should give up on this... i'll go talk to joe.

Olivia hoped the guys would want to give up the vigil and get the heck out of the woods. They could think up Plan B.

Another text from Brad: can't find joe...come help me.

Olivia's stomach lurched. She stumbled through the brush. Branches scratched her face as she ran for the road. She jogged along the pavement, trying to see the spot where Brad was searching for Joe.

"Brad!" she called.

"Here! In here." Olivia heard Brad's voice and headed to the sound. She entered the woods at the point where she could hear twigs snapping.

Brad was in about fifty feet from the road. When Olivia reached him, he held up Joe's phone.

"This is all I found," Brad said, his face pinched with worry.

"Where is he?" Olivia said, her voice tight and high, her eyes darting all about the woods.

"I've been calling for him. I walked around. All directions," Brad said.

"He can't just disappear." Olivia's voice cracked. "Did you see anybody else around here?"

Brad shook his head. They stared at each other.

"Liv, walk up the road. Call his name. I'll keep searching in the woods," Brad said.

Olivia nodded and turned back to the street. She jogged, calling "Joe" every few steps as she made her way along the road. She ran about a half mile before deciding to turn back. She saw Brad in the distance walking towards her. When she got closer, she could tell by his face that he hadn't found Joe.

Olivia was panting. "What are we going to do?"

"Maybe he went back to the car," Brad suggested.

Olivia didn't think so. "He would have passed your line of vision if he decided to come out of the woods and go back to the car. You would have seen him, Brad."

"He could have gone through the woods. I'll go back and check the car just to be sure. Stay here in case he shows up?" Brad said.

"Okay." Olivia nodded. She walked to the place where Brad had been positioned so that she would have a good view of the front of the Sullivan's house. She stared at it letting her eyes rove over every inch of the building and the yard.

Olivia couldn't sit still and decided to cross the road. She walked slowly past the trees that lined the wide patch of lawn separating the neighbors' house from the Sullivan's place. She stayed on the neighbors' side as she peered through the branches at the gray cape, studying it for anything that seemed different from their earlier visit. She examined each of the windows.

She was nearly at the end of the driveway opposite the edge of the garage, still on the neighbors' side, when she sensed something stir near the Sullivan's deck. Olivia froze. A German shepherd emerged from the far side of the garage, sat down at the bottom of the deck's stairs, and riveted its eyes on the back door of the house.

Olivia tried to slow her breathing. She didn't want the dog to sense her. She worried that someone would come around the garage after the dog and would see her standing behind the trees. While she grappled with whether or not she should stay where she was or risk the dog's attention by moving away, the back door of the Sullivan's house opened. Olivia held her breath.

A little boy emerged from the house. He was about five years old with dark blonde hair. He was dressed in shorts and a Red Sox t-shirt and he carried a huge dish overflowing with dog food. The German shepherd sat erect at the bottom of the steps, his tail wagging. The boy put the dish down in front of the dog.

"Okay, eat," he told the dog, and the shepherd lunged at the dish and started devouring the meal. The little boy squatted beside the dog, patting his side. He looked up and turned his head in Olivia's direction. His eyes met hers. He raised his hand and waved. "Are you Olivia?" he asked.

Olivia's eyes widened. She nodded. "Who are you?"

"I'm Mikey. Why are you standing there?" he asked.

She shrugged. Mikey kept patting the dog.

"Joe's in the house," he said.

Olivia stepped out from behind the trees and took two steps towards Mikey, but stopped and glanced at the dog as it looked up at her.

"It's okay," Mikey told the dog, and the dog went back to eating. "He won't bite," Mikey said to Olivia. "He listens to me. If I say you're okay, he won't do anything. He's good."

"Is Joe alright? Can I go in?"

"Sure. Why wouldn't he be alright?"

Olivia looked at the back door. "What's he doing in there?"

Mikey was still patting the dog. "Making me a sandwich."

The back door opened and Joe came out carrying a tray with a glass of milk and a plate with a sandwich on it. Joe smiled when he saw Olivia standing there. "Liv, why don't you answer your phone?"

Olivia pulled her cell phone out of her pocket and looked at the screen: Missed call.

"What's...all this?" she asked, gesturing at the boy and the dog.

"I called you from the house phone. I can't find my cell. This is Mikey...Mikey Sullivan. And that's... Lassie." Joe smiled as he set the food on the deck's patio table.

Mikey climbed the stairs and plopped into one of the chairs. He dug into the sandwich, mumbling, "I know Lassie's a girl's name, but he likes it. Dog's are particular about what they like." He nodded to the dog as it climbed the stairs and took its position next to Mikey.

"How did you two come to meet?" Olivia asked Joe. She was on the deck now too. She reached down and patted Lassie behind the ears. Mikey took a big gulp of milk.

Mikey answered before Joe had a chance. "I found Joe in the woods," he managed between swallows.

"Scared the sh...ah...crap out of me, too, I might add," Joe said. "The two of them came up behind me. Like two ghosts...didn't make a sound until they were right beside me. I almost had a stroke," Joe said.

"Oh!" Olivia said. "I need to text Brad. We were frantic when we couldn't find you," she told Joe. "What were you doing in the woods?" Olivia asked Mikey while she sent a text to Brad.

"Waiting," Mikey said.

"Waiting for what?" Olivia asked.

"Mom to come back," he said.

Olivia exchanged glances with Joe. "Where is she?" she asked Mikey.

Mikey shrugged. "Don't know."

"How long has she been gone?"

"Since the other night," Mikey said, continuing the attack on the sandwich.

"So you've been here alone?"

"No. Lassie's with me. And we were only here for a little while. We've been in the woods. At the camp."

Olivia looked at Joe for clarification.

"Mikey and his dad built a camp in the woods back there." Joe gestured to the land behind the Sullivan's house. "Mikey took me there so I could see it. He and his dad stayed there together, camping out some nights.

Seems they own quite a bit of the land back there. Mikey and Lassie were hungry so they came back to the house. That's when we met," Joe said.

"Dad called and told us to run away," Mikey said. "Mom said stay with Lassie at the camp. She said she'd come back as fast as she could."

"Did your mom say to stay away from the house?" Olivia asked.

Mikey nodded. "Yup. But we got hungry. And we got tired of waiting."

"Were you watching us from the upstairs window when we were here earlier?"

"Yup. I went in the house to change my shorts."

"Was it day or night when Mom told you to stay at the camp?"

"Almost night...it was after supper," Mikey said. "Dad called when we were eating. He said he was hurt. Mom said we had to go and stay at the camp. So we took pillows and blankets and walked there. But mom forgot her phone in the house. She went back to get it. She didn't come back. Lassie and me slept in the camp last night. I think mom went to get dad."

"So you and Lassie slept at the camp last night. Alone," Olivia asked.

Mikey nodded.

"How old are you?" Olivia asked.

"Five, going on six. My birthday's coming." Mikey

turned to Joe. "Joe, can I have another?" The sandwich was gone, crust and all.

"Sure, come on." Joe, Olivia, and Mikey went into the kitchen. "You want one, Liv?" Joe asked as he prepared to make another sandwich.

"No, thanks," she answered.

"I called the police," Joe lowered his voice. "Reported that our friend is alone here. They'll be along shortly."

Olivia nodded. "Good."

Lassie stayed on the deck, snoozing. Mikey sat at the kitchen table while Joe put some mustard on two slices of bread. Olivia started to clear the dirty dishes, but put down the glass and plate she had picked up. The thought crossed her mind that this could be a crime scene and she wondered if they had compromised any evidence by coming into the kitchen. "Joe? Do you think we should be moving things around in here? Touching stuff?"

Before Joe could answer, Lassie started growling outside, a low guttural sound that came from deep in his throat.

"It must be Brad coming," Olivia said.

"Or the police," Joe offered.

Mikey went to the back door and spoke to Lassie through the screen. "Stop, it's okay." The dog ignored him and bolted off the deck. It stood in the driveway barking. Olivia looked through the screen door over Mikey's head. The dog was stiff legged, growling, with eyes fixed down the driveway. The scruff on its neck and back was raised. The dog wasn't paying any attention to Mikey.

Mikey reached for the doorknob, but Olivia put her hand over his to stop him from opening the door. Mikey looked up at Olivia. She put her finger to her mouth and whispered. "Shh. Stay in here with Joe." She tiptoed through the kitchen.

"Joe," Olivia said, and pointed to the side of the house as she passed him on the way to look out the window of the dining room. Joe watched Olivia enter the dining room which was on the side of the house near the driveway. He started to put down the knife that he was using to make the sandwich, but changed his mind and held onto it instead. He waved at Mikey to come over to him.

Olivia hugged the wall as she made her way to the window. Still hugging the wall, she peered out from behind the curtain. She gasped and pinned herself flat against the wall. Her hands went clammy and sweat trickled down her back. Her heart struck her chest like a jack hammer.

It was the man from the accident scene. The guy who had appeared out of nowhere that night. He was coming down the Sullivan's driveway. His head was slowly turning from side to side, surveying the area while keeping the growling dog in his peripheral vision.

Olivia crept to the kitchen. She put her finger to her lips again to warn Joe and Mikey not to talk. She waved them closer to her. She leaned to Joe's ear. "It's the guy from the accident. The one who scared me to death. He's walking down the driveway." Olivia's face was pale. "Where the hell are the cops?"

Joe leaned down to Mikey and whispered, "Where's the door to the basement?"

Mikey pointed to the front room.

"Is there a door in the basement that goes out to the yard?"

Mikey nodded.

Joe pointed to the front room of the house. He put his hands on Mikey's shoulders and moved him along. "Stay quiet. Don't talk."

The three of them inched into the dining room on their way to the front living room, pausing before passing the side windows that faced the driveway. Lassie had advanced and was threatening the man with deep snarls and snaps. The man stopped. He was glaring at the dog.

"Joe," Mikey said. "What's that?"

Joe and Olivia looked at the dining table where Mikey's hand pointed.

Olivia stomach lurched and she sucked in a gasp of air. She clamped her eyes shut. Joe pulled Mikey around and hugged him away from the sight.

In the middle of the dining table was a severed finger, the fingernail polished light pink, a bit of blood and bone visible at the end. The finger had been placed on a small, china saucer.

"Let's get to the basement," Joe whispered, his face white, his skin covered in a sheen of sweat.

"I'm not leaving Lassie," Mikey said. His arms folded over his chest.

Olivia, shaking, bent to Mikey's ear. "Lassie can handle this guy, Mikey. But we can't. He's bad." Mikey gave Olivia a stern look. Olivia continued, "Lassie's helping us. I'm not kidding. This guy wants to hurt us. Lassie's helping us get away. I promise we'll come back for your dog."

The man in the driveway reached into his pocket for something.

"Come on," Joe grabbed Mikey's arm and directed him to the door that led to the basement. He tried the knob but it was locked. Cursing, Joe fumbled with the bolt and pushed against the door. It wouldn't budge.

Through the side window, Olivia could see the man in the driveway. He had his cell phone to his ear. He was backing up. He wheeled and jogged to his car.

"Joe," Olivia said. "He's leaving." She hunched over and went to the picture window. "He's back in the car. He's driving away." She straightened. "He's gone."

"We need to move. Now." Joe scooped Mikey into his arms. "Get the door," he said to Olivia.

Olivia unlocked the front door of the house and held

it open for Joe and Mikey. They ran for the side of the property that was away from the driveway. Joe carried Mikey in his arms. They hustled to the tree line, where they took cover. Joe put Mikey down and, breathing hard, bent over at the waist, sucking in air.

"Joe, are you okay?" Olivia asked, taking his arm.

He nodded, puffing, his eyes closed. He lay down on the pine needles covering the ground.

"Joe..." Olivia's eyes were wide with worry.

"I just need to rest." Joe's voice was weak. Olivia crouched beside him.

She pulled out her phone to call Brad. He answered right away.

"I saw the guy. I pulled over up the road so I couldn't be seen. I saw him drive away. I saw you run. I'm coming."

"Brad's coming," Olivia said. "Joe?" She touched his face.

"I'm okay. Too much excitement for me, that's all." He was still lying on the ground with his eyes shut, but his breathing was less labored. Mikey stood over him weeping. Olivia reached up and tugged on Mikey's arm to have him kneel beside her.

Brad pulled his car to the side of the road and lowered his window.

"Come on, get in, in case he comes back," Brad said. "Where's Joe?" Brad saw Mikey. "Who's this?"

Mikey turned to Olivia. "Lassie ran behind the house." Olivia nodded.

"Joe, come on. Brad's here. Can you get up?" Olivia asked.

Brad opened the car door and got out in a hurry. "What's wrong with Joe?"

Olivia answered, "He just got winded. I'm going to get the dog."

"There's a dog?" Brad questioned. He bent to help Joe stand.

"Stay here, Mikey," Olivia told him.

"No. Lassie won't come to you," Mikey said.

There wasn't time to argue, so Olivia took Mikey's hand and they crossed the grass back to the driveway. The dog was not in sight. Mikey whistled and Lassie came bounding from behind the house. He jumped and circled Mikey in a happy dance.

"Come on, we need to go," Olivia said, but before they could head to Brad's car, a police cruiser pulled into the driveway. Finally, Olivia thought.

Brad turned his car around and parked in front of the Sullivan's house. Joe was sitting in the front passenger seat. He opened the car door but he didn't get out. His face was ashen.

Two officers emerged from the cruiser. Olivia greeted them and pointed to Joe. One look at Joe and the cops summoned an ambulance.

The EMTs checked Joe's heart rate and blood pressure and gave him some fluids. They suggested a ride to the hospital to double check everything but Joe flatly refused.

By the time Olivia was finishing up talking with the officer, Joe had some color back in his face.

The second officer had called the station to request a detective and some lab personnel in order to process the severed finger. He had gone into the house to gather preliminary information when ten minutes later he radioed his partner to send the EMTs into the house immediately. The rest of his message was garbled and Olivia couldn't make out what he said but the other officer shot into the house ahead of the EMTs, his gun drawn.

Commotion ensued with the arrival of another squad car, two detectives in an unmarked vehicle, and a second ambulance. Olivia, Brad, and Joe stood next to Brad's car watching the assemblage, the adults exchanging questioning looks. Mikey sat in front of them on the lawn patting Lassie.

"What's going on?" Brad asked no one in particular.

Olivia strained to overhear what an officer was relaying back to headquarters. Her eyes widened. She leaned over to Joe and Brad. "Mike Sullivan's in the basement," she whispered. "He's hurt. Unconscious but alive."

"He was in the house this whole time?" Joe asked.

Emergency workers wheeled a stretcher towards the house.

Olivia turned her head to Brad and kept her voice low. "That guy who showed up...the guy in the driveway...he was the man at the accident scene."

Brad stared at Olivia.

"Was he looking for Mike Sullivan? Did he know Sullivan was here" Olivia asked. Her voice was shaky.

Brad shrugged. "Who knows? What connection does that guy have with Sullivan?"

Olivia and Brad exchanged glances.

"Are you okay, Joe?" Olivia asked. Joe was sitting in the car again.

Joe nodded. "I'm fine." His head was pressed against the seat headrest. "Just resting."

Another police car arrived. A woman stepped from the backseat. Mikey spotted the woman and yelled, "Auntie!" He ran to her and they hugged. A detective spoke to the aunt.

One of the first officers to arrive returned to Olivia, Joe, and Brad and told them that they had no more questions for them but would most likely be contacting each one in a day or two.

"Is Mr. Sullivan going to be okay?" Olivia asked.

"The EMTs are taking care of him. They'll be moving him to the hospital shortly," the officer told her.

The three of them said goodbye to Mikey and climbed into Brad's car for the drive home.

Brad looked into the rearview mirror at Olivia. His face was somber.

"What the hell happened back there?" Brad questioned.

Joe was still quiet, sitting with his eyes closed. Olivia filled Brad in on what had occurred at the house while he had been searching for Joe.

"Brad," Olivia said. "That guy. The finger." She shuddered. "Whose finger was it?"

"Who knows," Brad managed. He looked pale. "Mrs. Sullivan's?"

Olivia felt sick. "What if Mikey was there alone? When the guy showed up at the house," Olivia said.

"Thankfully, he wasn't." Brad stared at the road.

"It was that awful man from the accident scene," Olivia said. "What was he doing at the Sullivan's? He must have been looking for Mikey and his mom. Did he have something to do with Mike Sullivan's accident?"

"Could he be working for Siderov?" Brad asked.

"Do you think so?" Olivia continued, "Where did Mrs. Sullivan go? She would never leave her child alone in the woods so long." She swallowed. "Do you think she's dead?"

Brad's worried eyes held Olivia's.

"What the hell is going on?"

They were quiet for the remainder of the ride home. When they arrived back in Ogunquit, they dragged themselves into Olivia's house. Brad insisted on making dinner and cooked up some chicken for Joe and himself and made a veggie stir fry for Olivia. They devoured the food along with a bottle of white wine. Joe had perked up a little and was almost back to himself. There wasn't much conversation, each one replaying the events that took place at the Sullivan house.

"What an awful day. I haven't had that much excitement for years," Joe said. "And I hope I don't have any more excitement for many years to come."

"We're all exhausted," Olivia said. "I hope Mike Sullivan pulls through."

"He warned his family to run away," Joe said. "Somehow he made it back to the house despite his injuries. But no one was there."

"And the finger," Brad said. "A warning to Sullivan? A threat?"

"The guy in the driveway," Joe said. "What's his connection to all this? He must be after Mike Sullivan."

"This can't be because Mike talked about the Siderov's safe room," Brad said. "Mike must have some connection to the guy from the accident. Could it be drug dealing?"

"I can't believe that," Joe told them. "Mike wasn't tied up in something like drugs. I'd bet money on that. Has to be something else."

"I'm going to call Detective Brown tomorrow," Olivia said. "I want to be sure the Concord Police have informed him about what happened."

"I better go check on the bookstore," Brad said. He started to clear the dishes, but Olivia shooed him away. "You made the meal. I'll clean up. Go ahead. Go check the store."

"And I'm going home and going to bed," Joe said, pushing himself up from the table.

Olivia walked them to the front door, where she gave them both a long hug. She went into the kitchen and started cleaning the dishes and pans from dinner. She barely had enough energy to finish the task.

THE NEXT MORNING she called the Portland State Police Department. Detective Brown was away on business, so Olivia made an appointment to see him at the end of the week.

19

Olivia had arranged to speak with Rodney Hannigan at his law firm in Boston's financial district. She decided to take the train into the city and avoid the possibility of being followed on the highway. After the episode at the Sullivan house the previous day, she didn't think she could handle any more excitement.

The brass plate on the polished wood door leading into Hannigan's private office was engraved with "S. Rodney Hannigan."

Olivia didn't believe that Rodney was the "S" on the cross necklace, but she wanted to observe his reaction to the questions she would pose to him to rule out any lingering trace of doubt that he could be involved in Martin's death.

Rodney ushered Olivia into his corner office, which

was furnished with dark wood furniture and oriental carpets. High above the city, two walls of the office were glass, affording a spectacular view of Boston and the harbor beyond.

"S. Rodney Hannigan?" Olivia asked. "What does the "S" stand for?"

"Schroeder. My mother's maiden name. You see why I go by Rodney." Hannigan gestured to the sofa. "Please," he said. He took a seat in a wing chair that was positioned next to the sofa.

"Thanks for meeting me," Olivia said. "I just thought we should talk in person. Although, I'm not quite sure where to start. Or even what to ask." She smiled weakly and looked down at her hands.

"Olivia," Hannigan said. "I need to thank you once more. I can't imagine how terrible it was for you to come upon the accident. And again, I thank you for being with Martin when he passed. It comforts me to know that he wasn't alone. I'll be forever grateful that you were with him." He took a deep breath.

Olivia nodded and said, "You know that I believe that my aunt's death is unexplained, even though the coroner said she had a heart attack. She was fit and strong. She was riding a bicycle at the time of her death...something she never did. And she had a gun in her possession...also something completely out of character." Olivia paused. "I'm trying to connect some dots.

My aunt died under unusual circumstances. Certainly Martin's death has unusual circumstances surrounding it." Olivia didn't mention the tongue, but they both knew what she meant. "And Martin had my name in his wallet." Olivia paused. "The two deaths must be linked. Have the police made any headway into the investigation?"

"No, nothing, really. They call occasionally with an update that amounts to nothing at all. I feel that the case is being moved to the back burner. They have no leads. Martin's death will remain an unsolved homicide, I'm afraid."

"Rodney, did you pick Martin up from the airport the night he returned from London?"

"No, I was in New York City that week working on a case. We were in meetings until around 2am on the day that Martin died. I had only been in my hotel room about an hour when the Ogunquit Police phoned me to report the terrible news. I took a cab to LaGuardia immediately and flew to Boston. I rented a car at the airport and drove to Maine." He shook his head. "I drove like a madman, but I don't know why. I knew Martin was already dead."

Olivia nodded. She believed him. "What about what Martin said to me...'red Julie'...have you thought any more of what it could mean?"

Hannigan lifted his hands from the arms of the chair and turned the palms up in a gesture indicating that he had no idea. "Red Julie...I just...I don't have a clue. I don't think Martin knew anyone named Julie."

"More dead ends," Olivia said. She wondered how she would ever figure any of this out.

They were both quiet for a minute. "Did you find any emails from Martin to my aunt? Could they have known each other?"

"There were no emails from an Aggie," Hannigan said.

"Her full name was Magdalene Miller Whitney... but everyone called her Aggie."

Hannigan shook his head. "Whitney? Did you tell me that? I assumed her last name was Miller...the same as yours. I wonder if I overlooked something in the emails." He said, "Wait. Magdalene? She's not that real estate agent?"

Olivia smiled. "No, not her. They do share the same first name, though."

"That real estate agent contacted Martin every four months or so looking to list his house," Hannigan said. "She's an abrasive woman."

"Yes, she can be very abrasive." Olivia thought for a minute. "Martin's secretary, Paula Adams, said that Martin was a collector."

Hannigan looked surprised. "Yes. Yes, he was. Is that significant?"

"My aunt owned the small antique shop on the corner of Shore Road leading down to the cove," Olivia said.

"The Olde Stuff Shoppe?" Hannigan asked, straightening up.

Olivia brightened. "Yes. That was Aggie's shop. Had you visited it?"

"I didn't, no. But Martin enjoyed collecting things and he stopped into the shop every now and then. He made quite a few purchases there. I didn't know the owner's name was Aggie."

Olivia leaned towards Hannigan, and stood up excitedly. "They knew each other. There's a connection between them." Her heart was pounding. At last, they had found a link.

"Yes, it seems so," Hannigan responded, his face looking lighter.

"They knew each other," Olivia said almost to herself as she started pacing the room. She stood in front of the windows looking over the city, before turning back to Hannigan. "They're connected, Rodney. Through Martin's purchases at the shop. That's the link between them."

"Yes," he nearly whispered. Hannigan's eyes met Olivia's. "But why are they both dead?"

Olivia moved back to the sofa and sat. She suddenly felt weak. Her throat was tight and dry. Why are they both dead? She wished someone else would figure it out.

But there wasn't someone else. It was like a weight pressing her into the ground. She swallowed hard.

"What could have happened...what did they know that caused them both to die within a month of each other?" Hannigan asked.

Olivia tried to focus her thoughts. "What did Martin collect?" she asked.

"He loved wooden figurines, Hummels, hand crafted antique music boxes, antique jewelry boxes. Objects from Bavaria, Austria, Switzerland."

"Paula Adams contacted a dealer in Munich who Martin had bought collectibles from when he was there on other trips. We wanted to know if Martin went to see him when he was overseas this time. The dealer hasn't replied yet. Paula emailed me and said that she received an automated message saying the dealer was away and would be returning in a few days," Olivia said.

"That's a good idea to contact the dealer," Hannigan said. "If he saw Martin that week, maybe he can give us some additional information. Maybe he can shed some light on what Martin was doing."

"Did Martin collect any jewelry?" Olivia asked.

"No. No jewelry. Only the things I mentioned."

Olivia pulled the gold cross necklace from her pocket. "This is the necklace that I told you Martin had. Is it familiar to you?" she asked. Olivia watched his face.

Hannigan leaned closer and took the necklace in his

hand. He shook his head. "No, I haven't seen this before. It is quite beautiful. Except for that skull in the middle." He turned it over in his hand. "S," he said, seeing the engraved letter on the back of the cross.

"Martin put this in my pocket at the accident scene," Olivia said.

Hannigan's eyes widened, questioning. "Did he? I've never seen it before. What was Martin doing with this? Why would he put it in your pocket?" Olivia thought Hannigan seemed sincere in his denial.

"Another question without an answer," Olivia said.

They sat in silence for several minutes.

"Can you tell me more about Martin's interactions with the owners of the Victorian and their attempts to purchase his house?" Olivia was clutching at anything she could think of that might help to add pieces to the puzzle.

Hannigan stiffened. "As I told you, Siderov never spoke directly with Martin. However, he had a real estate representative who hounded Martin repeatedly. You see, the Ogunquit house was in Martin's name only. He was the sole owner. The owners of the Victorian desperately wanted to purchase the Ogunquit home. Martin loved that house, wanted to retire there, and would not consider any offers. The offers became astronomical, completely out of line with what the house was worth. Martin felt that the owners were engaged in some kind of a power play: you know, wealthy powerful man is rebuffed and then wants, at any cost, what has been denied him."

Olivia nodded. "Yes, sounds like them."

"You know them?" Hannigan raised his eyebrows.

"The son and I went out once. I didn't care to continue the acquaintance. He didn't care for that response. Neither did his father, who let me know how he felt when I went to the gala at their home. Which, by the way, I wouldn't have attended if I wasn't roped into going."

"Sounds like their tactics," Hannigan said. "They want something. They don't get it. They become aggressive in their attempt to take what they want. Very entitled. I don't think they are refused often." He paused. "I would be careful of them, Olivia."

Hannigan looked at the necklace in his hand. "This looks very valuable," he said, and raised his eyes to Olivia's as he passed the necklace back to her. "Martin had this?"

Olivia nodded. "Why would he put it in my pocket? If he wanted to give it to me, why wouldn't he have just handed it to me?" Olivia asked.

Hannigan was quiet. He shook his head.

"Unless he didn't want anyone else to see it," Olivia said.

Hannigan's face was serious.

"Why do you think the Siderovs wanted Martin's house so badly?" Olivia asked.

"We assumed at first that he wanted to have it for guests or to expand his property. Then we thought he just became crazed over owning it because Martin wouldn't sell," Hannigan said.

"When I was at the gala, Siderov's son called the house a 'monstrosity'. He became visibly angry and agitated when he talked about Martin's house. I found it odd...an overreaction," Olivia said.

"A strange group of people," Hannigan responded.

"Are they still pursuing the purchase with you?" Olivia asked.

"The representative contacted me shortly after Martin's death to present another offer. I really don't want the house, but I'll be damned if I sell it to them. I told the representative never to contact me again or I would pursue a restraining order with the courts...against all of them."

"How did the representative take that?" Olivia asked.

"Not well. He made a remark that I might come to regret holding onto the house. I blew it off, but in retrospect, and in light of this conversation, perhaps I should have taken it as a threat."

"Has there been any contact since?" Olivia asked.

"None."

"I have an appointment with Detective Brown later

this week. May I pass this information on to him?" Olivia asked.

"Please do."

"Do you have the real estate representative's name?"

Hannigan rose and took a silver pen from his desktop. He wrote onto a pad of paper, pulled off the sheet, and handed it to Olivia. He had written: Michael Prentiss, Prentiss Property Management.

"This isn't local. I've never heard of them," Olivia said.

"I never kept a contact number as I wasn't interested in speaking with them."

Olivia put the paper in her jacket pocket. "Is anyone staying at your house now?"

"No, it's empty. I have no intention of using it without Martin. And renting is a hassle I don't need at the moment."

"When I was at the gala, I saw several decks on your house that overlooked the Siderov property."

Hannigan nodded.

"Is there access to the decks from the outside of the house?" Olivia asked.

"Yes," Hannigan said. He thought for a moment. "Is there something you wish to see from the decks?"

"Maybe. I was thinking it couldn't hurt to watch the Siderov place. Although I really don't know what I'm expecting to see."

"I can give you a key to the house," Hannigan told her.

"No, I just want to use the decks. Someone being in the house might arouse suspicion."

"Olivia...I'm not sure this is a good idea. What if these people are dangerous?"

"If they are dangerous, I think we both have reasons to find out just how dangerous they are."

"Just tell the police. Let them investigate," Hannigan suggested.

"My aunt died of a 'heart attack'. Martin died...well..." Olivia's words trailed off. "The police don't seem to be helping."

Hannigan nodded, his face a mix of sadness and anger.

Olivia held out the necklace. "This was in Martin's possession just before he died. I don't know why he gave it to me. I don't know what he wanted me to do with it." She extended her hand. "It belongs to you now."

Hannigan shook his head vigorously. "No. I don't want it."

"Sell it then," she said. "It must be worth a good deal of money." Olivia just wanted Hannigan to take it from her, to free her from the obligation of figuring things out.

"I don't want that necklace anywhere near me. It wasn't anything Martin would own. I don't know why he had it, but it wasn't his. And if it had something to do with his death..." His voice trembled.

Olivia's hand dropped into her lap. Her energy was gone. She didn't know what else to do.

"Please don't give up." Hannigan's face was serious. "It means something. We both know it."

Olivia nodded.

"Use the decks on the house," Hannigan said. "See if you can discover anything about the Siderovs. But be careful, Olivia. Call me. Call me if you need anything," he said. They shook hands and Hannigan walked Olivia out.

She believed the depth of his emotions. He couldn't be involved in Andersen's death.

20

A bell tinkled when Olivia opened the door of Streeter Real Estate and stepped inside. A stylish male receptionist greeted her with a warm smile. "Welcome to Streeter Real Estate. How may I help you?"

"Hi. I was wondering if Magdalene was around. I don't have an appointment but was hoping to catch her if she was in."

"I'm not sure if she's available. She might be on the phone with a client. Let me pop into her office and see. Who can I tell her is inquiring?"

"Olivia Miller."

The man stood but stopped in mid turn. He cocked his head slightly as if he was considering something. "Olivia Miller? Aggie Miller-Whitney's daughter?"

Olivia nodded, surprised. "She was my aunt. My legal guardian. You knew her?"

"She did some legal work for me. She was a fine lady. I'm sorry for your loss."

He went to check on Magdalene. He came out of her office almost immediately with Magdalene right on his heels. "Olivia!" she called cheerily as she bustled into the waiting area.

Oh no, Olivia thought. She thinks I want to sell my house.

"So nice to see you. How have you been doing?" Magdalene said, her voice soaked with saccharine. "You haven't opened the shop yet."

"No. I've been busy getting things ready."

"Come into my office." She took Olivia by the arm. "What would you like? Tea? Coffee? Ice water with lemon?"

"Nothing, really," Olivia said.

"Now, now. It's so hot outside. What about some nice cool water?" She called over her shoulder, "Andrew, would you bring Olivia some water with lemon and some mint tea for me, dear?" She moved her lips close to Olivia's ear. "Isn't he handsome? So stylish. And smart and efficient, too. Wouldn't I love to have him barking up my tree?" She let out a heavy sigh. "But, alas, he doesn't like women." She shook her head. Olivia chuckled inwardly, as if Andrew being gay was the only thing keeping him from having a romantic interest in Magdalene.

"Please, sit." Magdalene gestured to the small sofa. Olivia sat down and Magdalene settled her considerable girth into a chair next to the sofa.

The office was elegantly decorated with cherry wood furniture, cut glass lamps, original paintings by Ogunquit artists, and the sofa and chairs upholstered in shades of cranberry and forest green. It gave the impression of understated success, which surprised Olivia, since Magdalene's manner and dress was anything but understated.

Andrew came in with a tray and placed Olivia's water and Magdalene's tea on the coffee table alongside linen napkins. He put a glass plate with small butter cookies in the center of the table. "Can I bring you anything else?" Andrew asked.

"No, dear. Very nice. Thank you," Magdalene told him with a bright smile. He left the room and she clucked her tongue against the roof of her mouth. "All men should be like that."

Olivia chuckled.

"What? You don't think so? Just wait til you're older." She lifted her tea cup and sipped. "Now, Olivia. Have you been thinking about selling the house? Or the business, perhaps?"

"No. I'm keeping them," Olivia said firmly.

Magdalene's face hardened. "What brings you in then?"

"I was speaking with Rodney Hannigan yesterday..." Olivia started but was cut off instantly.

"Rodney Hannigan! I've been trying to meet with him for some time. Well, not specifically with him. With Martin Andersen. Until his passing, of course. But I have sent my condolences to Mr. Hannigan and offered my services should he ever wish to sell that magnificent home."

"Yes, I believe he mentioned that." Olivia did not relay the part that Hannigan thought Magdalene was a pest.

"And what did you talk to him about?"

"He said that he had been repeatedly approached by an agency that was very persistent in trying to acquire their beach property."

Magdalene sat up straight, as if she needed to defend her territory against interlopers. "Did he name the agency?"

"Yes, and I wondered if you knew of them? It was Prentiss Property Management. Michael Prentiss was the man who contacted them."

Magdalene's face was screwed up as she thought. "Prentiss. No. I'm not familiar with them." She went to her desk and tapped at her laptop. "Prentiss," she said. "New York City? Well, then, I have some competition.

New York City." She looked at Olivia. "Is Mr. Hannigan amenable to the offer?"

"No," Olivia said, and Magdalene's face relaxed with relief.

"Good. Well, a client from New York is interested in that property, are they?"

"No," Olivia told her. "Prentiss is representing the Siderov family."

Magdalene looked as if she had been slapped. "What?" Her voice was shrill. Her jaw set and her eyes narrowed. "How dare they?"

Olivia looked confused. "What do you mean?"

"How dare those Siderovs use an outside agency. From New York? What does a New York agency know about the seacoast property of Maine? The Siderovs should have come to me, for heaven's sake." She sniffed. "Well, I believe that I will pay Mr. Siderov a visit."

Olivia looked pained. "Oh, no, I don't think that's a good idea."

Magdalene turned sharply to Olivia. "Olivia, I do know how to run my business."

"I just mean that I don't want to be brought up to the Siderovs," Olivia said. "And I'm sure Mr. Hannigan would prefer not to be mentioned."

Magdalene moved her hand about in the air. "Oh, my. I certainly know how to be discreet."

Olivia raised her eyebrows. "I...they..."

"What?" Magdalene asked. "Come, come. What are you stumbling over?"

"I just think that maybe they aren't the usual customers. They...seem...well, I wonder if they could be dangerous," Olivia said.

"Olivia, do you have some reason to suspect them to be so?" Magdalene asked with an edge of impatience.

"Not specifically."

"These people are incredibly wealthy," Magdalene went on. "Just the sort of client I prefer. They could be the means to many fruitful contacts."

"Well, if you find out anything about Michael Prentiss and his company, would you let me know?"

"My I ask what your interest is in all of this?" Magdalene said.

"My interest is in the Siderovs' desires and means," Olivia said stiffly. "I want to know if they're up to something. If you or any of your contacts can shed some light on them, I hope you'll share the information with me."

"Of course I will. I'll ask around. Discreetly, mind you." Magdalene pushed herself out of the chair. The meeting was over. "Thank you for stopping by, Olivia."

21

"Why do you talk me into doing these things?" Brad said. "It's just like when we were little kids."

They walked along Perkins Road and when they approached the brick driveway to Martin Andersen's house, they looked ahead and behind for any cars or walkers headed in their direction. The coast was clear, so they jogged down the driveway and to the left side of the massive contemporary structure.

A wide bluestone and granite walkway edged around the house to the side facing the ocean. The walkway led to a splendid patio in the middle of a wide expanse of manicured lawn. Granite containers spilled with petunias and impatiens.

The edges of the patio were landscaped with sea grasses, hydrangeas, and Rosa rugosa. Chairs and lounges were scattered around the patio. A small lap pool glistened in the early evening light. A teak wood staircase rose to the first level deck along the side of the house facing the Siderov property.

"This is fantastic," Brad said, taking it all in. "That Hannigan guy is certainly keeping the place up."

"Come on, Brad. Let's go up to the first level deck," Olivia said.

They each carried a small duffel bag. On the deck, they crouched down and gazed at the view from their perch.

"No wonder the Siderovs want this place. Almost every inch of their property is visible from here. The view must be even better from the third level deck," Brad said.

"Let's go see," Olivia suggested. They took the staircases to the third level. "Look at this." They had a perfect view of the lawn, house, and driveway of the Siderovs. They sat low on the floor of the deck, peering through the slats in the railing.

"Ha," Brad said. "No privacy at all for those bastards." He took out two pairs of binoculars from his duffel. Olivia lifted two cameras and a zoom lens from her bag.

"Let's settle in," she said.

"Next time we come, let's bring cushions to sit on. This wooden deck isn't the most comfortable thing in the world," Brad said.

Olivia smiled and handed him a sandwich. "Here, this will help you pass the time more comfortably."

"You think of everything." Brad munched. "What do we expect to see?"

Olivia sighed. "Who knows? Probably nothing."

Over the next three hours, the light of the day faded and the Siderov estate became veiled with darkness.

Olivia and Brad passed the hours chatting and observing the property, watching servants walk a dog and water hanging flower baskets on the veranda of the Victorian. There was a delivery of fresh flowers from a florist truck. Neither the Siderov father nor son made an appearance.

"I wish we could see inside," Olivia said.

Brad yawned. "Not unless you acquire x-ray vision any time soon." He slid backwards along the deck so that he could lean up against the wall of the house. "You should have taken the key to the house that Hannigan offered you."

"Why?" Olivia asked.

"I need the bathroom," Brad replied.

Olivia rolled her eyes and chuckled. "Guess what? So do I."

"Should we call it a night? It's 11:30 already. I have to get up at five tomorrow morning. Some of us have to work, you know, Liv," Brad teased.

Olivia put the cameras back in her bag. "Yeah, let's go. I don't even know what I'm expecting to see here."

"We'll try again tomorrow night," Brad told her. "We aren't giving up after one try." Olivia watched him put the binoculars into his duffel.

"My butt's killing me from sitting on that damn wood," Brad said. He waddled along the deck to the stairs in a crouch position so he couldn't be seen from the Siderov place. He looked so much like a duck that Olivia started to laugh. She clasped her hand over her mouth to keep the sound from traveling.

"I'm glad I'm entertaining you," Brad muttered.

Olivia nearly gagged on her stifled laughter. Tears rolled down her cheeks as she followed Brad along the deck in the same crouched stance.

THE NEXT NIGHT of spying went the same as the first. Brad and Olivia saw nothing of interest. They sat on the third level deck for hours, with Brad complaining that he forgot to bring a cushion to sit on.

"Go get a cushion from the lounge chairs on the patio," Olivia told him.

"Nah, I might miss something," Brad said.

"Same routine as last night," Olivia said. "The maid

brings the dog out. The houseman waters the flowerpots on the veranda. Nothing else happens."

"The florist's truck didn't come tonight. That's different."

"Yeah, well, I don't think they need a floral delivery every day," Olivia said. "I wish I could see inside that house."

"I heard that last night," Brad said.

"I want to know what's going on. Where's Siderov? Where's Alexei? Don't they ever leave that place?"

"Well, there is a way you could probably find out," Brad said.

Olivia raised an eyebrow. "How could I?"

"Go out with Alexei again. Return his call."

Olivia groaned, and said, "You do have a point. I might be able to get into the house again if I went out with him. At the very least, I might learn more about their comings and goings. And after a while; who knows, he might even spill something."

Brad sat up, his face serious. "I was joking."

"Even so...it might produce results. And you wouldn't have to sit on the deck anymore."

"Liv...I don't want you seeing him. They're crazy. It could be dangerous," Brad told her.

"Maybe."

"Maybe what?" Brad said.

"Maybe I should see him a couple more times."

"Has he contacted you?" Brad asked.

"A couple days after the gala...he texted me."

"What did he say?"

"He said something like he needed to speak to me, it was important," Olivia said.

"Did you respond to him?"

"No."

"Wouldn't he wonder why it took you so long to answer him?"

"I could say my phone died. It...it fell in the toilet. That's why I couldn't reply."

Brad made a face. "That's lame. He wouldn't fall for it."

"Then I'll say I hadn't been feeling well, but now I'm better and I'd like to meet for coffee."

"Leave it. It's a bad idea. Joe would have a fit."

Their conversation was interrupted by the sound of a truck approaching the Siderov place. They turned to see. It was a delivery truck.

"Another flower delivery?" Olivia asked.

The guy got out of the van carrying two medium size packages. He rang at the front door. The maid answered and the man entered the house with the boxes.

"Who delivers so late?" Brad asked.

"The van doesn't seem to have anything written on it," Olivia said. "No company name."

The guy came out of the house and went back and forth to the truck a few more times carrying boxes.

"Maybe they're getting ready for some event," Brad offered.

Olivia considered that. "Last night flowers were delivered. Wouldn't flowers be delivered the same day if there was an event? To keep everything fresh?"

"I don't know. Maybe Siderov just likes flowers around the place," Brad said.

"Can you see if the truck says anything?" Olivia asked. They both raised binoculars.

Brad answered, "I don't see anything written on the side."

Olivia was craning to see while staying low on the deck. "I don't see a telephone number or a website or anything written on the van."

"There isn't anything," Brad said, lowering the binoculars. "Why wouldn't a delivery company display a name and number? Wouldn't you want to attract business?"

"If you were a legitimate business," Olivia said.

The guy came out of the house carrying a big box and placed it in the back of the van. Olivia lifted her camera and focused on him. She managed several shots before he climbed in and started the engine. As it drove away, she focused on the van itself, trying to get the license number. She took several photos before it was out of sight.

"Now what?" Brad asked. "Should we stay longer?"

"I guess not. We don't even know if Alexei and his father are at home."

"We'll come back tomorrow night," Brad said.

Olivia craned her neck. "Look. Two guys just stepped onto the veranda."

Brad raised his binoculars. "One looks like Siderov."

"That's Detective Brown. Talking to Siderov." Olivia lowered the binoculars. "Why would Detective Brown be there?"

"How'd he get there?" Brad asked. "There isn't a car in the driveway."

"I'm going down. I want to get closer." Olivia put her binoculars on the deck.

"Liv," Brad said sternly. "No."

She packed the cameras in her bag. "I need to hear what they're saying."

"What will you do? Just walk up to them? There are security cameras all over."

"Maybe I can hug the tree line. Somehow get around to the other side of the house. Get closer to the far side of the veranda."

"I'm going with you."

"No. That won't work. If I get caught, I can say I came to talk to Alexei. Stay and watch with the binoculars."

"This is serious," Brad said. "You think the Siderovs could be connected to trouble. This isn't something to take lightly. Maybe the events are all unrelated. Maybe it's just a bunch of coincidences that have no link to each other. But maybe everything is linked together and the Siderovs are dangerous people. We just don't know. You can't put yourself in danger. Think about Joe. What if something happened to you? How could he cope? And so soon after Aggie."

"I know. You're right." Olivia groaned. "I wish I could hear what they're talking about."

"Come on, let's go home," Brad said. He and Olivia went down the stairs from the deck and followed the walkway leading back to the driveway and out to the street.

22

Olivia was in the pharmacy, picking up a few things. As she passed the prescription counter, a man turned around. "Olivia." Olivia looked up to see Alexei in front of her. She wasn't happy about it.

"Alexei."

"How are you?" he asked. He looked wan and tired.

"Good. I'm good." Olivia wanted to slink away.

"I'm sorry I upset you at the gala...after showing you the house," he said, paying the pharmacist and taking his bag. "I wish I could have spent more time with you." He stayed next to Olivia as she wandered the aisles.

"I know you had to see to your guests," she said. She took her things to the checkout counter.

"Do you have time for a drink someday?" he asked.

Olivia paid the cashier. She and Alexei stepped out onto the sidewalk.

"I don't know. I have a lot of work to do."

"I'd like to talk to you," Alexei said. He ran his hand over his forehead. The whites of his eyes were bloodshot and his facial features seemed pinched.

"Are you all right?" Olivia asked.

"I've had a headache all day," Alexei answered.

"I was out for a walk along the rocks near your house the other evening," Olivia lied. "Was that Detective Brown I saw at your house?"

Alexei's eyes widened. "You were on the rocks?"

Olivia ignored the question. "Detective Brown has been investigating Martin Andersen's death. Your father knows Brown?"

"Not really."

Olivia pressed for information. "Do you know why he was there?"

"Something about a license." Alexei checked his watch. "I know that I've gotten off on the wrong foot with you. I've been under a lot of pressure...a lot of stress lately. I'd like a chance to start over."

Olivia didn't know what to say. Alexei was draining, but she was starting to feel bad for him again.

"Would you meet me for coffee or a drink sometime?" he said. He looked up and down the main street as if he were expecting someone. Beads of sweat showed on his forehead. "I need to chat with you. It's important."

"Maybe," Olivia told him. She wanted to get away from him.

"I'll give you a call. I need to get going."

After Alexei had crossed the street, Olivia groaned. Why did Alexei seem so nervous? Please don't call me.

23

"Andrew, dear," Magdalene called from her office. When he did not respond to her, she heaved herself out of her chair and waddled into the hallway. Andrew had the phone to his ear and raised his index finger to indicate he would be off the phone momentarily. She arrived next to Andrew's desk just as he disconnected from the call.

"That was my friend in New York. He reaffirms what your colleagues have told you. Initially, Prentiss Property Management was an independent company but it now appears to be a branch of some other corporation. There doesn't seem to be any recent record of them actually processing any real estate transactions. Their business is mainly property management now. And when my friend called the parent corporation to try to speak with Michael Prentiss, he was told that Mr. Prentiss had passed away."

Magdalene pursed her lips. "Recently?"

Andrew nodded. "Yes. I looked it up online." He paused for effect. "It appears to be a homicide."

"What?"

"Prentiss was found in his townhouse. Shot in the head."

Magdalene's eyes widened.

"Perhaps someone was unhappy with him? A client, possibly?" Andrew asked.

Magdalene knew who Andrew was suggesting. Her mind was working. She tapped distractedly on Andrew's desk, then straightened up.

"Well, enough time spent on Prentiss." She checked her Rolex for the time. It was almost nine at night. "Andrew, tomorrow morning call the Siderovs for me and..." Her voice trailed off. "Oh, no, never mind. First I need to stop by that new listing I have. Anyway, an unexpected visit to the Siderovs from a neighbor might be the best way to approach them," she clucked.

"Do you think that's a good idea?" Andrew asked. "Perhaps that is one client who should be avoided."

"I'm sure Mr. Siderov would enjoy a nice chat," she said, dismissing Andrew's concern. "Since he has lost his representative, he may be in need of another one." She started down the hallway to her office. "Call Olivia Miller for me before you leave tonight, will you, Andrew? Let her know what we discovered about Prentiss. She may find it interesting."

~

OLIVIA SAT at the desk in the antique store, staring at her laptop. The sun had gone down and the shop was getting dark. She was trying to figure out Aggie's online portion of the business and needed to contact customers to explain Aggie's passing and why their orders had been delayed.

She had spent most of the day tracking and organizing the inventory and packing up items for shipment. She had missed dinner and had a massive headache brewing. Flipping screens to check her email, she found a new one from Paula Adams.

OLIVIA,

The Munich dealer responded and did indeed meet with Martin that week. Martin had photographs of a recent collectible purchase that he made in the States and wanted the dealer to give his opinion about the piece's authenticity. The dealer said he told Martin that the item was a forgery, an excellent one, but in his opinion it was not authentic from what he could tell from the photos. Give me a call when you can.

Paula

As Olivia reached for her phone, it started to vibrate. She lifted it from her pocket and looked at the phone's screen to see who was texting her. It was from Rodney Hannigan: can you meet me at my beach house?

Olivia texted a return message: whats going on?

found something you need to see it's important i need to leave soon can you come now? Hannigan responded.

Olivia answered: i'm at the store be there in a few minutes

Hannigan's discovery and its urgency started Olivia's heart beating hard against her chest. What could he have found? Will it answer our questions? Will the police be able to use it?

Olivia put her phone on the desk, shut down her laptop and shoved it into her backpack. She closed the store windows, grabbed her keys, flung her backpack over her shoulder, and locked the door of the shop. She hurried down the sidewalk.

On the desk inside the shop, her cell phone rang with the incoming call from Andrew.

ANDERSEN'S DRIVEWAY was illuminated by lights strategically placed above the garages. There was no car parked in view. The house looked dark from the street side, so Olivia stepped along the walkway that she and Brad had used to reach the decks. There were lights on in the big room off the lower level deck.

Olivia climbed the stairs and knocked on the glass door.

"Come in," a man's voice called. "It's open."

Olivia put her hand on the knob and turned it. As she stepped into the room, the hairs on her arms stood up and a fleeting sensation of alarm shot through her body, but she dismissed the feelings as anticipation of what Hannigan had to show her. She stepped into the living room and closed the door.

Alexei walked around the corner from the hall and stood before her.

The surprise of seeing Alexei kept her silent, but her eyes narrowed and her head tilted slightly to the side, questioning his appearance in Andersen's house.

"Hello, Olivia," Alexei said.

"Alexei," she said. Her throat felt tight.

"Come in." He gestured to the sofa.

"Where's Mr. Hannigan?" she asked, trying to keep her voice calm. She stood where she was.

"He isn't coming."

"He texted me," Olivia said even though she knew she had been tricked. Her muscles tensed and her heart was booming.

Alexei shook his head. "I texted you. Mr. Hannigan seems to have misplaced his phone."

He moved further into the room. Olivia did not want him to get any closer. She whirled and grabbed the doorknob. She yanked on it. The door would not open. She stopped trying to force it and just stood there facing the outside, her back to Alexei.

"Mr. Andersen installed all the latest electronics in the house." Alexei's voice was bored. "You just push a button on the control panel and all the doors and windows lock."

Olivia took a deep breath and slowly turned to face Alexei.

"What do you want?" Her voice sounded thin.

"Please sit down. Relax," he said. He took a seat in a club chair that was next to the sofas. He slouched a bit and leaned back.

Olivia sat down on one of the sofas at the end furthest from Alexei. He didn't look at her. His gaze was out the huge windows where the darkness now shrouded the view. They sat in silence until Olivia's anger began to override her fear.

"What's this about? Because I didn't go out with you again?" she demanded. Alexei did not respond. He didn't even look at her.

Olivia swallowed. "You were in my house that night weren't you? The night I found you in my backyard?"

Alexei raised his eyes. "Yes." The word floated on a long exhale of his breath.

"Did you find what you were looking for?"

Alexei's face was like a stone. He turned his gaze back to the windows. "If I did, you wouldn't be sitting here."

Olivia started to unzip her backpack. Alexei sprang like a cat and ripped it from her hands.

"Stand up," he ordered. She slowly stood.

He patted her down. "You should have stayed out if it," he muttered. He pushed her backwards so she sat down hard on the sofa. He threw her backpack and it landed on the opposite matching sofa. He went and stood by the big windows with his back to Olivia.

Olivia's mind raced. She looked about the room for a possible weapon. She tried to take slow deep breaths so she could assess the situation more calmly. She didn't know what Alexei was up to but she wanted to be ready for anything.

Olivia heard the garage door opening below her.

Alexei straightened and turned around. Footsteps could be heard on the steps leading from the garages to the main floor of the house. There was more than one person coming.

A burly man with long greasy hair came into the living room from the hallway. No one spoke and no one looked friendly. Dmitri Siderov entered next. He glared at Olivia with cold, deep set beady eyes. Olivia thought he looked like a reptile.

"Ms. Miller, how nice of you to drop by," he sneered.

"I wish I could say that it was nice to see you again. But I can't. Because its not." Olivia tried to keep her voice even. Alexei shot her a look of warning.

"Ms. Miller. So confident and bold." Siderov smiled. "But that's a challenge that we like." His smile vanished. His eyes flashed steel. "It's amazing how quickly confidence can disappear."

He turned to Alexei. "You managed to get her here. Good for you." His voice was mocking. Alexei remained quiet.

"What's this about?" Olivia tried to steady her voice.

Some noise in the hall caused Olivia to turn her head. Another man came into the living room. He had a deep scar that ran from his left temple to the jaw line. His hand held tight to the arm of a woman he pushed along.

The woman, whose eyes were fixed downward, was

dressed in jeans and a cotton shirt. Her light brown shoulder length hair was disheveled and partially hid her face. She had flip flops on her feet. She looked exhausted, maybe high.

The man snapped his fingers and pointed to the floor. She sat down clutching her knees, not looking up.

Siderov sat down on the opposite sofa and rested his elbow on the arm of the couch. "Thank you for placing that ad in the newspaper, Miss Miller. It validated our suspicions." A false smile spread across his mouth.

Olivia's head tilted. "Did you lose a necklace, Mr. Siderov?" she said, her voice laced with sarcasm.

Siderov's faced clouded and the fake smile disappeared. "You have become somewhat of a gnat, Ms. Miller. Prying into other people's business. Imagining things that are fiction. Making claims that are untrue." He brought his hands together with the fingers tapping. "Just telling you to stop would be useless, as it seems that you are the persistent type." His jaw muscles twitched as he clenched his teeth. "Unfortunately." He paused. "For you." He flicked a piece of lint from his pants.

Olivia wished she had texted Brad or Joe about where she was going. She realized that no one knew where she was.

"And where is my other object?" Siderov demanded.

"I don't know what you're talking about," Olivia said.

Siderov let out a deep sigh. "As I thought."

"I texted my friends that I was coming here," Olivia lied. "They know."

Siderov chuckled, but there was no mirth in it. "No matter. We're leaving," Siderov said and rose from the couch.

"I'm not going with you," Olivia said, glaring at him and sitting straighter. She knew it was useless to defy them but she was going to fight whatever they had planned.

Siderov waved his hand dismissively. "Prepare her," he said to the greasy-haired man.

The man pulled a syringe from his jacket pocket and walked towards Olivia. Olivia's heart sank. She jumped up.

"Stay still," he ordered. He reached out for her arm, but she jerked it back. She took two steps away from him.

The man with the scar moved across the room from behind to head Olivia off. As the man with the syringe advanced, Olivia stepped onto the coffee table and jumped to the side of the room where only Alexei stood.

The woman on the floor lifted her head slightly to watch what was happening.

There were four men in the room, but Olivia didn't care. As they advanced on her, she kicked over the sofa side table and picked up a heavy glass vase. Olivia threw it at the greasy-haired man.

Noticing a pen on the glass side table, she grabbed for it. The scar-faced guy grasped her other arm and Olivia reached up and slashed at his face with the pen. The attack caused the man to lose his grip on her.

In a flash, the greasy-haired man moved closer and punched Olivia in the face.

Explosions went off in her head. She staggered and went down. The man sat on top of her and jabbed the syringe into her arm.

Olivia lay crumpled with her cheek resting against the beautiful hardwood floor. Her vision started to blur and despite trying to get up, her muscles would not respond.

She shifted her eyes to the woman who was sitting on the floor on the other side of the room. The woman's head was tilted down but her eyes were raised and they met Olivia's.

Olivia felt like she was floating. She tried to focus. The woman sitting on the floor looked familiar. While Olivia wondered where she had seen her before, something on the middle shelf of the bookcase next to the woman caught Olivia's attention. She forced her eyes to stay open.

On the shelf was a red camera bag with gold piping stitched around the front flap. A last name was embroidered in gold thread on the flap. Olivia knew what it said without being able to clearly see the words, because she recognized the bag. She knew who it belonged to. It was Aggie's. Aggie had been in this room.

Olivia's vision went black and her head slumped on the floor.

24

Olivia's skin felt damp and cold. Her mind was engulfed in a black fog. It was as if she was swimming up from a murky swamp. Her eyelids moved like heavy drapes slowly opening. They slammed shut again from the piercing bright lights that cut into her optic nerve like a knife.

When she tried to move her arm it was like one hundred pound weights were attached to it. He mouth was dry and her lips felt numb. She brought her hand up to her face and pressed her fingers against her eyelids and temples, trying to rub out the stabbing, pulsating pain. She opened her lids just a slit to gradually accustom her eyes to the white brightness of the room.

She lay on a hard, smooth, cold concrete floor. Flicking her eyes around the bare room without moving her head, she observed two plain cement walls. She saw no one. She listened. She heard nothing.

Rolling over onto her back, Olivia turned her gaze away from the two banks of cold, fluorescent lights embedded in the high ceiling. The act of rolling over made her aware of how sluggishly her muscles were responding. From her position on her back, she could see a third wall just like the other two. The fourth was a wall of bars. A cell.

Olivia focused her attention on listening for any sounds that might provide more clues as to where she was and who was around. A faint metallic humming was all she could hear.

Moving to her side, she tried to push herself into a sitting position. The ten foot by ten foot room spun around her and she pressed her palms against the floor to steady herself. Her stomach lurched and she swallowed hard. Forcing herself to take some deep breaths, she waited until her equilibrium was reestablished and the room stopped spinning.

She raised her eyes and crawled over to the edge of the cell to examine what was beyond the bars. A larger empty room with more walls of concrete and fluorescent lights was outside of her holding cell. Olivia thought it looked like the inside of a bunker or a huge basement. There were no windows and she got the feeling that she was underground. There were three drains in the larger room's floor. There were splotches of reddish, rusty stains here and there on the walls and leading to the drains. Some of the stains were darker than the others.

Olivia's stomach turned to ice. She knew what the stains were. Blood. Her throat tightened. Her eyes searched the room for an escape. All she saw were the straight, high concrete walls. Convinced that she must be being watched, she scanned the walls and ceilings for a video device, but saw none. I know they're watching me even if I can't see a camera.

A heavy moan from outside of Olivia's cell caused adrenaline to shoot through her body and she froze in place on the floor of her cell, straining to locate the source of the sound. Several seconds passed and Olivia heard a scuffing noise coming from outside her cell to her right...then silence. Olivia waited. A cough. Olivia leaned her head against the bars and looked to her right, but could see nothing. Another cough. A woman.

"Is someone there?" Olivia whispered. Olivia waited. No one responded. She tried again, a little louder this time.

"Is someone out there?"

A weak, raspy voice answered, "Yeah." The person coughed again. "I'm here."

"Are you in a cell?" Olivia asked softly.

"Yes." The person had a fit of racking coughs.

"Are you okay?" Olivia said. She heard shallow, wheezing breaths, but no one replied.

Before Olivia could speak again, the loud clang of metal against metal filled the air. She jumped. She heard heavy footsteps coming closer. Olivia scooted back away from the bars.

The greasy-haired man who had injected her at Andersen's house stepped to the front of her cell. His face was expressionless as he stared at Olivia. He held a butcher knife in his hand, the sharp edges glinting under the bright lights. The corners of his mouth moved up slightly, twitching into a faint grin, and then his face went blank again. He stared at her for a full minute.

"Bitch," he said.

He turned away slowly and lumbered to what Olivia assumed was the next cell. Olivia did not edge forward, just stayed sitting in the middle of her lockup. She couldn't see the man.

Olivia guessed that the man was staring at the woman on the other side of the wall as he had done with her, but a horrible sound like a war yell came out of the brute as he roared and banged the knife on the bars of the next cell like a crazed banshee. The woman prisoner let loose with a high-pitched anguished wail.

Olivia covered her ears with her hands, but she could still hear the screaming. When it stopped, the man lumbered away. Then the metal on metal sound. The rooms were quiet, except for the wretched sobbing of the woman in the next hold.

What the hell? Olivia's hands were shaking. She hugged her knees and rested her forehead against them. How am I going to get out this? Think. Think.

I'm probably not going to get out. Her eyes filled with tears. Joe. Brad. At least you're both safe. Olivia wiped her eyes on the hem of her shirt. She lifted her head and scanned her cell and what she could see of the room beyond.

She set her jaw as rage bubbled up in her chest. She stood. I won't make it easy for these bastards.

25

Joe added chopped carrots to the salad and tossed all of the ingredients to mix them. He had banana bread baking in the oven and it filled the room with a delicious odor. There was a knock on his kitchen door and Joe looked up to see Brad standing behind the screen.

"Come in, Brad," Joe called.

Brad entered the kitchen.

"Hey," Joe said. "I just got in a little while ago. I stayed late working on the Wells house. I'm starving. You probably ate already, but would you like to stay and have a second supper?" Joe asked. "Got plenty."

"I need to get back to the store. I have an event tonight. It sure smells good though," Brad said.

"I can make up a plate for you...you can eat it later," Joe offered. "What's your event?"

"I have a three piece bluegrass band playing at the bookstore tonight. I'm doing a music theme this week," Brad said. "Joe, have you heard from Liv today? I've been trying to reach her for the past few hours but she doesn't answer her phone. But neither do you, for that matter. I tried your phone a couple times too. I got worried and decided to come over."

"Oh, sorry. I must have left my phone in the truck," Joe told him. "I haven't heard from Liv, though. Not sure what she's up to."

"She usually answers my texts right away. I stopped by her house before I came here, but no one answered the doorbell," Brad said. "So I came to see if you knew where she was."

"I haven't seen her today. Maybe she's at the antique store?" Joe said.

"That's going to be my next stop."

Joe's face creased with worry. "Why wouldn't she answer her cell?"

"Maybe she forgot to charge it is all," Brad said. "No need for concern."

But Joe was worried and it was written all over his expression. He took the bread out of the oven and set it on the stovetop to cool. "I'm going with you." He covered the salad with wrap and turned the crock pot down. "Let's go," he said, wiping his hands on a dish towel.

Brad looked in the shop window. The 'Closed' sign showed through the glass and no one answered the door when they knocked. "I don't see anyone. The lights are off in the back room."

"Where could she be? She's always either here or with one of us," Joe said.

"You have a key?" Brad asked.

Joe fumbled through his key ring looking for the right one. Aggie had given him a key to the shop in case of emergency.

"Did Liv have a friend planning to visit?" Brad asked.

"Her good friend isn't coming until August."

They exchanged glances.

"You don't think that Alexei guy called her again?" Joe asked.

"He has been trying to get in touch with her, but she never answers his calls. I don't think she would. We talked about it recently and she said she would keep clear of him."

Joe found the key and inserted it in the lock. They stepped in and flicked the light switch. The two of them peered around the shop for anything that might suggest Olivia's whereabouts.

"Her phone," Brad said, picking up Olivia's phone from the work table. "Well, that's why she's not answering." He returned it the table.

"But where the hell is she?" Joe said. "She never just disappears without telling me what's up."

"She's a grown woman. She doesn't have to keep us abreast of her comings and goings," Brad said. "Maybe she... had a date or something."

"Oh, come on," Joe said.

"It's not that farfetched, Joe."

"She doesn't do that. She tells me. Always." Joe's expression darkened. "Something's wrong."

"Maybe it was the spur of the moment. Someone came by...asked her to go for a drink," Brad offered.

Joe shook his head. "No."

"There has to be a simple explanation. We can't assume the worst," Brad tried to convince Joe and himself.

Joe shook his head again. "I can assume the worst. Something's wrong. I'm calling the police." He reached in his pocket for his cell and remembered he left it in his truck. He borrowed Brad's phone. When the dispatcher answered, Joe expressed his concerns.

"I'll pass the information on to the officers, but they usually won't get involved for twenty-four hours. You said there isn't any indication of a struggle either at her home or at her business. It's impossible to immediately determine if someone is missing or just hasn't kept in touch or they forget to call to say where they are. I'm sure you'll hear from her soon," the dispatcher said. "She probably just forgot to tell you. She'll turn up, sir." The dispatcher cleared his throat. "It happens all the time. She's only been out of touch for a few hours. I wouldn't worry."

"Olivia doesn't just disappear. That's not her. She isn't like that," Joe said. "That's what has us concerned. It would be completely out of her personality and character to just disappear like that. In fact, she doesn't leave for even a few hours without telling me where she's going."

"Well, sir, I'm sorry, but the officers don't get involved when an adult has only been out of contact for a few hours. You can go down to the station in the morning if you still have concerns."

Joe ended the call by pushing a button on Brad's cell. He was fuming. "Do you believe this?" He started pacing around the shop.

"Maybe she had another idea about the recent goings on and she's checking it out," Brad offered hopefully.

"Is her car at her house?" Joe asked.

"It wasn't in the driveway."

"Let's go see if it's in the garage." They walked back up the hill to Olivia's house. The garage had a keypad attached to the door frame and Joe punched in the code that raised the door. Olivia's Jeep was sitting in the bay.

"Maybe she just got home," Brad said. He knocked on the door leading from the garage to Olivia's kitchen. No one answered. Joe removed his key chain from his pocket and unlocked the door.

"Liv?" he called as he entered. It was quiet in the house. Brad and Joe walked through the rooms, looking to be sure Olivia wasn't inside hurt or sick.

"I feel like a peeping Tom," Brad said.

"Her keys are missing. She always leaves them right here," Joe said, indicating the small kitchen desk built into the wall. "So we know she probably was at the antique shop today because she left her phone there. And her keys are gone, which she would have needed to get into the store. But the keys weren't left at the store and the place was in order and the door was locked." Joe was pacing again. "So she probably left of her own accord."

Joe stopped walking and stared at Brad.

"What?" Brad asked.

"I don't know," Joe answered.

They were both quiet for a minute.

"Maybe she tried to call you. You left your phone in your truck," Brad offered.

Joe's face brightened. They locked Olivia's back door, lowered the garage door, and jogged across the grass to Joe's truck, which was parked in his driveway. He flung open the driver side door and pulled his phone off the console. He looked at the phone's face.

"No missed calls, except one from you," he told Brad. His arm dropped to his side. "I'm worried, Brad," Joe's voice quavered. His face looked all rubbery, like he was about to lose it.

"It's okay." Brad was worried too, but he was desperate to reassure Joe. "I'm sure she's fine. Maybe she went shopping."

Joe gave Brad a look. Olivia hated shopping.

"Well, maybe she went for a swim," Brad said.

"It's late...it's dark," Joe said. "She'd be home by now if she went for a swim. She wouldn't swim alone in the dark." Joe sat down on the truck's runner. He put his head in his hands. "What are we going to do?"

Brad walked the length of the truck and back up again. Back and forth several times. He stopped in front of Joe. "Maybe Alexei called her and she went out with him. She wanted to, so that she could try to find out if he or his father was hiding something."

Joe lifted his head.

Brad continued, "I told her not to. But who knows; maybe he called and..."

"Did you take her phone from the shop?" Joe asked. "Can you look at her calls and texts?"

"I left the phone on the work table. Wait. Maybe she's on another stakeout at Martin Andersen's house."

Joe looked hopeful.

"We decided not to go there tonight because I had the event at the bookstore...we were going to wait until tomorrow night. You know how she is...maybe she couldn't wait."

Joe stood. "Let's go see. Oh, but your event. I'll go see. You go back to the store."

Brad ran his hand through his hair. "I want to go with you, but I don't have anyone at the store who knows what to do. Maybe I could cancel it."

"You know you can't. It's too late for that."

Brad looked at his phone to check the time. "Oh no, I should be there right now. I'm late already." He made a call to the bookstore to tell his employees what to do until he arrived. "Joe, call me as soon as you get to Andersen's house."

"I will," Joe told him.

"I'm going to run back to the bookstore," Brad said.

"I can drive you," Joe offered.

"Too much traffic. It will be quicker to run." The traffic at night on Shore Road was often bumper to bumper with people arriving for vacations or coming into town for the restaurants and shops.

"I have a bike. Take that," Joe said.

"Yeah, okay. A bike would work," Brad said.

They went into Joe's garage.

"What the hell is this?" Brad asked.

"It's an adult tricycle," Joe told him. "It's brand new. I never use it."

"I can see why," Brad said. "Why don't you take the

bike to Andersen's instead of the truck? You can bypass the traffic and get there faster. I'll just run to the bookstore. It won't take me long."

Brad started down the driveway and looked back. "Call me. Let me know if she's there."

Joe nodded and wheeled the bike into the driveway.

26

Olivia woke up with a start. She had dozed off leaning against the back wall.

She heard men's voices. A sudden bang and hum from above her head jolted her to instinctively stand up. A metal door was rolling down in front of the bars of her cell.

Olivia ran to the bars, trying to see out before the door completely cut her off from being able to view anything beyond her own four walls. She couldn't see anyone but she could make out the sound of men talking from somewhere in the large room. The door reached the floor with a shudder and slam.

Olivia stepped back. She hated enclosed spaces and she started to hyperventilate. She crouched down and put her hands on the floor to steady herself and tried to slow her breathing. With a bang above her, the lights of her hold switched off and she was plunged into total darkness.

"No!" she screamed. She could not see her own hand in front of her face. She stood, panicked, and rushed to touch the wall. She was disoriented and felt along the walls until she found the bars. Reaching through them, she pounded against the outer door.

"Open this door!" she shrieked. She was nearly hysterical from the fear of being enclosed alone. She started to sob, and reached down to pull her shoe off so she could use it to pound against the metal door. She fell to the floor as she tried to yank off the shoe. Olivia sat in the blackness, panting. Get hold of yourself. Don't lose control. Calm down, calm down.

She put her shoe back on and tied the laces. They want me to freak out. I won't play into their hands. I won't. Olivia thought she heard something outside the door. She crawled closer and put her ear as near to the door as she could. She heard voices but could not make out what they were saying. She heard a noise like metal sliding along metal. She heard a woman speak. Then she heard her screaming. The screams faded as if the woman was being taken away. Oh no. Oh no.

JOE RODE the bike down along Shore Road, staying as close to the shoulder as he could so that he was able to pass by the cars which were bumper to bumper in a line on the street. The bike didn't have a headlight on it, so Joe balanced a flashlight in his hand while also holding onto the handle bar so that he could see the road better and so he was visible to others in the darkness. The bike didn't have anything on the back except a small reflector and Joe worried that a car might bash into him from behind if the traffic started to flow.

He turned down the road that led to the cove and followed past the restaurants and stores until the road curved again to the right, leading to the section of private homes.

When Joe arrived at Andersen's house, he rode the bike down the driveway and pulled it onto the grass next to some bushes. He turned off the flashlight and stepped quietly along the walkway leading to the left of the house. He stopped and listened. He gazed up to the three levels of decks above him but could see nothing.

The house was dark from Joe's angle. He moved further up the walkway. Now he could see a light in a room off the first deck. He hesitated at the bottom of the stairs that led to the first level. He knew Olivia didn't have a key to the house, but maybe she met Mr. Hannigan and was inside the house with him. Or maybe the lights were on a timer. Maybe Olivia was on the deck doing her surveillance.

Joe called softly, "Liv?"

Nothing. For a minute, he wrestled with whether or not he should go and knock at the door. He put his foot on the stair and started up. When he reached the deck and saw that it was empty, he sidled up to the glass door and peeked into the expansive living room. Something caught his eye. Joe squinted and moved his head up close to the glass. On the far sofa was Olivia's backpack. But where's Liv?

Joe raised his hand to knock on the glass just as a man entered the living room from inside the house. The man halted abruptly when he saw Joe's face at the door.

OLIVIA SAT ON THE FLOOR, having pushed herself into a black corner of her lockup. Being in the corner made her feel more secure because she had the two walls close to her shoulders. She wished she could sleep but rest evaded her. She rubbed her forehead and thought about Joe and Brad. They must be worried. They must wonder where I am. She stretched her legs in front of her to get the kinks out of them. She was sore and achy and her head pounded from what she thought must be after-effects of whatever was in the syringe.

The metal door boomed and a motor whirred. The door lifted slowly, allowing light to enter the cell a bit at a time, as if it was dawn and the sun was inching over the horizon.

Olivia stood, grateful for the light but fearful of what would come next. When the door was fully retracted, two men appeared from the right: the short, stocky man with the scar and the greasy-haired man.

The scar-face made a motion with his hand and the bars slid back. They both scrutinized her. The one who gestured for the bars to open signaled for Olivia to come forward. She stayed where she was.

After a moment he said firmly, "Come."

Olivia moved forward. The greasy-haired man showed handcuffs to her but she did not extend her arms.

"I don't need handcuffs," she said.

"Come, come," the scarred-faced man said and waved his hand slightly. "We'll decide that."

The greasy-haired man took hold of her arms and twisted them behind her, forcing the handcuffs on. The scar-faced man wheeled to the left and strode to a door at the far end of the bunker room. The greasy-haired man gestured for Olivia to follow the first man. He gave her a push and walked behind her.

Olivia glanced at the floor and the wall as she walked

stiff-legged and was thankful there didn't appear to be any fresh stains on them.

~

BRAD STOOD behind the counter of his bookstore, listening to the bluegrass band play. A large crowd had showed up for the event and all the tables were full. People were standing around the edges of the room, enjoying the music and drinking coffees.

Brad wished that it was over and that he could talk to Joe. He checked his phone again, which he had been doing every few minutes for the past forty-five. Where the hell is Joe? Why doesn't he call?

A customer approached and ordered an espresso. Brad put his phone down and tended to the request. He felt both exhausted and agitated. He wanted nothing more than for everything to be all right. Why doesn't Joe call?

27

Olivia followed the man into a room about the size of a two-car garage. It too was bare walled and had no windows. There were two straight back chairs in the middle of the room. Four beat-up, cushioned chairs were along the far wall. Olivia's heart beat fast and her hands felt clammy.

The scar-faced man spoke. "Sit," he said, indicating the hard chairs.

Olivia sat down in the closest one.

The greasy-haired man stood at attention in front of the door where they had entered. Scar-face knocked on a heavy door near the cushioned chairs.

A tall, slender man with eyes like a dead shark entered the room. Olivia's eyes widened. Her pulse beat like a drum. It was the man from the accident scene, and he was followed by Dmitri Siderov. Siderov sat in one of the chairs by the wall and crossed his legs. His eyes fixed on Olivia for several minutes, his face blank.

He sighed and said, "I believe you have something of mine, Ms. Miller. Two things, actually."

Olivia knew he must be referring to the necklace, but what was the second thing? She had no idea what he was talking about.

Siderov glanced down and picked at one of his fingernails. "And you won't leave here until I know where they are." He looked up at her. "We can make things quite unpleasant for you." His voice was matter-of-fact. He stood and moved quickly for the door, which the sentry opened for him. "I'll be back."

Scar-face and Dead Eyes took positions on either side of the door through which Siderov left. No one spoke and they did not make eye contact with Olivia. Olivia wondered what the hell Siderov thought she had of his.

"I need to go to the bathroom," she said. No one looked at her. "I don't feel well." The scar-faced man glanced at her.

"Should I just throw up on the floor then?" She coughed.

"Take her." Dead Eyes indicated to Scar-face.

Scar-face's eyes narrowed into slits. He waved for Olivia to come to him. He opened the door and pushed her out into the bunker room. He grabbed her arm and moved her along one of the walls until they came to a door. He took hold of the handle and flung it open to reveal a small bathroom. Olivia stepped over the threshold and held her handcuffed hands out from behind her back.

"Just go," he muttered.

"I need these off to go," she said.

At first he didn't move, but then he reached into his pocket and took out the key. He released the handcuffs.

Olivia bent down by the toilet clutching her head. She looked up and said, "Can I have some privacy?"

The guy just stared at her.

She pretended to have dry heaves into the toilet and turned her head to him. "What am I going to do? Walk through a concrete wall to escape?" She stood up and walked over to the door. "Shut it...or I'll puke on your fancy shoes."

The guy pushed her back and slammed the bathroom door.

Olivia pretended to have dry heaves again while she looked around the bathroom. No window. No tub. Just a small medicine cabinet with a mirror attached to it and a dirty towel on a towel rack.

Olivia pulled the towel off the rack. She coughed and heaved some more for the guy's benefit. She positioned the towel over the mirror and while she wrenched it off the cabinet she used her foot to push on the handle that flushed the toilet, the flushing noise masking the removal of the mirror.

Part of the mirror came off in her hands and she immediately smashed it on the porcelain sink, shattering the mirror into pieces. She slipped a piece of it into the back pocket of her jeans.

The door of the bathroom flew open. Olivia held out a piece of the mirror wrapped in the towel like a knife in front of her.

The guy halted when he saw the sharp glass of the mirror pointing at him.

"Stupid bitch," he yelled as Olivia ran at him with the glass, slashing at him like a wild woman.

Olivia managed to cut his hands and face before he had her in a lock hold. He threw her onto the floor outside the bathroom. He swatted the glass out of Olivia's grasp and he wrapped his massive hands around her throat and choked the air out of her.

Olivia's eyes bulged and she kicked and bucked off the floor, desperate to suck in precious oxygen. As she started to lose her vision, the door to the other room flung open and Shark Eyes shouted, "Enough!" He kicked the strangler in the back.

"I said stop, you idiot!"

The hands came off Olivia's throat and she gulped air into her lungs with a horrible wheezing noise. Her hands, bloody from breaking the mirror, clutched at her neck, smearing blood all over her skin.

"Get up," Shark Eyes ordered.

She rolled onto her knees and attempted to stand. Scar-Face grabbed her under her arm and hoisted her to her feet. She bent at the waist, still trying to suck more air.

"Go get cleaned up, you fool," Shark Eyes sneered at Scar-face. "You don't decide when she dies."

Shark Eyes dragged Olivia back to the room and pushed her into one of the chairs, where she continued to wheeze and gasp.

BRAD COULDN'T STAND it anymore. He punched Joe's number into his cell and listened to it ring...and ring. Joe's voice mail message came on. Brad hit the counter with his hand. Where is he? Now what?

Brad tried to remember if Joe had taken his phone with him when they parted ways earlier. He was sure Joe had it in his pocket when he left him. Why doesn't he answer? Everyone carries a phone but no one can pick the hell up.

Brad looked around the room. Some of the patrons had left and the band was wrapping up with its last song.

He had been looking forward to hosting this event but now he was counting the seconds until it was over.

SIDEROV BURST INTO THE ROOM, banging the door against the wall. He glared at Olivia. She had managed to catch her breath, but her throat was tight and constricted. Her right hand was bleeding freely from the shards of the mirror and she had wrapped the bottom of her shirt around it. Her neck was smeared with blood and her shirt and pants had patches of blood on them. Siderov's eyes shot daggers at each of the men in turn.

Scar-face, who had attempted to strangle Olivia, entered the room from the other door. Siderov gave him an icy stare.

"Get out," Siderov hissed. The man backed out and closed the door.

"Get Alexei down here," Siderov barked to no one in particular.

He wheeled on the greasy-haired man and ordered, "Bring in the woman."

In a matter of minutes, the greasy-haired man was dragging a woman into the room. It was the same woman who had been at Martin Andersen's house when Olivia was tricked into going there. Olivia recognized her as the woman who had tried to run from the van the night she was washing her paintbrushes in the shop's sink.

The woman was pushed into the chair next to Olivia and sat slumped there with her left hand resting in her lap. The hand was wrapped in gauze and blood was seeping through the bandages. Siderov moved closer to the two women.

"One of you has two items of mine," Siderov said. "Things I want returned. And the other of you has information that I require."

The woman remained slumped and silent.

Olivia said, "What makes you think we have what you want?"

"Unless you are relaying the whereabouts of the objects, then keep your mouth shut," Siderov told Olivia. He cleared his throat. "As I said, one of you has objects that belong to me." He glared at Olivia. "I want them back."

"What are they?" Olivia asked.

Siderov smacked Olivia across the face, nearly knocking her out of her chair. The woman lifted her eyes to peer at Olivia without moving her head.

"We will be back in fifteen minutes. Both of you better have the answers I desire." Siderov gave them each a look of menace. "Or things will become unpleasant."

He turned his face to the other woman. "More

unpleasant than losing an appendage." He stormed out of the room with his two goons trotting after him. Olivia and the woman were alone, but Olivia suspected they were being watched.

"Are you okay?" Olivia whispered. The woman made an almost imperceptible nod.

"I'm Olivia," she said. There was no response.

"What's your name?" Olivia asked. The woman shook her head.

"Look, they'll be back soon. Please talk to me," Olivia told her. "I need to figure out what to do."

The woman raised her head. Her eyes were empty. "Do? What can you possibly do? We're already dead."

Olivia whispered, "I'm not going to believe that. Do you know what Siderov thinks I have?" Olivia asked. "What he wants back?"

The woman shook her head. Olivia didn't know whether or not to believe her and she wanted to ask more questions, but decided what Siderov was looking for probably wasn't going to assist them in escaping.

"You can't give up. There are two of us. I'll think of something," Olivia said. "Can you tell me what you know about them...this place?"

"I don't know anything," the woman said.

Olivia glanced at the door. "We're running out of time. I need to think...make a plan."

The woman said, "We are out of time."

"We can't just give up and die here."

"I'm already dead," the woman said. She made eye contact with Olivia. Her face was ashen.

Olivia looked at the woman's hand. "What happened to you?"

The woman lifted her hand from her lap and turned her blank eyes to Olivia. "They cut off my ring finger."

Bile rose in Olivia's throat. The finger on the dining table at the Sullivan's. "Why?" she asked softly.

The woman snorted. "They want my husband. They cut my finger off to bring to him. So he could see it. My wedding ring. My finger. To prove they have me here." Her shoulders slumped and she looked down.

"Oh," Olivia breathed. She swallowed. "You're Liz Sullivan. Mike's wife."

Liz's face crumpled. She closed her eyes and nodded.

"They want my husband. They're going to punish him."

"Why?" Olivia questioned.

"He came to do some work here the other day. He called me from his car. He was running away. He saw something here. They shot him in the shoulder. But he got to his truck. He told me to hide."

Olivia's heart sank into her stomach and ice flowed through her veins.

Liz went on, "They said...," her face contorted,

"they're going to kill our son. If I don't tell them where Mike is." Tears poured from her eyes. "They have our son here." She choked on the words.

"Mikey?" Olivia said.

Liz's eyes bored into Olivia.

"Mikey's not here. I saw Mikey." Olivia lowered her voice. "He's with your sister now. I saw your husband, too. He's hurt but he's alive. He's in the hospital. The police are watching out for them. They're safe."

Liz tilted her head, considering. "What?"

"It's true. My friends and I found them. Well, it was more like Mikey found us. But they're okay. They're safe."

Liz stared at Olivia. "They told you to tell me this. To get me on your side. To trick me."

"No, Liz. They're okay. I'm not trying to trick you."

"I don't believe you," Liz whispered.

The door banged open. Alexei strode in with a Doberman Pinscher on a leash. The dog lunged at the women, yanking against the leash, and it snapped the air, gnashing its teeth. Alexei ordered the dog to sit.

"You have my father's property," he said to Olivia. "And you," he said to Liz, "you need to tell us where to locate your husband."

Olivia and Liz stared at him.

"The dog can be very persuasive," Alexei said.

A light went off in Olivia's head. She turned to Liz and

looked her in the eye while telling Alexei, "Don't call him 'the dog'. Dogs are particular about what they like to be called. Especially, Lassie. Right, Liz?"

Liz looked confused but after a few seconds her eyes widened and the corners of her mouth twitched up. Her lower lip was trembling and she bit it to keep from crying. Mikey. Mikey said those very words about Lassie all the time. Olivia had met Mikey. Mikey was safe.

"What did you say?" Alexei questioned Olivia.

Olivia's lip turned up in a sneer. "I said the dog is particular."

Alexei wasn't sure what she meant and his face turned stony. He brought the dog closer to the women and allowed it to bark and snap at them. Olivia jumped out of her chair and stood behind it.

"Get out of here, Alexei."

Snarling and growling, the dog leaped at Liz. It smacked against the chair and knocked her to the ground. Olivia lifted her chair and pushed it at the dog to get him away from Liz. The dog lunged at Olivia with such force that the strain on the leash nearly knocked Alexei off his feet. The Doberman clenched onto Olivia's arm and she screamed and kicked, falling backwards. Liz jumped from the floor but was at a loss for what to do and stood there gaping, cradling her bandaged hand. Alexei had to pull on the leash with all of his strength to move the dog back.

"You bastard," Olivia hissed, clutching her arm.

Siderov and two of his men burst into the room.

Fury blazed in Siderov's eyes as he boomed at Alexei, "Who gave you permission to enter this room?" He barked orders in Russian and Alexei and the dog retreated to the far wall.

Liz hooked her good hand under Olivia's arm and helped her to her feet.

"Sit!" Siderov screamed at the women. "Tie them to the chairs," he barked at the men, who rushed forward and roped Olivia and Liz to their seats.

Olivia assumed that things weren't going according to Siderov's plan and that he seemed like a man who did not like to appear to be losing control of a situation. She knew he was going to take it out on them.

"THEY SEEM NERVOUS," Liz whispered to Olivia. "They haven't seemed so ...disorganized."

Olivia nodded in acknowledgement. She was glad to hear that something might have them on edge. On the other hand, she worried that it might make them careless...or desperate.

"Shut up," Siderov spat. Sweat beaded up on his brow

as he advanced on the women. "I'm running out of time. Who wants to tell me the things I need to know?"

Olivia and Liz were silent.

Siderov waited a full minute. He took a deep breath. "Then it appears it is time for some encouragement." He wheeled around, strode to the chairs along the wall and sat.

"Ms. Miller," Siderov said in a calm voice. "I thought your arrogance would interfere with your ability to be forthcoming with me, and I was correct."

Olivia looked at him with hate filled eyes.

"So I took out some insurance."

Olivia's heart beat fast.

"Your old man friend is a guest here as well."

Her heart jumped into her throat.

Siderov let his words hang in the air before he continued. "I am going to make what's left of his life very uncomfortable. Unless you give me the information I have requested."

"You can have that damn necklace. I don't know what else you want. I don't know anything." Olivia's voice was shrill.

"Then you will have the opportunity to see your friend," Siderov sneered. "I will deliver him to you in pieces."

Olivia wildly strained and rocked in the chair, trying

to free herself. "Shut up! Shut up, you bastard!" she yelled. "Joe!"

"As time is of the essence, encouragement will also be issued in this room," Siderov continued. "Whoever tells me what I want to know is the winner. The loser...well, the winner gets to see what would have happened if she lost." He stood. "Go get the instruments," Siderov ordered.

The greasy-haired man hurried out of the room.

"And you," Siderov said to Shark Eyes, "begin on the old man."

"No!" Olivia shrieked, tears spilling from her eyes.

Shark Eyes strode away through the door.

Siderov directed his comment at Liz. "And you, Mrs. Sullivan, it's time to lose another of your parts."

Liz shrank in her seat.

Siderov smiled sickeningly and stood.

"Alexei," he said. "I hope you're paying attention. Since you can't do anything right, maybe you'll learn something. Let's have some fun while we wait for the instruments."

Olivia looked to Alexei and their eyes met. She shook her head slightly, tears streaming down her face. He turned away.

Siderov pulled out a switchblade from inside his jacket and approached Olivia. Liz watched in horror.

Siderov glared at Olivia, then reached behind and slit the ropes that bound her to the chair.

"Stand up," he ordered.

Olivia rose from the chair.

"So much like your foolish aunt," he sneered.

Olivia's blood boiled with a blinding rage and she spat into Siderov's face. Siderov's cheeks flared red. He punched Olivia in the stomach and she doubled over, a blast of pain exploding through her core.

Siderov snapped his fingers in the air. "Alexei, let's see what your stupid dog can do." He gestured to Olivia and took several steps back.

Alexei's face was grim and he stood stock still. He said, bitterly, "Yes, Father, let's see." He leaned down and held his hand in front of the dog's face, said something to it, and pointed with his arm outstretched...at his father.

The dog shot off its haunches like a missile straight at Siderov, clamped onto the stocky man's neck, and brought him to the floor. Siderov's screams caught in his throat.

Olivia stumbled backwards out of the way. Alexei watched blankly for several seconds as the dog worked on his father.

Olivia pulled the mirror shard from her back pocket and bent to saw at the ropes binding Liz. Alexei strode across the room and Olivia stood quickly to threaten him with the shard. Alexei ignored Olivia as he bent and scooped up Liz, chair and all, and rushed toward the door. "Hurry," he urged.

They crossed the room and Olivia reached for the handle, intending to swing the door open for them. "Alexei, where are they holding Joe?"

A blast thundered through the concrete room as a bullet discharged from Siderov's weapon and plunged into Alexei's back. Liz's screams pierced the air. Alexei jerked, stumbled, and slumped to the floor still holding Liz and the chair, his eyes wide and questioning.

"Alexei!" Olivia cried. She clutched at his arm as he slid over onto his side, the gun's report still echoing off the walls.

Alexei's eyes were fixed and empty. Olivia knelt beside him, and looked over her shoulder to locate Siderov. The Doberman was lying still on the floor in a pool of blood.

Siderov, blood streaming from the puncture wounds the dog had inflicted on his neck, lumbered towards Olivia, his eyes glassy as he leveled the gun at her. He pulled the trigger.

There was no time to move or to think. Olivia waited for the bullet.

The gun clicked.

Siderov flung the weapon to the floor and continued his advance.

Olivia, shaking, rose to meet him. "Monster," she choked. "You shot your own son."

Siderov took the final two steps to Olivia. His eyes were like black holes. His breath was ragged.

His right hand came up to strike Olivia and as she raised her left arm to block him, Siderov's other hand plunged his switchblade into Olivia's stomach.

She gagged. She pressed her left hand against her abdomen, her eyes wide, disbelieving.

Siderov smiled triumphantly, blood and sweat glistening on his skin.

Siderov wheezed, "I ...decide...who dies."

Hate and fury hardened Olivia's face. "No. You. Don't," she said through gritted teeth. She gathered all that was left inside her, straightened, and with a swift, forceful motion of her right hand, Olivia lashed the mirror shard across Siderov's neck and cut his throat.

He stumbled back. He swayed. He fell to his knees and wobbled for a moment before falling headfirst to the cement floor. Blood pumped from the gash as his life drained away.

Olivia dropped the shard and clutched her bloody stomach with both hands. She slid in slow motion to the floor.

~

Olivia! Olivia!" Liz screamed, craning her neck to see

what had happened. Liz was still strapped into her chair, lying backwards on the floor next to Alexei's body. Olivia opened her eyes and stared at the ceiling. Her hearing was muffled. The lights above her seemed to alternately brighten and fade.

One of Siderov's thugs ran up to the door, looked at the carnage and raced across the room to the opposite side and out into the bunker room.

Olivia's body tingled. Blood soaked through her shirt and dripped onto the floor. She started to shiver and her eyelids shut. Joe. Where's Joe? Her lips moved but no sound came out.

Running feet could be heard in the hallway and four men rushed into the room. The police officer tended to Liz, the detective checked Siderov and Alexei. Two men knelt beside Olivia. One touched her cheek. She opened her eyes and looked at their faces. Joe! Brad! She blinked.

"Joe, Joe," she murmured. Siderov lied. Joe wasn't his prisoner. She reached for his hand. "You're...all right."

He nodded, his cheeks wet with tears streaming from his eyes.

Brad knelt beside her and stroked her hair. "Here comes the cavalry," he whispered to her.

Olivia swallowed. "Your timing's...a bit...off," she told him. Her voice was a hoarse whisper.

"We'll have to work on that," Brad said.

Olivia's eyelids were so heavy, she let them close. She

coughed and her breath came in wheezes.

"Olivia Suzanne Miller," Joe said gruffly, choking on his fears. "You stay here. Don't be going anywhere. Help's coming. Don't...don't you dare leave me."

Olivia opened her eyes into slits. "I'm...not going... anywhere," she mumbled, huffing. "You're... stuck...with me."

Olivia moved her head slightly, trying to see Brad's face. It seemed to float above her, in focus one second and out of focus the next. She blinked and squinted, but the effort it took drained all of her remaining energy. She tried to speak to him but her lips only trembled and just a wisp of air puffed out of her lungs and her words remained unformed. She was fading into herself. *Stay with me, Brad. Don't let me go.*

Olivia's body began shaking violently. Joe squeezed her hand as her eyes rolled back in her head.

JOE AND BRAD rode in the ambulance with Olivia to York Hospital, Joe watching Olivia's face and cursing the traffic all the way. An intravenous line was attached to Olivia's arm and gauze sheets were pressed against the knife wound in her stomach. The paramedic had injected her with something and placed an oxygen mask over her nose and mouth.

Between the mirror shard, dog bite, Alexei's blood spatter, and the switchblade, there wasn't much of Olivia's body that either wasn't covered or dabbled in blood. She looked like she had just come out of a war zone.

"We should've gotten there sooner," Joe said, a hitch in his voice. He looked as if he had aged ten years.

"She's okay, Joe," Brad reassured weakly. His eyes were wet. "She's strong. She'll come out of this fine."

"Been a hell of a year for her." Joe shook his head.

"Hell of a year for you too," Brad said.

"I'm not the one with my blood on the outside of my body." Joe caught the sob that tried to escape from his chest. "My poor girl." The words crumbled in his throat as he passed his calloused hand over his face. He leaned forward to see out the ambulance window. "Where's the damn hospital?"

The lights of York Hospital showed through the window. The ambulance bounced over a bump in the driveway leading into the emergency room entrance. The doors of the ambulance flew open and the stretcher was pulled out. Joe and Brad followed it into the hospital. People in scrubs were waiting and they shot questions at the paramedics as the stretcher was wheeled down the hallway into surgery. The doors slammed in Joe and Brad's faces and they stood there, shell-shocked.

A short, round woman with kind eyes hurried up to them. "You're her next of kin?"

"Well, in a manner of speaking," Joe replied.

"Sir?" the woman questioned.

"This is her friend." Joe gestured toward Brad. "I'm her neighbor and her...." Joe's voice trailed off, not knowing how to explain that Olivia was as dear to him as his own child, that he would give his life for her, that if she died he did not know how he would go on. What was the word for that? "I'm her..."

Brad said to the woman, "Her aunt passed away last month. She has a cousin, but no other blood relatives. This man has acted as her father for years."

The woman held a clipboard out to Joe. "Will you fill this in, then?" She led Brad and Joe to a small waiting room and explained where they could get coffee and that someone would update them on Olivia's condition periodically. She asked if she could get them anything. They shook their heads.

A long night and morning of waiting ensued. Joe sat like a stone for hours. He would not leave the waiting room. Minutes ticked by. A television hinged to the wall showed a sitcom but the sound had been muted. Brad bought coffee from a machine and the two cups sat untouched on the table. A few other people came and went.

Around five o'clock in the morning, a tall auburn-haired woman dressed in scrubs entered the waiting area. Brad stirred from dozing in the chair and Joe's breath caught in his chest when he saw the woman sit down across from them.

Joe desperately wanted news of Olivia but now that this person was here to speak with them, he wasn't sure he wanted to hear what she had to say. At least while sitting and waiting there was hope, and he didn't want that hope replaced with misery.

"I'm Dr. Higgins," the woman said, leaning forward in her chair. Her voice was kind. Joe met her eyes. "The surgery went very well. Olivia is doing fine."

Joe burst into tears.

The doctor smiled at him and said, "I'm glad I have good news to share. Miraculously, none of her major organs was injured in the attack. She needed some blood and the wound required repair and stitching up. The tissue will heal and she will be as good as new in no time. She's in the recovery room. She'll be ready to go home in about forty-eight hours."

Joe wiped his cheeks with the backs of his hands. Brad swallowed hard and brushed at his eyes as he passed Joe the box of tissues from the side table.

Joe managed a hoarse, "Thank you."

"She'll be drowsy, but you can see her now if you'd like," the doctor said.

Joe nodded and they stood.

"The nurse will show you where to go. I'll be in to check on her later."

Joe and Brad found the floor and the room where Olivia was in recovery, and when they tiptoed around the corner and saw her, she was lying on the hospital bed with her eyes closed. Her brown hair was spread out on the pillow like a halo around her head and her skin was pale and luminous from the combination of the loss of blood and the glow of the room's bright lights.

She opened her eyes and saw them. The effects of the anesthesia made the edges of dream and reality blur, but she knew they were real. Her two men, standing solid before her. Her heart full of love. The corners of her mouth turned up. "Hey, you two," she said softly.

"Hey, yourself," Joe whispered. He touched her hand with his fingertips like he was afraid she would break if he held her. She took hold of his hand. She looked up at Brad and reached for him. He was still carrying the tissue box and he put it on the bed next to Olivia and gripped her hand. A huge lump in his throat kept him silent.

"Do you have a cold?" Olivia asked Brad. Her voice was heavy and her words slurred.

He looked at her quizzically.

"Your eyes. They're red," she said. "You brought a tissue box."

"Oh. No," Brad said. "Just...allergies," he lied and

blinked back tears.

Joe lifted her hand and kissed it. "You want anything, sweetheart?"

"I'm a bit thirsty," she said.

He lifted the cup of water from the table and held the straw steady so she could place her lips on it. She sipped and rested her head back on the pillow. Some water dribbled onto to her chin and she lifted the tissue box to take one out to dry her face. Her movements were slow and sluggish. She held the box in front of her eyes and studied it.

"Liv?" Joe asked, wondering why she was staring at the box.

She put the box back on the bed. "Something came into my mind. But then I lost it." Her voice was croaky from the tube that had been dropped down her throat during the surgery. Joe tilted his head and looked at her, questioning.

"What were you thinking?" Brad asked.

"Not sure," Olivia said. Her eyes were half closed. "When can I go home?"

Joe responded, "The doc said you can probably go home in forty-eight hours."

"Okay." She nodded. "Don't leave me." She fought to keep her eyes open, but her body's need for rest won out and she drifted away into sleep.

28

Just before noon, Joe returned to the hospital from having gone home to shower and shave. He brought Olivia some pajamas, clothes and toiletries from her house and had her backpack and laptop and some flowers that he and Brad had spent quite a bit of time choosing from the florist shop.

Brad had to return to work but he demanded that Joe call him every hour with updates. When Joe finally found the room Olivia had been moved to, he saw her sitting up in bed, her hair in a ponytail, talking to Detective Brown, who was sitting in the chair next to her.

Olivia's face brightened when Joe entered the room. "Joe!"

"You look terrific," Joe told her and kissed her head. "These are from Brad and me." He set the vase of flowers on the window sill.

"They're beautiful. Thank you."

"Detective." Joe nodded to Brown and said to Olivia, "I brought your laptop and some of your things." Joe put the bag on the floor and Olivia beamed at him.

"You recovered my backpack," she said.

"I did indeed," Joe said.

"Detective Brown is questioning me about the other night," Olivia told him.

"So soon?" Joe asked, concerned about Olivia having to relive it all.

"It's best to take the information when it's fresh," the detective said. "Before she has a chance to hear things from others."

"Should I wait outside?" Joe asked.

"No," Olivia told him. "I'd like you to stay with me."

"It won't take too long," said Brown.

Joe pulled up the extra side chair and listened as Olivia recounted the events of the previous night, explaining how Alexei had texted her from Hannigan's phone and that she went to the house expecting to meet Hannigan there. Joe's emotions alternated between horror for what Olivia endured and fury at the people who inflicted it on her.

Brown wrote in his notebook. "I know it's difficult to have to tell this. I appreciate your going through it with me." He closed the notebook and looked at Olivia. His face was serious.

"You should know that Alexei Siderov survived the gunshot."

Olivia's eyes widened in shock. Joe looked pained.

"He's in no condition to give us any information right now, but we hope to talk with him soon." He paused. "Most likely, we will need you to testify when we go to court."

Olivia nodded.

Joe piped up. "What about Mike Sullivan, Detective? Do you know how he's doing?"

"Mr. Sullivan has been in a medically-induced coma. He was in tough shape. He hasn't been able to give us any information. He is expected to pull through."

"Thank heavens," Olivia murmured. "What about Liz Sullivan?"

"She'll be fine. She's been seen by a plastic surgeon," Brown told them. "When will you be discharged?"

"The day after tomorrow," Olivia said.

"I'll have to collect the necklace that Andersen passed to you. As evidence."

"Of course," Olivia said.

"Why don't I give you a call the afternoon you're discharged and see how you're feeling? Maybe I can come by to pick it up then. The sooner the better, I'm afraid."

"I could bring it by the station later today, if that would help," Joe offered.

"No, no. That's not necessary," Brown said. "I might

need to ask Olivia a few more questions anyway." He stood. "I'm glad to see you're doing so well," he told her. "Thank you for your time."

Joe stood and came around the end of the bed to shake Brown's hand.

As soon as Brown was out the door, Joe said, "For Pete's sake. They can't even give you a few hours to rest." He shook his head. "I just don't like that guy." He took the seat that Brown had been in.

"He's okay, Joe. It has to be done," Olivia said softly. She seemed to have lost her energy.

"Can't believe one of those bastards survived," Joe muttered angrily. "He should have died."

"Joe...we shouldn't think that way," Olivia whispered.

"A trial? Ugh," Joe said.

Olivia was quiet.

"Are you doing alright, Liv?" Joe asked, concerned.

"Just tired from the telling, I guess." She turned her head to Joe. "I need to hear how you and Brad showed up with the posse at Siderov's."

"Not now, sweetheart. Why don't you rest?"

"I want to hear. Tell me. I can listen while I rest. Please, Joe."

"I'll give you the condensed version. Then when Brad is here, you can get us to fill things in," Joe told her.

She closed her eyes and nodded. "Tell," she said.

"Brad came to my house looking for you," Joe said. "He had been trying to reach you for hours. We went to the shop, went to your house. Brad had to go back to work the event at his bookstore, so I took the bike and went to Hannigan's house to see if you were there doing surveillance. There was a light on in the living room and I decided to go up and knock. I saw your backpack on the couch and I got panicked. Detective Brown came into the living room just as I was about to bang on the glass. He was searching Hannigan's house, looking for anything that could shed some light on Andersen's death. I told him my concerns, grabbed your backpack, and we went to the Siderov's to speak to them. Of course, while riding the bike to Hannigan's my phone fell out of my pocket and Brad couldn't reach me."

Olivia opened her eyes and chuckled, but had to clutch her stomach from the pain. "Ugh. You and that phone, Joe."

"So Brad called the Ogunquit police and made up a story that he saw a man dragging me into Hannigan's house." Olivia opened her eyes in astonishment.

Joe continued, "Well, I wouldn't answer his calls and he knew I went to Hannigan's and he was worried. The police met Brad at Hannigan's just when Brown and I were leaving for the Siderov's so we all went together."

Joe paused and cleared his throat. "The housekeeper

answered the door. She looked frightened, nervous. One thing led to another and we ended up breaking into the basement."

Joe looked over at Olivia. "The end," he said.

Olivia turned her head. "I'm surprised the police would agree to go to the Siderov's based solely on your worries."

"They had some suspicions of their own as it turns out, and with you missing – well, it gave them cause." Joe paused, then said, "There was a drug warehouse in the basement of the Siderov's house."

Olivia's eyes widened. "What?"

"They were storing drugs, shipping them through Canada to couriers who took them overseas. Allegedly, of course. They were also suspected of money laundering, racketeering, theft of antiquities and major works of art. Not to mention the murder of at least nineteen people. Those are the things the police know about. There may be more."

"You're making this up," Olivia said.

"I kid you not," Joe answered.

"Good grief," she said.

"You got that right."

Olivia struggled to sit up. "So what were Aggie's and Martin Andersen's connection, besides him being a customer of hers? What did they know? How was Aggie involved with the Siderovs?"

Joe shrugged. "Unknown."

Olivia frowned.

"I assume the police will try to link that necklace Andersen gave you to the Siderovs," Joe said. "And as far as 'red Julie'...no clue."

Olivia looked off into space and sighed. Her face brightened. "Joe! I almost forgot! When I was at Hannigan's, I saw Aggie's camera bag on a bookshelf. She had been at Andersen's house. We need to get it. We need to look through the pictures on her camera."

"Her camera bag?" Joe stared at her. "Why was it there?" Joe wondered.

"Maybe she and Andersen were watching the Siderov's house?" Olivia said. "Would you hand me my laptop, Joe?"

Olivia sent an email to Rodney Hannigan telling him that she was okay and that while she was being held at his house against her will, she saw a camera bag belonging to Aggie. As she would have to lie low for a few days to recover from surgery, Olivia asked if Joe might be able to borrow the key from Detective Brown and go by and pick up the bag sometime soon. She included Joe's cell phone number in the email.

Olivia shut down her laptop and Joe moved it aside. She leaned back on her pillow. "Joe, maybe we'll find some pictures on Aggie's camera that will give us some information."

Joe nodded. "And maybe that bastard Alexei can give some answers as well. And if I find out he had something to do with Aggie's death..." His voice trailed off.

29

By the time the hospital managed to discharge Olivia, it was well past noon. Brad and Joe loaded Olivia and all her things into Brad's car and they made the short drive back to Ogunquit. As they pulled into her driveway Joe said, "I don't know why you have to be so difficult."

"Well if I wasn't, then it wouldn't be me," Olivia said.

"I agree with Joe," Brad said.

"That is no surprise," Olivia answered.

"You shouldn't be alone right after getting out of the hospital," Brad told her. "The nurse said so."

"Joe is right next door," Olivia said.

This argument had been going on since they pulled out of the hospital driveway. Olivia wanted to be in her own house and in her own bed. She knew Joe and Brad had work to tend to - and anyway, she didn't want to be fussed over.

"Liv...forget it. I'm not going to Wells today," Joe said. "And maybe not tomorrow either. If you won't come to my house, then I'm coming to yours. I'll bring my paperwork over and I'll do it at your kitchen table. After that, I'll leave you alone for a while, but I'll be back with dinner and I'm sleeping in the guest room tonight. You aren't going to be alone your first night out of the hospital. That would be just plain dumb."

Olivia sighed. "Fine."

They helped her into her house. Brad got pillows and blankets from the spare bedroom and made a nice nest on the couch for Olivia. Joe put her clothes away and freshened the water in the vase of flowers. He brought her some books and made sure her laptop was in easy reach. Brad made a pot of tea and placed it on the coffee table.

"You're both good to me." She smiled at them as she settled on the couch and snuggled under the fleece blanket. Even though it was a warm day, she felt a little chilled. She sipped the tea. "Thank you," she said. Brad put her cell phone and the television remote on the end table.

"I'll call you later," Brad told her. "I need to get back to the store. Don't give Joe a hard time."

"Tell him not to give me a hard time," she said. "He's like a clucking hen."

"I heard that," Joe called from the kitchen. He carried in a plate of toast and jam. "I'm going home to get my paperwork. I'll be right back. Try to stay out of trouble until I get back."

Brad and Joe walked to the door. "Call me if she gets too unbearable," Brad said to Joe.

~

JOE WORKED at Olivia's kitchen table while she dozed, used her laptop, nibbled at whatever Joe brought her to eat, and strolled around the house a little.

"I better get better fast otherwise I'll go stir crazy."

Joe answered without looking up from his papers, "You've only been home for four hours." Joe's phone rang and he answered. A realtor friend of his called to tell him about a property coming up for sale and he asked Joe if he wanted to come take a look. It was right near the center of Ogunquit on Beach Street and Olivia urged him to go.

"I'm fine. Go. You'll be back before my next round of bad luck descends. I'd ask to come along but I know what the answer will be."

Joe reluctantly made arrangements to meet the

realtor for a brief look at the house. "I'll be back in an hour or two. I'll bring dinner back."

"Don't rush. Really. Nothing can happen to me sitting here on the sofa," Olivia told him. Joe kissed her and headed out to walk up to the center of town.

∾

OLIVIA STARTLED AWAKE WITH A JOLT. She had napped sitting in the living room chair and wasn't sure if what woke her was in her dream or not. A strong breeze was blowing outside and the shade was banging against the open window.

Olivia held her stomach with one hand and with the other pushed herself up out of the chair. She walked over to the window to shut it and saw that black clouds were rolling in from the west. She went around the rest of the rooms to shut the windows in anticipation of rain.

When she was in the den, the doorbell rang. Olivia's stomach was getting sore, so she kept her hand on the bandages as she tried to hurry to the front door.

"Detective." Olivia was surprised to see Detective Brown standing on her front porch.

"Sorry I didn't call first. I was driving by and thought I'd take the chance to see if you were home so I could pick up the necklace." A gust of wind brought the scent of rain.

Olivia nodded and stepped back. "Come in."

The detective walked into the living room. "Thanks. Are your friends around?" Brown asked.

"No, Brad is working and Joe had to go out," Olivia said. "He won't be gone long.

The necklace is in my room," Olivia told him. "Please sit down. I'll just be a minute to get it." She gestured to the living room chairs. "Can I get you something to drink?"

"Oh, no, thanks. I'm all set."

Olivia started for the hallway.

"How are you feeling?" the detective asked.

"I'm okay. Just starting to feel a little tired and sore, but not bad at all," Olivia said as she left the room to get the necklace. She walked gingerly down the hall to her bedroom, holding her stomach.

"Glad to hear it," Brown called to her from the living room. "You'll be good as new to start Stanford in the fall."

Olivia stopped short. Her breath caught in her throat. Stanford? *The only person I told I was going to Stanford was Siderov.* Her blood turned to ice.

Instead of going to her room for the necklace, she edged into the den and went to the walk-in closet to open the wall safe. She switched on the closet light and punched in the combination code. Swinging open the door to the safe, she reached in. Olivia heard her phone ringing in the living room.

As she withdrew her hand from the safe, something at the door of the den caught her attention and she turned around to see Brown staring at her.

JOE WAS WALKING through the house on Beach Street when his cell phone rang. He glanced at it but didn't recognize the number, so he put it back in his pocket.

"Take the call, if you like," Joe's friend said.

"I don't know who it is," Joe replied. "They can leave a message." He and his friend finished going into all of the downstairs rooms and headed up the stairs to the second floor. There were four bedrooms and two baths, all in different states of disrepair.

Joe and his friend stood on the front lawn, looking at the outside of the house. "I like this place. I think I could do a lot with it," Joe said. "It has an excellent location. It would all depend on the price."

"I'll give you a call as soon as it's officially listed," his friend said. "I think the family wants to unload it quickly. They may be very happy to have an immediate offer."

"I hope we can work something out. Let me know."

Joe and his friend shook hands. Joe headed up Beach Street to the center of town thinking about where he would stop to get takeout to bring home for dinner. He wondered what Olivia would like to eat so decided to call her. As he pulled out his phone, he changed his mind in case she was napping. Remembering the earlier call, Joe checked if there was a voice mail. He punched in his password and a man's voice came on.

Joe, this is Rodney Hannigan. I just returned home from Logan Airport and saw Olivia's email. I lost my phone before I left on business for a few days and had to get another one. I had no idea all of this happened. Thank heavens Olivia is alright. Detective Brown has not tried to contact me; in fact, he does not have permission to enter the beach house. I never gave him a key. He never told me he was going to investigate the house. I called Olivia but she didn't answer. I am very concerned that Brown entered the beach house without permission. I don't like this. Maybe I'm an alarmist but until he explains how and why he entered my house, may I suggest you use caution in any dealings you have with him. Please give me a call when you can.

Joe's heart thudded against his chest. He punched Olivia's cell number into his phone and waited. It rang and rang and her voice mail kicked in. He hit the end button and put the phone in his pocket. Brown. What's that son of a bitch up to? Joe took off running down Shore Road in the direction of Olivia's house.

"WHAT DO you have in that safe?" Brown commanded, advancing across the room.

Olivia glared at him. "Nothing of importance to you."

"I'll judge that," he said, moving fast to the closet.

Olivia slammed the door of the safe and spun the dial.

"You need to leave," Olivia said.

"I know your aunt had something that belonged to the Siderovs. Something relevant to this case," Brown said. He grabbed Olivia by the shirt front and pulled her close. "Open the safe," he hissed.

"Now it makes sense," Olivia said.

"What are you talking about?"

"I wondered why my aunt didn't go to the police. Now I know."

Brown put his hand on Olivia's neck and tightened his grip. He pressed his face next to hers. "Open it."

"What happened to my aunt?" Olivia croaked.

"Shut up."

Olivia's head hurt and she felt weak and woozy.

Sparkles danced in front of her eyes and she squinted, trying to force the dizziness to pass. Trying hard not to pass out, Olivia looked over Brown's shoulder and focused on the long, white shelf that Aggie had placed on the wall above her desk. On it were pictures and trinkets from when Olivia was little.

Aggie had framed a drawing Olivia had done when she was about four, and the picture was on the shelf leaning against the wall. There was a cat sculpted out of clay, a pair of little sneakers Olivia had worn, a red box that Olivia had constructed out of a tissue box which was made to hold some of Aggie's jewelry. It was held together with tape and glue and had a flap on top that opened and shut. It was covered in rhinestones.

Olivia had carefully folded a piece of red velvet cloth and covered the bottom of the box with it. On top of the velvet, Aggie had put a snapshot of her and Olivia on the first day of summer when Olivia was thirteen. It had been unusually warm and they had spent the day boogie boarding in the ocean, lying on the beach and eating ice cream.

Aggie said it was one of the best days of her life and that by keeping the snapshot in that special box it would keep the magic of that day in her life forever.

Brown pressed harder on Olivia's neck and shook her. She shifted her gaze back to his face.

He banged her head against the safe. "Open it,"

he raged.

Olivia lifted her arm in slow motion, turned the dial and stepped back.

Brown pushed on the handle and swung the door open. The safe was empty. He smacked Olivia across the face and she hit the opposite wall of the closet and slid down to the floor.

She gasped and clutched her stomach.

"Where is it?" Brown sneered.

Olivia, grimacing, leaned slightly to the side and reached behind her.

"You mean this?" Olivia slipped the handgun that had been in the safe from her waistband and held it out in front of her.

"Bitch," Brown cursed.

"Back up," Olivia ordered.

Brown hesitated and took several steps back. Olivia pulled herself up from the floor and steadied herself by leaning on the wall. Her temple oozed blood from where her head had hit the safe.

She gestured with the gun for Brown to move back and she stepped out of the closet and into the den.

In one swift movement, Brown's hand flicked to his side and he raised his police side arm and pointed it at Olivia.

She and Brown stood leveling guns at each other.

"Now, what?" Brown said.

"Get out of my house."

"I don't think so."

Brown lunged for her gun. Olivia sidestepped him and brought the gun up and smacked him across the face with it.

The man wrenched it from her hand and Olivia tried to get around Brown to run for the living room. He caught her by the arm and dragged her to where her gun lay on the floor.

When he picked it up, he flicked it open and checked the barrel. Empty. He shook his head and tossed it on the den sofa. "Where is it?"

Olivia's stomach lurched as the little strength she had drained out of her. "I told you...it's in my room," she mumbled. Her face was white.

"Not the necklace," he menaced. "You know what I want."

"No," Olivia said, her teeth clenching. She inhaled sharply and spat each word out. "Why don't you tell me? Murderer."

Brown's eyes were filled with hate. He growled, "I'm running out of time." Sweat beaded up on his forehead and upper lip. He dragged Olivia by the arm to her bedroom, where she retrieved the necklace and passed it to him.

Brown shoved Olivia down the hallway to the living room and pushed her into one of the chairs. Nausea flooded her body. Blood seeped into her shirt from the surgical wound.

The doorbell rang. Olivia and the detective exchanged glances.

"Liv?" Brad called from outside the door.

Brown glowered. "Get rid of him. Tell him we're going over some more details. Make him leave." Brown spoke through clenched teeth. "Or I'll kill him." Brown brandished his weapon before returning it to the holster beneath his jacket. "Get up. Open it."

Olivia shuffled to the door and opened it a crack. "Hi."

"Hi. I made you a blueberry cake," Brad said. "You okay? You look pale." He was holding a cake plate covered with a metal dome. Brad moved to enter the house.

Olivia stepped to block him. "Detective Brown is here. We're going over things."

"Again?" Brad said. "You should be resting."

Brown appeared behind Olivia. "It's necessary."

"You're bleeding," Brad said when he saw the blood stain on her shirt. He pushed into the room. He took her arm. "Sit down. Should we call the doctor?"

He walked Olivia to the chair and made her sit.

"Brad, it's ok. It happens. I just change the bandage. The doctor said to expect it. I'm okay," she lied.

"Really?" He was balancing the cake plate on one hand. Brown was hovering next to him. "Your temple...it's bleeding." Brad took a tissue and dabbed at it.

"I bumped my head in the bathroom. It's ok. I got dizzy, but I caught myself before I fell," Olivia said.

"This is why we didn't want you alone," Brad scolded.

"It's nothing," Olivia told him. "I need to ask you to go. I'm getting tired and I have to finish up with Detective Brown."

"Okay." Brad was unsure. He looked at Brown, who nodded at him, and then back at Olivia. "Where's Joe?"

"He went to look at a house on Beach Street. He'll be right back." She leaned her head back on the chair. "I really need you to go, Brad. So I can finish up with the detective and then I can rest." She lifted her head and her eyes bore into Brad's. "You know what a wimp I am," she said pointedly.

A disbelieving look passed over Brad's face and he was about to say something when Olivia said, "Thanks for the cake, but I'm allergic to blueberries. It was nice of you to bring it though. You know Joe will devour it. Maybe you could come by tomorrow for a little while."

Brad's eyebrows rose. "Okay," he said slowly. He put the cake on the coffee table. He looked back and forth between Brown and Olivia. "I...okay...be sure to get some rest...I'll come back tomorrow." He backed away several steps, staring at Olivia, turned for the door and let himself out.

Olivia let out a deep sigh. "There, he's gone."

"Now where is it?" Brown asked.

"I gave it to you," Olivia slurred. "Get out." She felt like she was going to vomit.

"You know I'm not leaving with just the necklace."

"Why don't you tell me what it is you want? You can have whatever it is. Just leave us alone."

Brown rubbed his forehead. He moved to the fireplace and leaned against it for a second. He straightened and his fist pounded on the mantle, making Olivia jump. He whirled around, his eyes flashing. His chest was rising and falling. "Your aunt was in possession of a valuable antique Swiss music box. It was engraved wood with inlaid mother of pearl." His hands were clenched by his sides. "She sold it to the wrong person."

Olivia looked puzzled.

"It was intended for Siderov, but Alexei got to your aunt's shop too late." He shook his head. "Shouldn't send a boy to do a man's job," he muttered. He was pacing. "It seems she had already sold it to Andersen and no amount of money could get her to withhold the sale in order to sell it to Siderov." He wheeled towards Olivia. "She shouldn't have done that," he sneered.

"A music box?" Olivia asked incredulously. "All of this for a music box?"

Brown studied Olivia's face. "You're as stupid as she was."

Rage bubbled up inside of Olivia. She pushed herself out of the chair and stood on wobbly legs. The room was spinning again. Olivia's shirt was wet with blood. "I don't know where it is," she seethed. "If she sold it to Andersen, why are you looking for it here? Stupid?"

"They hid it from us!" Brown shrieked. He flung his arm out, smashing over a lamp. His face was purple with fury. His shirt was wet from his sweat. "That's why they're both dead!" His eyes, bulging out of his head, locked on Olivia for a full minute.

She swayed slightly and put her hand on the back of the chair.

Brown's jaw set. He had made a decision. "You're coming with me." He crossed the room and grabbed Olivia's arm.

Olivia's head felt like a balloon full of helium. "No. I'm not," Olivia mumbled. She flopped to the floor like a rag doll with Brown still holding onto her arm. He stared at Olivia collapsed at his feet.

Confusion raced over the man's face. Brown bent and scooped her up and headed for Olivia's garage. He turned the knob and pushed open the door leading from the kitchen into the garage. Brown opened the back door of Olivia's Jeep and plopped her on her back onto the seat.

Olivia opened her eyes. She took a deep breath, bent her knee, and as Brown was hunched over backing out the car, she let loose and booted him in the face with her foot, catching his nose with her heel.

Brown screamed and clutched at his face, stumbling back from the Jeep. Blood poured from his nose.

Olivia leaned for the car door and yanked it closed. The pain in her gut radiated like knives up into her chest and down through her thighs but she forced herself to reach over the front seat to hit the button that locked all the doors.

With a groan, she crumpled into a ball on the floor of the car. Olivia felt she was floating out of her body. She closed her eyes. A moan slipped from her lips.

"I'll kill you!" Brown was wild. He pulled out his gun and shot out the passenger side window.

The blast was deafening. Glass shattered and flew. He yanked on the passenger side door but it wouldn't open.

Brown whirled around to look for something to smash the remaining glass out of the window so that he could get at Olivia.

When Brown turned, there, face to face in front of him, stood Joe, holding a compression nail gun in his hand.

Joe lifted the nail gun and pressed it to Brown's forehead - in less than a fraction of a second, the nail plunged through the skull and into Brown's brain.

Brad ran from the side yard into the garage carrying a metal pipe. He saw Brown slumped at Joe's feet on the cement floor of the garage.

Joe was shaking. Brad put his hand on Joe's shoulder

and squeezed.

Brad opened the back door of the car to see Olivia on the floor.

"Liv!"

She turned her head and seeing Brad, a weak smiled brightened her face.

"Did he hurt you?" His voice was tight with anger.

"I'm okay," Olivia managed.

Brad put his arms around her and lifted her out of the Jeep.

"How's our timing this time?" he asked her.

"Much better," she said softly, resting her head on his shoulder.

"So you're a wimp now, huh?" Brad asked.

"It was only temporary," Olivia whispered.

30

Brad called the police and an ambulance. The paramedics arrived first and one tended to Olivia, where she was lying on the sofa. Brad and Joe stood over him as he inspected her surgical incision.

"Are you in pain?" the paramedic asked Olivia.

"Only when I move or take a breath."

"It looks worse than it is," the paramedic explained. "Some of the stitches at the bottom of the incision have let go, but I can bandage it up and there shouldn't be any more bleeding. Tomorrow you can call your doctor and make arrangements to be seen. The light-headedness and nausea are normal reactions to too much activity so soon after anesthesia and surgery." He began to dress the wound and prepare the bandages. "If the blood seeps

J. A. WHITING

through these bandages, then I want you to go to the emergency room. You won't be alone tonight?"

Brad answered. "No, I'll be here keeping an eye on her."

The paramedic nodded and continued to work on Olivia. They heard sirens approaching. A team of police and detectives entered the living room and Joe took them to the garage. He didn't come back.

"I think Joe should call our lawyer," Olivia said to Brad. "Is he still in the garage?" Brad nodded.

Two detectives approached and one took Brad aside for questioning while the other pulled a chair up alongside Olivia. The paramedic was finishing with the bandages.

"I'm Detective McDonald. I need to talk to you about tonight's events."

Olivia scowled.

"You're Olivia Miller?"

"Where's Joe?" Olivia asked.

"He's with one of the officers," McDonald replied.

"Is the officer a friend of Brown's?" Olivia's voice had an edge to it.

"The officer is questioning him."

"Does Joe need a lawyer?" Olivia asked.

McDonald didn't answer right away.

Olivia's eyes flashed. "Your detective friend tried to kill me. I believe he had a hand in killing my aunt." Olivia narrowed her eyes. "How do I know you're not going to try to kill me, too?"

The paramedic finished with Olivia and stood. "She needs to rest," he told the detective, as he gathered his medical supplies.

The police chief overheard what Olivia was saying to the detective and walked over to them. "Ms. Miller, how are you doing? I'm sorry about all of this." He waved his hand in the air. His face was drawn. "You can trust Detective McDonald."

"How do you know that?"

"He's my son-in-law."

"How do I know I can trust you?"

The chief shrugged. "You don't. I guess you'll just have to have faith in some people." His shoulders slumped as he crossed the room to see Brad and the other detective.

McDonald asked Olivia to describe the evening's events. She went through things, beginning with Brown arriving at her door until she locked herself in her Jeep in the garage.

"He shot out the car window. I was afraid he was going to shoot me next. The sound was deafening. My ears are still ringing," Olivia said, bringing her hand up to cup her ear.

The police chief had returned and pulled up a chair. He was listening to Olivia's description of what had happened.

Olivia rubbed her temples. "I can't tell you any more. I didn't see anything after that." Olivia leaned back. Her stomach was churning and her vision was blurring. "I need a break. If you want to ask me anything else, it will just have to wait until tomorrow."

She raised her head and looked about the room at the people milling about. Some were taking photographs; others were writing in notebooks.

"Where's Joe?" Olivia demanded. "I want to see him." Nobody answered.

"Brad," Olivia raised her voice. "Will you go find Joe? And will you hand me my phone, please?"

Brad excused himself from the detective and brought Olivia her phone. He headed out to the garage to see what was happening.

Olivia called the number of the lawyer who handled their affairs. He had been a friend of Aggie's for years. When he answered, Olivia told him what had happened, and he agreed to be at her house in fifteen minutes.

The lawyer arrived and Joe emerged from the garage. He sank into the living room chair. The police were none too pleased to have one of their own killed with a nail gun.

"I'd like all this business behind us," Joe sighed. "But I'm afraid that a reason of self-defense doesn't fly that well when someone kills a detective."

Olivia's face was creased with worry and anger. "Then

they shouldn't have a dirty cop in their midst." Her voice was hoarse. She thought of Brown's hands gripping her throat.

"Brown was a good actor," Joe sighed. "It's not the police department's fault."

Olivia sat up straight. Her eyes were wide. She remembered what she saw in the den when Brown was choking her. "Brad...on the shelf in the den is a red box that I made for Aggie when I was little. Would you get it for me?"

"Sure thing," Brad said, getting up from the living room chair.

"What's with the box, Liv?" Joe asked.

"I thought of something earlier." A cloud passed over her face. "When Brown was choking me in the den." Her throat constricted at the thought of Brown's hands on her. "I just remembered." She swallowed hard to clear the tightness in her throat.

Joe looked quizzically at her. Brad bought the box in and handed it to Olivia.

"Thanks," she said. "I hope I'm right." The law enforcement officers watched what was going on. Olivia closed her eyes and said softly, "Please let me be right."

She opened the lid of the box and peered inside. There was the picture of Olivia and Aggie taken years ago at the beach. Olivia lifted the small square of red cloth that was under the photo. A smile worked at the corners of her mouth. She held the red box out to Brad. They exchanged glances and he looked inside of it.

"What? What's going on?" Joe asked, getting up from his chair and walking over to Brad. Brad reached in and removed a red flash drive and a small silver key.

"It's Aggie's," Olivia said. Her eyes glistened with tears. "It's Aggie's flash drive. I made the box for her. When I was little. It's a red jewelry box." She looked at Brad and Joe and a smile spread across her face. "Red jewelry box. Red Julie."

Brad and Joe stared at her with their mouths partially open. They blinked at each other.

"Really?" Joe asked.

"Red Julie...jewelry, not Julie," Brad said. "That's what Andersen was trying to tell you."

Olivia nodded and said, "That's what he was saying to me. 'Look in the red jewelry box'. He knew Aggie hid this here. She knew I would find it. Eventually."

"It's been here all along," Joe said. "Right under our noses."

Olivia gestured to the flash drive in Brad's hand. "Let's see what's on it."

Joe hustled to get Olivia's laptop. Brad called the police chief over. Olivia slid her legs back against the couch so Brad and Joe could sit down with her. Brad inserted the drive and opened the latest saved Word document. It was saved as 'Livvy.'

Olivia and Joe peered over Brad's shoulder. The three of them held their breaths.

LIVVY DEAR

If you are reading this, then something has happened to me. Bring these pictures and documents to the FBI. NOT THE POLICE. You can trust Martin Andersen.

The music box is in the treasure chest.

I love you.

OLIVIA COVERED her face with her hands and hunched over, rocking. Brad put his arm around her. She straightened up. Her face was wet and she wiped the tears with her sleeve.

"I'm okay."

Brad's face was lined with concern.

"Liv, honey, what does she mean 'the treasure chest'?" Joe asked gently.

"I'll show you in a minute. Keep looking on the flash drive, Brad," Olivia urged. "I'm okay."

Brad scrolled through the pictures that Aggie had saved. Numerous pictures were of Siderov and Brown exchanging objects and riding in a van together. There were pictures of the suspicious florist making deliveries to Siderov's house.

The last pictures showed Siderov, Alexei, and Brown pulling two men out of a van and, holding, what looked like guns, to their backs, pushing them towards the Victorian. It was clear that the pictures had been taken from Andersen's decks.

Further down was a list of sales for the antique shop with scanned copies of bills of sale. One showed Aggie's purchase of a music box and another was for the sale of that same box to Martin Andersen. There were pictures of it.

Brad turned the computer so that the police chief and two of the detectives could see the information that Aggie had saved for them. Their faces showed the strain of betrayal.

The police chief cleared his throat. "We'll need the flash drive."

Brad nodded.

The lawyer instructed Brad to copy the files to Olivia's laptop before he removed the drive and handed it to Detective McDonald.

"The treasure chest is in the basement. We need to go down to the basement," Olivia said.

"Liv, you need to stay put," Joe said, but as soon as the words were out of his mouth he knew they were useless.

"I'll carry you," Brad told her. He lifted her from the

sofa and they went to the basement, accompanied by two detectives and the chief.

"It's the old Christmas trunk," Olivia said. "We called it the treasure chest."

Joe moved an old straight-backed chair next to the old steamer trunk that Aggie kept the Christmas decorations in and Brad eased Olivia onto it.

"Check the decorations. Aggie must have wrapped it in some of the decorations. Look and see," Olivia requested.

Joe, Brad, and two police officers carefully lifted out decorations, one by one. Tree skirts, boxes of ornaments, bags of ribbons and tinsel.

Joe held a box marked "ornaments" and lifted the cover. "It's here." He was holding a wooden music box. He set it on the concrete floor. Everyone stared at it.

"That's the cause of all this?" Brad asked.

"Smash it," Olivia said angrily. "Just smash it."

Joe lifted it up again and handed it to the chief.

The music box, the old chest, and the basement were photographed by a member of the police department. They dusted different things for fingerprints, which Olivia thought was useless.

They all returned upstairs, where the box was inspected more closely. There appeared to be a place on the bottom where a key could be inserted.

Olivia's eyes widened. "Chief, the key. There was a key in the red jewelry box. Brad, where did you put it?"

"It's on the coffee table," Brad answered.

The police chief put on surgical type gloves and carried the music box to the coffee table. Everyone huddled around to see.

The chief placed the bottom of the small key into the grooves on the box. He wiggled it to adjust the fit. There was a click from the box.

A small door in the bottom of the box sprang open and, making a tinkling sound, hundreds of sparkling diamonds dropped from inside the box onto the table.

The six people around the coffee table simultaneously sucked air in audible gasps. They stared transfixed by the bounty before them.

"What the...?" Joe said.

The chief' stood transfixed. He couldn't take his eyes off the diamonds. "We'll be needing photos of all this."

31

The next morning Olivia was returned to the hospital, where they fixed her up for the second time. This time on the car ride home Olivia didn't complain about having someone stay with her. It wasn't because the events of the last few days had frightened her into wanting company. It was because she was glad they were all alive and she liked just being able to look at them.

When she got home, she ate three pieces of blueberry cake and downed a big glass of milk.

"Thought you were allergic to blueberries," Brad said.

"It was temporary," Olivia said.

"I see," Brad said.

"Brad and I were hoping to have the cake all to ourselves," Joe told her.

"Too bad for you." Olivia smiled.

~

Smuggling diamonds was added to the long list of crimes allegedly committed by the Siderovs. Alexei was interrogated by the police and he revealed that Brown had been an accomplice of theirs for some time.

The FBI was investigating and they discovered a foreign bank account in Brown's name containing close to four million dollars. Joe and Brad had no charges filed against them.

The Sullivans were reunited with Mikey and Lassie. Mike Sullivan recovered from his wounds. While working at the Siderov place, Mike had entered the storage room filled with drugs. One of Siderov's men saw Mike leaving the room and pursued him. Mike was shot in the shoulder but he made it to his truck.

He tried to drive to his home, but passed out and hit the tree a few miles from his house. Liz Sullivan's wound from losing her ring finger required attention from a plastic surgeon but it healed well. The emotional wounds from the trauma would take longer to deal with.

Detective McDonald invited Olivia, Joe, and Brad to the station so that he could tell them what Alexei had reported to the FBI. McDonald, Olivia, Joe and Brad sat at a wooden conference table in a small, muggy room at the police station. Rain pelted the window.

"The cross necklace belonged to Siderov," Detective McDonald told them. "The night Martin Andersen returned from London he drove up to his beach house. That same night, Alexei, Siderov and two of Siderov's employees showed up at Andersen's place and demanded the music box. Martin pulled a gun on them. He killed one of them and shot and wounded the other one as he escaped to his car. Martin and Siderov fought in the garage. Martin pulled the necklace off of Siderov's neck in the fight. Siderov shot Martin in the stomach and Martin shot Siderov in the shoulder. A car chase ensued with Martin losing control and flipping his car over right before the highway entrance."

The detective paused and took a sip of his coffee. He took a deep breath. "Then Siderov cut out Andersen's tongue."

Olivia grimaced. "I must have pulled off the exit ramp right about then," she noted.

The detective nodded. "Siderov heard your car and took off before he could locate the necklace. Siderov was afraid Martin would survive his injuries, so he sent his man back to finish Andersen off. That was the guy you saw, Olivia. The authorities showed up before he could act." The detective looked solemnly at Olivia. "And it's a good thing the police arrived when they did. No doubt he would have shot you too."

A chill went through Olivia's body.

Detective McDonald continued. "Alexei also revealed that Siderov planned to send one of his men to the hospital to kill Mike Sullivan to keep him from talking about the drugs he saw at the house."

"Just eliminate anyone in their way," Olivia said. She shook her head slowly.

"So how did the diamonds get in that music box? How did Aggie have it?" Joe asked.

"The Siderovs and their contacts used unsuspecting antiques dealers to move their inventory. In this case, the diamonds were placed in the music box and given to a dealer who had a legitimate business but who also moved illegal items. That dealer sold the music box to Aggie. Right after the box was shipped to her, the Siderovs were contacted and told when the package would arrive at Aggie's shop. Usually one of the Siderovs or their representative would appear at the shop and would pay full price for the item."

"Aggie must have known that Martin Andersen would be very interested in the music box and obviously contacted him about it. She knew he was a collector," Olivia said.

"So it seems," the detective said. "Alexei was too late to the store to make the purchase of the box. Occasionally this happened, and Siderov would arrange for one of his men to pay a visit to the purchaser of the item. The item would be located and taken into possession. If the purchaser got in the way, he would be eliminated. Martin knew he was in danger after Aggie died."

"What about Aggie?" Olivia asked softly. "Did Alexei know anything about her death?"

The detective nodded. "Alexei reported that Brown and another of Siderov's men went to Aggie's house on the night she died. They broke in but couldn't find the music box. Aggie tried to escape them by sneaking out of the house and taking the bike. Aggie and Andersen had joined forces and had figured too many things out. Siderov wanted them eliminated because he knew one of them had the box and was keeping it from him. We assume that as soon as Martin found out Aggie was dead, he figured he would be next, and so took off for London."

"What happened to her?" Joe asked quietly. "We need to know." Joe reached for Olivia's hand.

The detective cleared his throat. "When they caught up to Aggie, they injected her with a combination of cocaine and digitalis, which caused the fatal heart attack. Vials of the drugs were found in the Siderov home."

Joe stared out the window. His eyes were hollow, his face drawn and pale. Olivia swallowed. Her cheeks were flushed with anger. Her eyes glistened with tears. Brad looked down at his hands.

"I'm sorry," the detective said. They sat in silence for several minutes.

"There's one other thing," Detective McDonald said. "Alexei Siderov died last night at the hospital. Sepsis. From the gunshot wound."

Olivia's eyes went wide. She squeezed Joe's hand.

"Good," Joe whispered. "They can't hurt anyone else now," was how Joe looked at it. "Monsters and murderers; let them reap what they sow."

DURING THE FOLLOWING MONTH, Olivia regained her strength. Her doctor suggested that she and Joe make appointments with a counselor to address the grief of losing a loved one to violent death and to deal with the feelings of guilt that could arise from having taken a life, even in self-defense. Olivia and Joe went to talk to counselors, but after three sessions each they stopped going. They figured that the road to healing was a road they would travel together.

Joe and Olivia were both grateful that the monsters responsible for Aggie's death were now dead. And neither one of them felt remorse for having had a hand in some of it.

Following weeks of high heat and humidity, an early

August day dawned clear and cool, and Joe, Olivia, and Brad drove to the cemetery to visit Aggie's grave. They placed red carnations, her favorite flower, in the bronze vase next to her headstone. Olivia told Aggie that it was over now.

A tide seemed to break in Joe and his body was racked with anguished sobs. Olivia held him in her arms as the grief poured out of him, a heavy stone of grief deep in her own heart.

BRAD TOOK a night off from the store and they bought pizzas, made a salad, and sat around Joe's fire pit watching the sky darken and the stars twinkling over the Atlantic. At midnight, they raised glasses of champagne and toasted the gift of being alive.

Joe raised his glass. "To Aggie, for making my life the happiest I ever knew...for bringing me love...and for bringing me Liv." They clinked glasses.

Olivia cleared her throat. She started to speak, but her voice broke. She rose from her chair and gave Joe a bear hug, resting her cheek on his shoulder. She turned to Brad and hugged him like a drowning woman. When Olivia stepped back from him, she held his eyes for a moment and smiled. She returned to her seat and brushed her hand over her eyes.

Brad took his turn. "To you two...for making this home."

Joe downed his champagne, sighed and stood up. "I'm off to bed. Better days are coming." He kissed Olivia's head and squeezed Brad's shoulder. "Goodnight, Children."

"Goodnight, Joe," Brad and Olivia said.

The two sat in silence, sipping their champagne.

"I think I'm going to take up karate," Olivia said. "I've said that before, but now I really mean it."

"It's probably a good idea," Brad said. "Can't hurt."

"I should probably learn how to shoot, too."

"Or at least learn how to load the gun," Brad teased.

"It's been a strange few months," Olivia said. "I'm glad they're over."

"Amen to that," Brad said. He looked at Olivia. Her hair shimmered in the moonlight. "You know, Liv, I think that a true friendship is a great gift."

Olivia turned to look at him. Her heart sank at the word friendship.

"The past few weeks have shown me that it's important to go with intuition, to believe in yourself and what you think is true. That life is short and precious." Brad hesitated, but went on. "There's something even more precious than friendship."

Olivia blinked at him. Her heart did a flip. "What's that?"

Brad got out of his chair and knelt next to Olivia's. He touched her cheek. Moving his face close to hers, Brad paused for a second, breathing in her scent. He closed his eyes and touched his lips to hers.

His lips on Olivia's mouth were as a light as a butterfly and they sent sparks flying through her veins. She reached up her hand and placed it tenderly on his shoulder.

Brad kissed the side of her neck and lifted his head. "I intend to woo you, Olivia Miller."

"Please do," she said softly. Olivia could not believe how this man melted her heart. The best friend she ever had.

"Will blueberry cake be involved?" she asked.

"Most definitely."

She took his face in both her hands, leaned in, and kissed him.

THANK YOU FOR READING!

To hear about new books and book sales, please sign up for my mailing list at:

www.jawhitingbooks.com

Your email will never be sold, shared, or spammed.

If you enjoyed the book, please consider leaving a review. A few words are all that's needed. It would be very much appreciated.

AUTHOR'S NOTE

I have taken liberties with the geography and landscape of the town of Ogunquit, Maine in order to suit the story, not to try to improve the area, since it is perfect just the way it is.

ALSO BY J. A. WHITING

OLIVIA MILLER MYSTERY-THRILLERS

SWEET COVE COZY MYSTERIES

LIN COFFIN COZY MYSTERIES

CLAIRE ROLLINS COZY MYSTERY

PAXTON PARK COZY MYSTERIES

ABOUT THE AUTHOR

J.A. Whiting lives with her family in Massachusetts where she works full time in education. Whiting loves reading and writing mystery and suspense stories.

Please visit her at www.jawhitingbooks.com

51160623R00229

Made in the USA
Lexington, KY
01 September 2019